D1440830

A COWBOY AND HIS BOSS

A Johnson Brothers Novel, Chestnut Ranch Romance, Book 5

EMMY EUGENE

Copyright © 2019 by Emmy Eugene

All rights reserved.

No part of this book may be reproduced in any form or by any electronic or mechanical means, including information storage and retrieval systems, without written permission from the author, except for the use of brief quotations in a book review.

ISBN-13: 978-1660309122

CHAPTER ONE

G riffin Johnson couldn't tie a bow tie to save his life, and he glared at his neck in the mirror. The other brothers seemed to have perfected it somehow, but Griffin didn't see how.

He'd had his mother tie it for Seth's wedding in November. And then for Travis's nuptials in March.

Russ and Janelle were getting married right here on the ranch, and Griffin was supposed to be in Russ's bedroom five minutes ago.

He was not asking his mother for help for a third time. He could do this.

He tried to loop the two ends over one another like he'd seen in the Internet video, but he felt like a four-year-old trying to tie his shoes for the first time.

"This isn't happening," he muttered, abandoning the task. He was the only Johnson brother without a relationship, and he'd thought he'd at least beat Rex.

But he'd gotten back together with an old girlfriend, and he'd had a date for the wedding for over two weeks.

Griffin had tried dating a few people in the small Texas Hill Country town of Chestnut Springs, but nothing seemed to stick.

And the most recent woman he'd been out with was one of Janelle's best friends and her Maid of Honor. Griffin had to escort her down the aisle and everything, as Russ had asked him to be the Best Man.

Griffin loved his brother, or he'd have said no. He didn't want to attend the wedding at all. Not that he'd ever miss it, because Russ had been through the wringer to get to this point. And he was deliriously happy, and Griffin was happy for him.

The fact that he was leaving for Camp Clear Creek in the morning had sustained him through the last week.

He'd been a camp counselor there for a couple of years now, and he loved summer at Lake Marble Falls. He liked working with the boys, he loved being outside, and he enjoyed all the activities the Texas Hill Country had to offer.

Rex would say that Griffin couldn't wait to see Toni Beardall, but Griffin had dismissed him every time he'd even looked like he was going to mention Toni. His younger brother could be relentless, and Griffin had learned how to deal with him the best. If he didn't completely shut down Rex, the man could really rev up his mouth. It was always better to cut him off before then, and the only other person who could do it effectively was their mother.

Griffin left the bedroom where he'd been getting ready and went downstairs to the master suite. He knocked and said, "Russ, it's me. Let me in."

The door opened, and noise spilled into the hallway. All the brothers were already inside, along with their father, and the air smelled of leather and cologne.

Seth already wore his dress hat, as did Travis. Their oldest brother pulled out a box and said, "Okay, we're all here." He cut a look at Griffin, who still didn't have his tie right. "We got you these."

Russ took the box and looked at his brothers. "What's this?"

"Open it," Travis said.

Russ pulled the black ribbon off the box and opened it. "Oh, wow." He lifted out a perfectly silver cufflink in the shape of a J. Griffin had actually found the cufflinks, and he grinned as Russ put them on.

"I need help with my tie," Griffin said, and Travis turned toward him. He had the tie whipped into shape in only a few seconds, and Griffin turned toward the full-length mirror to make sure if was straight.

"We need to get outside," Seth said. The brothers huddled up, and a powerful sense of belonging moved through Griffin. In an hour, more than half of them would be married, but he believed they'd always be brothers. That bond wasn't changing just because Russ was about to say I do.

"Boys," Momma called, and Griffin grinned along with everyone else.

"How old do you think we'll be before she'll stop calling us boys?" Seth asked, and they all laughed together.

"Comin', Momma," he said, but he didn't lower his arms from Griffin's shoulders. He looked around at them. "I sure am glad to be your brother." He smiled, and Griffin's own emotion welled in his chest.

"All right, men. Let's go before Momma comes in here."

"Ready, Daddy?" Russ asked, looping his arm through their father's.

"You're coming with me, Pops," Rex said, joining the pair of them. Daddy smiled at his boys, and he left the room with Rex.

"You okay with Libby?" Russ asked.

Griffin nodded, his emotions laced tight as he went out into the kitchen behind Seth. Russ had been working on the backyard at the homestead for the past five months in anticipation of this wedding, and the patio now had air conditioning that blew down from the ceiling in the deck above it.

Tea lights had been strung through the rafters too, along with with several buffet tables that were laden with food and flowers.

Pretty, wedding music played out of the bluetooth speakers Russ had installed, and Griffin paused to take in the rows of chairs. Millie had tied white ribbons to them and set Texas bluebonnets through the knots.

Even Griffin could admit the space was beautiful. Perfect for a wedding.

"Johnson men," Millie said. "Over here."

Rex walked Daddy down to the front row, where

Momma waited, and then he joined the wedding party. Griffin felt better with Rex by his side, as the two of them had done pretty much everything together for the past five years. They'd even bought a house together, and Griffin knew he was about to live in it alone. Well, soon enough, as Rex had advanced his relationship in the direction of marriage.

For Griffin, he wasn't sure that was ever going to happen, and he lingered several feet from Libby without talking to her. Guests continued to come around the side of the house, where Russ had laid a cobblestone path that led from the driveway to the patio.

The altar at the end of the aisle arched above everyone's head, and held flowers and more lights. Everything was perfection, and if Griffin ever found someone he wanted to spend the rest of his life with, he was going to hire Travis's wife to plan the wedding.

Janelle's mother and father came out of the house, and Millie said, "It's almost time. Everyone line up with your escort, please." She moved among the wedding party, which consisted of all the Johnson brothers, the four ranch hands which worked the ranch with them, and Janelle's brothers on the male side. Her sisters, the sisters-in-law, and some of her friends completed the bridal party, and Griffin moved to the front of the line, his elbow already cocked for Libby.

"Evening, Griffin," she said pleasantly, and Griffin looked at her. She really was beautiful, and he wished they had more in common. But going out with her had been boring, and while he'd thought there was a spark of attraction the first time they'd had dinner together, it had fizzled by the end of the night.

He hadn't given up though, and he'd tried taking her to a spring dance in town. A movie. For a hike. In the end, she'd said, "I don't think this is working," and Griffin hadn't been able to argue.

It was his most amicable break-up, which was fortunate, as he had to walk her down the aisle for this wedding.

"Good to see you, Libby."

She smiled, and Griffin was proud of himself for being cordial and kind. Inside, he felt like someone had taken a melon-baller to his most vital organs, hollowing them out one painful scoop at a time.

Russ stood down at the end of the aisle, the arch over his head. Mille went to check on Janelle, and Griffin overheard her say, "We're waiting? One more guest?" She sounded stressed, and Griffin was ready to get this show on the road. It wasn't exactly cool the last week of May, despite the upgrades on the patio and the shade from the tents that had been set up.

"She's here," Janelle said. "She's coming around now."

"Great," Millie said. "Phone, please. You don't need that at the altar."

Griffin smiled at her no-nonsense tone, as he really liked Millie. Travis had built them a house right inside the entrance of Chestnut Ranch, and Griffin found it downright charming. This spring, Millie had put in rose bushes and let the entire side yard grow wild with bluebonnets, Indian paintbrush, and other native Texas wildflowers.

"She's right there," Janelle said, and Griffin looked to where Janelle nodded to the right of the wedding party.

His breath froze in his lungs as the gorgeous, curvy, brunette he'd been communicating with for a couple of months rounded the corner of the house.

Toni Beardall had an anxious look on her face, and she held up one hand as if to say, *Sorry, Janelle.*

She paused near the back row, looking for a seat, and she had to climb over several people to one lone seat in the middle of the row.

"Sorry," she said. "Sorry. Excuse me."

Griffin couldn't stop grinning. If he'd have known Toni was going to be at the wedding, he wouldn't have been dreading it quite so much.

"Do you know her?" he asked Libby. Janelle had held the wedding for her. Only for a moment, but it meant something.

"Sure," Libby said. "She's one of Janelle's clients. A good one too. Refers tons of people to us, and she runs a camp a little bit north of here, where we handle all their legal issues."

"Ah, got it," Griffin said, tucking Libby's arm closer to his side as the wedding march began.

"Here we go, people," Millie said. "Eyes up. Smiles on. Remember, this is about Russ and Janelle."

Griffin did what Millie said, because he was leading the party out. The guests stood and turned toward the aisle, and Griffin's eyes latched onto Toni.

A smile brightened her face when she saw him, and she lifted her fingers in a little, waggly wave.

Griffin couldn't look away from her, and he stumbled slightly. Panic reared in his throat, and he yelped.

"Griffin," Libby hissed at him, but what did she expect him to do?

He reached out to steady himself against the chair on the back row, embarrassment spiraling through him. Had he just yelped during the procession?

He faced the front, his goal in sight, and Russ's grin said he hadn't messed up too badly.

Griffin felt like every eye was on him, even after he passed them. But really, it was Toni's gaze that had seared him.

He led Libby to her spot, almost right behind the pastor who'd come out to the ranch to perform the ceremony, and circled around to his side. Only a few feet from Russ now, Griffin calmed a bit more.

He'd done what he'd said he'd do, and all he needed to do now was observe the nuptials. He'd hand Russ the diamond when it was time, and then he could eat.

His eyes moved instantly to Toni, and a flush moved through his body when he found her looking at him too. He couldn't believe his luck, and all the legends he'd heard about meeting the perfect woman at a wedding rushed into his mind.

Maybe, he thought to himself.

He'd never once confessed his feelings for Toni to anyone. Rex, of course, had suspected, but Griffin thought he'd done a good job keeping everything under wraps.

She hadn't left the camp, as Rex had suspected. Griffin had communicated professionally with her. She'd hired him without an in-person interview because he'd worked for the past two summers at Camp Clear Creek. He'd read all the emails she'd sent, and he was packed and ready to leave in the morning.

Seeing her tonight was just an added benefit.

"Dearly beloved," the preacher said, and Griffin tore his eyes from the gorgeous brunette in the back row as all the guests settled back into their seats.

The preacher talked about love throughout the ages, and Griffin found himself wanting that sort of romance in his life. Maybe he'd always been a bit of a romantic, and he was glad he wasn't standing next to Rex. He could practically hear his brother's scoffing in his head.

Russ and Janelle exchanged vows, Griffin handed off the diamond at the right time, and the preacher finally said, "I now pronounce you husband and wife." Russ grinned and dipped Janelle as the crowd cheered.

Griffin laughed and clapped along with everyone else, and Russ turned toward their guests and lifted Janelle's hand into the air.

Her two daughters preceded them back down the aisle, and Griffin had twenty minutes before dinner would be served. During that time, he'd agreed to help Millie move the chairs out and bring tables in, putting the chairs around them for dinner.

All the groomsmen did, and Janelle took a microphone from Millie. "Thank you to everyone," she said. "We love you all, and we're glad you're here to share our special day with us." She beamed up at Russ, and Griffin could feel their love penetrate the entire congregation.

"It's a buffet," Russ said. "So let's eat."

Griffin stayed on the edge of the other guests, tracking Toni as she said hello to several people he didn't know, and then made her way over to Janelle. She hugged her friend and then Russ, and then Toni looked around.

Griffin wanted to step right to her side and sit by her for the rest of the evening. His mouth was far too dry, and his palms much too sweaty, a sure indication that he *really* liked this woman.

He wove through the crowd, determined to be at least a little bit like Rex today, and take control of his own future.

"Hey," he said, easing to Toni's side. "Looking for a friend to sit by?" He cursed himself for the words the moment they left his mouth. A friend? He didn't want that.

"Hey, Griffin." Toni grinned at him and stepped into his embrace. "Wasn't that a beautiful wedding?"

He held her tight, pure bliss moving through him. He released her sooner than he would've liked, but he reminded himself that she was his boss, and he couldn't give away too much of how he felt right this instant.

"Sure was," he said. "Are you staying to eat?"

"Definitely," Toni said. "This is going to be our last good meal for a while." She trilled out a laugh, and Griffin sure did like the feminine sound of it.

"Tell me you didn't hire Isaac to cook again," he said. "Because we almost starved last year." He chuckled with her, and Toni shook her head.

"Nope, I got a new guy this year. Dalton Walters."

"Is he good?" Griffin steered her toward the end of the buffet line, intending to spend the next several hours with her. Rex caught sight of him, but Griffin ignored the grin on his brother's face.

"Better than Isaac," Toni said, picking up a plate. "Is there dancing at this wedding?"

"Yes," Griffin said. "Later, after dinner and cake."

Toni put a round of filet mignon on her plate. "Save me a dance?"

"You betcha," he said, hoping he sounded casual and friendly. He'd definitely need to look up the rules for dating at Camp Clear Creek, though something told him Toni would be off-limits once the job started.

CHAPTER TWO

Toni Beardall loved weddings. She loved fancy dresses and good food and men in cowboy hats. She had a strict no-dating policy for herself, though, and she hadn't been out with anyone seriously for years.

She had plenty of friends she spent time with, some of which were men, and she was happy enough with her life the way it was. She didn't have any children, and she'd been married once before.

Once, in her opinion, was enough.

But she did like basking in the love of other people, especially people dear to her. And Janelle Stokes—Johnson now—was especially special to Toni.

She'd helped Toni during a crucial time of her life, and they'd become lifelong friends as Toni went through her divorce, aka the worst experience of her existence.

The presence of Griffin Johnson just behind her,

putting shrimp and scallops on his plate, warmed her in a way she hadn't experienced in a while.

He was dangerous to her health, she knew that. He made her want to abandon her male-free lifestyle and find out if maybe her first marriage had just been a horrible mistake.

In her job with teens, she told them not to dwell on the past. Not to wallow in the mistakes they'd made. But to move forward, with a new plan, and learn to let go of the past.

She counseled them to do that, but actually doing it herself? Toni was terrible at following her own advice, that was for sure.

"Other than the food," Griffin said. "Is everything ready at camp? Do you need any help with anything?" He spoke in a smooth, delicious voice that reminded Toni of the dark chocolate she loved. She ate a piece every day, usually just before bed, to remind herself that life was good and worth living.

"I think we're set," she said. "I hired a new activities director this year. I think you'll like her."

"Yeah?" Griffin asked. "Is she going to do actual activities? Last year, Amber had mostly—"

"Crafts," they said together. "I know," Toni answered. "And yes, she's going to do actual activities. Annie's a former director for a Boys and Girls Club out of New Jersey."

"New Jersey," Griffin said. "Wow. What's she doin' down here? She knows she'll need to wear boots, right?" He chuckled and adjusted his plate in his hand to add two rolls on top of everything else he'd piled on.

"Annie's great," she said, not wanting to give away the woman's secrets. "She moved here a year or so ago, and she's been working as the activities director for a charter school."

"So she'll have things for both boys and girls."

"Definitely," Toni said. "I know that was a problem last year."

"Yeah, my fifteen-year-old boys really didn't want to make furry flip flops."

Toni laughed, put a pat of butter on her plate, and turned toward the sea of tables. Janelle hadn't assigned seats, and Toni had been lost for a minute, wondering where to sit, before Griffin had joined her.

Now, though, she let him lead the way through the maze and to a table where a man and a couple were already sitting. "Hey," Griffin said. "This is Toni Beardall, my boss. Toni, these two are my brothers. Travis and Seth. And Seth's wife, Jenna."

"Nice to meet you," Toni said as she set her plate down on the table. She sat next, smiling at his family.

"Your boss?" Travis asked.

"At Camp Clear Creek," Griffin said. "She's the camp director." He smiled at her, but Toni didn't really like being introduced as his boss. She definitely was his boss, though, and how else was he supposed to introduce her?

"How do you know Janelle?" Seth asked, and Toni's heart skipped a beat.

"She handled my divorce," Toni said smoothly, watching

Griffin. He didn't flinch at all. "Years ago. We've stayed friends."

"Oh, that's great," Jenna said. "Are you remarried?"

"No, ma'am," Toni said, keeping her smile hitched in place.

"Are you a temporary employee at the camp?" Seth asked. "Like Griffin?"

"I actually work there year-round," she said. "We do fall camps, as well as winter expeditions." She took a sip of the pink lemonade on the table, which was tart and sweet at the same time. It also added a lovely color to the tablescape, and Toni set her glass down. "I'm a counselor for teens in the slower times. I have an office in Horseshoe Bay."

"Oh, I see," Seth said. The conversation was easy, and Toni participated as they talked about the area where she lived, the Texas Highland Lakes, and the horses around the ranch.

Soon enough, dinner ended, and a woman spoke into the microphone again. "It's time to get your dancing shoes on," she said, a bright smile on her face. "We're going to have the father-daughter dance, and the mother-son dance first."

She turned, clearly looking for someone. "Janelle? Russ? Get your parents and get out here."

They both stood from the table behind Toni, and they got the right parent and took them to the patio, where the soft lights cast everything in a romantic glow.

Unconsciously, she swayed with them to the music, and then she stood when the woman in charge said, "All right, everyone. Find yourself a partner and join the happy couple."

"That's my cue," Travis said. "Come on, guys. Millie doesn't want the dancing to be a flop."

Jenna and Seth went with him, but Toni picked up her plate. "And that's my cue to leave," she said, flashing Griffin a smile. "I'm tired, and I have a long drive to get home."

"We have to be there bright and early in the morning," he agreed. He took her plate from her. "I'll walk you out."

Toni wanted to tell him he didn't need to do that, but he'd put their plates somewhere and guided her toward the walking path that led around the house before she could find the words.

Small, knee-high torches had been staked in the ground along the path, and Toni loved everything about this ranch. "This is your ranch, right?" she asked as they left the celebration behind.

"Russ is technically the one who runs the ranch," Griffin said. "But yes, all five of us boys own part of it."

"Twenty percent?" she asked.

"Yep."

A sea of cars and trucks spread before them, and Toni sighed. "I was late, and I had to park way down the lane." She looked at Griffin. "It's fine. I can manage."

"What kind of cowboy gentleman would I be if I left you to walk in the dark all the way down the lane?" He shook his head. "I'd never be able to face my momma again, that's for sure."

"All right." Toni wove through the cars in the driveway,

Griffin right behind her. Once they got out on the road,
though, he stepped to her side.

"It's so beautiful out here," she said. "The whole sky is
just wide open." She looked up at the stars, drinking them
all in. They held special significance for her, but she wasn't
going to tell Griffin that story quite yet.

Just the fact that she thought there would come a time
where she would share something so personal about
herself with him surprised her. She cut him a look out of
the corner of her eye and found him gazing at the
stars too.

"I love Texas," he said with a sigh. "Do you think you
can see a sky like this anywhere else?"

Toni heard the appreciation in his voice, and she liked
this softer side of the cowboy she'd known for a couple of
years.

"Maybe," she said.

His hand brushed hers, and her pulse rioted. But he
didn't try to hold her hand. Of course he wouldn't, and the
fact that Toni even thought he might was ridiculous.

She pulled her keys out of her dress pocket and clicked
the unlock button. The headlights on her SUV flashed, and
she needlessly said, "I'm right there."

Griffin guided her the last several steps, his hand big
and warm on the small of her back. Toni carried at least
twenty extra pounds—probably thirty, if she was going to
be completely honest—and she normally flinched away
from a male touch.

But with Griffin, she wanted to lean in. He reached for
the door handle and opened her door for her. "It was so

good to see you tonight, Toni," he said, and she was probably imagining the husky quality in his voice.

"Thanks for walking me all the way out here," she said. "I'm not normally late."

"I know." He gazed down at her, and the light from her car spilled onto his face. He was made of pure handsomeness, and as the moment lengthened between them, Toni grew a bit more antsy.

"Anyway," she said. "See you tomorrow." Without thinking, she tipped up on her toes and kissed his cheek. Fire burned through her as her mind screamed at her that kissing wasn't a very boss-like thing to do.

Her heart nudged her to kiss him again.

She stalled as Griffin's hand slid along her waist, holding her right in front of him. His other hand moved to her face, tucking her hair behind her ear. "Good-night, Toni." He bent down and touched his lips to hers, and Toni sighed right into him.

He'd taken an awkward moment and made it sweet. She wanted him to kiss her for a lot longer, but he pulled away almost as quickly as he'd leaned down. He fell back a step, and the shadows gathered on his face.

"See you tomorrow," he said, and Toni ducked into her SUV, her face burning. Every cell in her body burned, actually, and it wasn't until she was on the highway heading north that she realized what had happened.

"You kissed him," she said to the dark stretch of road in front of her. "What in the world...?"

She'd kissed him, and she'd *wanted* to kiss him, and she had no idea what any of that meant. Not for what would happen when she saw him tomorrow. And not for what it meant for her life overall.

She hadn't kissed anyone in a very long time, and the warmth and care in his touch lasted with her all the way back to Horseshoe Bay. As she went inside her house and shed her dress and shoes, she wondered if she should open the door to her heart.

If she did, would Griffin walk through it? Or had he just been caught up in the wedding magic? The beauty of the stars?

She didn't know, but what she did know was that she couldn't wait to find out.

❧

TONI ARRIVED AT THE ADMINISTRATION CABIN AT CAMP Clear Creek by six-thirty a.m. The camp counselors were supposed to be there by eight, and all other personnel, like the cooks, janitors, maintenance crew, her activities director and her aides, by nine.

They'd have a staff meeting that took them to lunchtime, when Toni would sign for the fifty pizzas she'd ordered. Her stress level was high, but it was accompanied by a general sense of excitement for another summer filled with campers.

She loved her job at Clear Creek, and she couldn't wait for the first group of kids to arrive on Monday. Just two days, and over them, her counselors would make sure their group of cabins were clean and ready for habitation. They'd go through the files for the first group of kids, a two-week camp that focused on outdoor activities as well as skill development.

Every camp was a little bit different, and Camp Clear Creek offered everything from boys-only weeks to high adventure camps for those who wanted all of the hiking, canoeing, and fishing they could get. They had girls-only camps, and arborist camps. They had week-long camps, two-week camps, and three-week camps, and they'd run through the end of August.

The three months in the summer was the busiest and most fulfilling time for Toni, as after that, she ran weekend camps through November, and then focused on her counseling for a couple of months, only doing an eight-day camp over the Christmas holidays.

Toni set out packets with her counselor's names on them, pausing for a moment when she put Griffin's on the table.

Now, in the light of day, she couldn't believe she'd kissed him, and she hoped today wouldn't be awkward.

She set out the muffins she'd bought that morning, along with a tray of the best sausage kolaches the Hill Country had to offer. Paired with juice and milk, the breakfast meeting for the counselors was set and ready.

Only a few minutes later, the first couple of people began to walk through the doors. Toni knew them all, as she'd personally hired them. They had a high return rate for counselors, and about sixty percent of the people coming that summer had been a camp counselor at Clear Creek for at least one year.

She knew the moment Griffin walked in, and it wasn't

only because of his sexy cowboy hat or the way his spicy cologne called to her female side.

He devoured her with a single look, ducked his head, and stepped over to a group of men who'd all worked at Clear Creek last year.

She chatted and moved around the room, getting to everyone, always keeping her eye on Griffin. When she finally approached their group, it was almost time to start.

"Hello, fellas," she said. "Glad to have you back with us this year."

"Couldn't be more excited."

"Glad to be here."

"This is my favorite summer job."

Toni looked at Griffin, who hooked his thumb over his shoulder. "Can I talk to you for a second?"

Her heart pounded as she nodded. "Go help yourself to muffins and kolaches," she told the others. "We'll get started in a minute."

Griffin retreated outside to the porch of the admin cabin, and Toni followed him. Was he going to quit? Rebuke her for kissing him? Tell her he didn't like her "like that" but he appreciated the gesture?

He retreated all the way to the porch railing before turning back to her. Toni's heart made literal booms in her chest as she waited for him to say something. He was the one who'd asked to talk.

"I just have a quick question," he said.

"Shoot." Toni folded her arms, hoping with everything inside her that she could answer it.

CHAPTER THREE

Now that Griffin had Toni alone, his brain didn't fire right. He'd been thinking about her for twelve straight hours, barely able to stop even while asleep. His stomach twisted, and his feet shuffled through the nerves.

"I'm just wondering what the dating rules are here at camp," he said.

"Dating rules?" she repeated. "Same as always. Boys and girls aren't allowed to be in each other's cabins." She gestured to the door separating them from the rest of the camp counselors. "We'll go over all of that in our meeting this morning."

"Oh, yeah, I know." Wow, he was an idiot. He hadn't phrased it right, and now he had to ask a second time. "Not for the kids," he said slowly. "I meant, you know, for the adults." He lifted his eyes to hers, diving all the way into her dark depths. "I meant, what are the rules for us... and...dating."

"Oh." Her eyes widened. "Us."

"Yeah," he said, taking a tiny step forward and reaching for her hand. "I thought last night was really...beautiful." Kissing her had felt oh-so-right, even if he'd only done it for a moment.

He'd watched her taillights disappear into the night, and then he'd just stared down the road where she'd gone until Rex had texted him, asking him where he'd disappeared to.

Out walking, he'd said, and then he'd hurried down the path to the bridges that crossed Chestnut Springs so he wouldn't be a liar. But really, he'd been out thinking about Toni.

"You did?" Toni asked.

Griffin narrowed his eyes at her. "You didn't?"

"I just...I figured you'd think it was a mistake."

Confusion riddled through him. "Why would kissing you—?" He glanced at the door and lowered his voice. "Why would that be a mistake?"

"I don't know," she said, but she shifted uncomfortably too, and there was definitely something there that she did know. She just didn't want to tell him. "I—" She silenced as the door opened and Cody Blackburn filled the entryway.

"Oh. Sorry. I didn't realize you were busy." He shot a glance at Griffin, who ducked his head so his cowboy hat would conceal his face. Heat burned in his neck and cheeks, and he had no idea what to do about it.

It was summer in Texas, so Mother Nature wasn't going to help cool him off. Maybe if he went down and jumped in the lake, that would help. But only his internal temperature, not his humiliation and embarrassment in front of Toni.

When will that end? he wondered. He'd already tripped in front of her too.

"I'll be right in," Toni said, checking the watch she wore on her wrist. "It's time to start, isn't it?" She sighed as Cody closed the door. She met Griffin's eye again, and thankfully, she didn't look disgusted or annoyed.

"Technically," she said. "It's against camp policy for counselors to have a romantic relationship."

"Technically?"

"I don't typically enforce that rule," she said. "I've had other counselors see each other, start relationships, that kind of thing." A wash of annoyance did cross her expression then. "I just tell them not to let it interfere with their work. They're still not allowed in each other's cabins, just like the teens. And it has to be discreet."

"Discreet," Griffin said, thinking he could abide by all of those rules.

She took a step closer too, her dark eyes shooting sparks at him. Griffin had always wanted a huge fireworks show with a woman, and he'd never had it. But with Toni, there was definitely a crackling electrical storm brewing between them.

"Very discreet," she said quietly. She backed up as if he'd caught fire, and she didn't want to get sucked into the flames. "Now, I run a tight ship, Mister Johnson, and we're now two minutes past the start time of our meeting."

"Yes, ma'am," he said, reaching to open the door for her. She stepped inside, and Griffin followed, a tiny smile on his heart that he didn't allow to form on his face. She wanted very discreet?

He could do that.

"Ladies and gentlemen," Toni called. "If you'll find your seats, please, we'll get started."

Griffin loved the vibrancy and energy of the first day at Camp Clear Creek, and the buzz in the air right now was nothing compared to what would flow through camp on Monday, when the first campers arrived.

He felt more alive as he threaded his way through the tables and chairs to the spot with his name on it than he had in the last ten months of working the ranch. He loved Chestnut Ranch; that wasn't the issue.

He worked enough jobs there that he was never bored. He loved his brothers, and all of his new sisters-in-law. He loved the Thursday dinners with his parents, and walking down Victory Street to get something from the Edible Neighborhood Jenna and Seth had established.

He just felt...stifled by all of it at the same time. Bored. Ready for something else in his life.

And he knew what else—a wife and family of his own.

He looked up at Toni as she started talking again, and he opened his folder along with everyone else. She'd changed the training from last year, and Griffin was grateful for that. He didn't need the same spiel year after year, even if the woman giving it was gorgeous.

He did find his attention wandering from the material to the presenter, because she had a beautiful voice, and beautiful hair, and beautiful curves...

"Griffin, will you read that section?"

He blinked as Toni looked at him, her beautiful eyes now trained on him. His heart sprinted in his chest, and he couldn't admit he hadn't been paying attention. Thankfully, the woman sitting next to him cleared her throat and pointed at her own paper.

He quickly found the spot on his and started reading about curfews. "Camp attendees should be out of the cabins by seven-fifteen for the flag raising ceremony and breakfast. Camp counselors will need to check on their assigned cabins no later than seven o'clock a.m. to assist with this endeavor.

"All cabins will be responsible for at least one flag raising ceremony during their stay at Camp Clear Creek. Counselors should work with youth to help them with the ceremony and morning devotional, but they should not take over and plan or do it all themselves. Camp Clear Creek is committed to training leaders and providing teens with the opportunities they need to develop leadership skills."

He looked up. "Should I keep going?"

"Just one more paragraph, please," Toni said without looking up.

"All campers, including counselors should be in their cabins by ten-thirty p.m. Quiet time begins at eleven p.m. and goes until six-thirty a.m. The only exception is those campers, counselors, or groups who have permission to go hammocking, though quiet time hours still apply."

He drew in a deep breath and looked at Toni again. She was smiling now, and Griffin couldn't help feeling like he'd just solved the world's hunger problem. "Thank you," she said. "Curfew is one of those things I feel like we have to constantly enforce. I don't want it to be something we're frustrated about, though, so just do the best you can. Sometimes nighttime is the greatest time for these kids. They do need time to just talk and build friendships."

She paused for a moment, looking around at the two dozen or so counselors. "How many of you went to camp when you were a kid?"

Griffin glanced around as almost every hand went up. His didn't, though. His parents hadn't sent him or any of his brothers to summer camp. The ranch *was* summer camp, hosted right at home by his gruff father. Daddy was really a softie underneath the harsh voice and unrelenting demands. Momma made chore lists and expected her sons to learn how to run a household too.

Because of her, Griffin could wash his own clothes, sew on buttons, and put dinner on the table. It might not be a fancy dinner, but he could feed himself and others if he had to.

"Almost all of us," Toni said. "And how many of you loved it?"

Most of the hands stayed up, and Toni smiled. Griffin's pulse skipped ahead of itself with the curve of her mouth. Oh, that mouth. He'd tasted it for just a few seconds last night, not nearly long enough for him.

But he'd been surprised at his own actions, and even more shocked that Toni didn't slap him away. She'd kissed him back, if only for a moment, and he sincerely hoped he could be discreet enough to build a relationship with her that would allow him to kiss her again.

Longer next time, he told himself. A lot longer.

Toni was talking about friendships and the importance the experiences here at camp could have on the teens that had signed up to come. "We've been fully booked for three months," she said. "This is a popular place to come, and I know that's because of you." She beamed around at all of them. "I really appreciate you, and I'm here for you this summer." Her eyes landed on his, and Griffin wondered if her words could have another meaning.

"Now, the rest of our staff will be here in a few minutes, and we're going to do introductions and a getting-to-know-you game then."

Griffin groaned internally, but someone in the room actually let the sound out of their mouth. He chuckled along with several others, including Toni.

"I know," she said. "They're not my favorite either. But, just like the teens we have coming here to build memories and bonds, we need to do the same."

As if on cue, the door opened and a woman entered. She froze when she discovered she had almost thirty people looking at her. "Oh," she said, her eyes widening.

"Come in," Toni said. "We're breaking up right now."

The woman came in, and she looked vaguely familiar to Griffin. She had dirty blonde hair that barely brushed her shoulders and thick black-framed glasses perched on her nose. She smiled at Toni, who went to greet her as several counselors got to their feet, Griffin included.

The only reason he kept looking at the new woman was because she was now talking to Toni, and that woman was like the sun to his planet. He revolved around her. He was attracted to her. She pulled him in with the magnetic force of her personality.

She turned toward him, as if the sun could feel the gaze of a distant planet, and gestured for him to come over. "Griffin, she says she knows you."

"I thought you looked familiar," he said, extending his hand to shake hers.

"I should hope so," the woman said, sending confusion through Griffin.

He glanced at Toni. "I'm sorry," he said as gently as he could. "I don't remember your name."

She scoffed and looked at Toni. "It's just like these handsome cowboys, isn't it? They go out with you, promise you stuff, and then forget you even existed." She gave Griffin a violent glare and walked away, leaving him dumbfounded—and having nowhere else to look but at Toni.

"Who is she?" he asked.

"Lilly Mae Moore," Toni said, falling back a step. She scanned the length of his body, as if she could sense whether Lilly Mae had told the truth or not. "You don't remember her? She says you went out for six months."

"That is not true," Griffin said, shaking his head. He felt Toni retreating from him, and he'd just gotten close enough to talk to her.

"Toni," someone said, and she let herself get distracted.

"Excuse me," she said, all business. She walked away, crushing Griffin's heart with every step she took in those sexy cowgirl boots.

"Lilly Mae Moore," Griffin mumbled to himself. He'd

gone out with her maybe five or six times, total. Over the course of a month or two, not six.

And what in the world had he promised her? He couldn't think of a single thing.

"Griffin," someone said, and he turned around to see one of his friends from last year. An instant smile lit his face, and he stepped into a big bear hug from Ian Traverse. "It's good to see another cowboy." Ian laughed, and Griffin joined in.

At least not everyone here was going to hate him.

CHAPTER FOUR

Toni refused to let herself glance around for Griffin. She knew where he was without looking anyway, and she hated those people who always seemed to be searching for someone better to talk to than the person they were with. She had to manage all of these people, all the personalities, all the idiosyncrasies, all the schedules, the sicknesses, the little affairs, of every person at this camp.

The health of the teenagers, whether that be their mental, physical, or spiritual health, mattered a great deal to Toni. To the parents sending their child to Camp Clear Creek, she was basically telling them she'd watch out for their kids and their well-being. She took that responsibility very seriously.

So she listened to Caroline McDuff, one of her returning counselors who wanted to talk about a couple of weeks off that she needed in July.

Already? Toni thought, but she nodded as she made a note of it on her clipboard. "I'll still need you to email those dates," she said. "And I'll have a form going out tonight for stuff like this, and you'll need to fill that out too." She looked at Caroline, a flash of feeling like a geriatric dinosaur moving through her as the perky twenty-something smiled and nodded.

But Caroline was a great counselor, and she worked really well with fourteen-year-old girls, who were a special breed of human not all adults could handle.

"I can do that," Caroline said. "Sorry, Toni. I didn't know my mother was going to get engaged and want to have a wedding in less than two months." And she didn't sound happy about it either.

"Oh, wow," Toni said, surprise moving through her. "Less than two months?" Griffin moved through her peripheral vision, and it took every ounce of willpower Toni possessed not to track him as he chatted with Ian.

"Right?" Caroline said, throwing her hands up. "Literally every person I've told about is surprised, and yet, my mother doesn't get it."

Toni had some things to say about her mother too, but she just smiled. "I'm sure you can have that cycle off. I just need to be reminded."

"Thanks so much," Caroline gushed, tucking her blonde hair behind her ear. "I'm so glad to be back." She moved away from Toni, who suddenly didn't have anyone to talk to. She hated being in the middle of the crowd but still a satellite, no one orbiting her. She was always looking for something or someone to attach to.

She looked down at her clipboard, her thoughts consumed by Griffin Johnson and that kiss from last night. How could he not remember a woman he'd dated? Her heart re-iced over the part he'd managed to thaw. He was just like all the other cowboys in Texas. Good-looking, and boy, did he know it. Charming, and he knew that too. Ready to steal her heart, crush it in his fist, and throw the weeping, wailing organ back to her as he left town.

No, thank you.

She drew in a deep breath and faced the room. "All right, everyone," she called in a loud voice. "Let's come back together." She looked around for her new chef, her new head janitor, the housekeeping supervisor, and her new activities director.

"Annie," Toni said. "Marco, Dalton, and Marion, can you four come up front, please?" She waited several seconds while everyone settled down into their spots, including all the maintenance people, the part-time help she'd hired for lawn care, the servers she'd provide for breakfast and dinner and aides for the activities. They sat in rows in the back of the room, squished together like sardines.

Wow, it took a lot of people to run a summer camp.

"Thanks for coming this morning, y'all." Toni beamed out at everyone. "I realize I know everyone, but that a lot of you might not know anyone here. I wanted to introduce some key people to the counselors, as they'll have to work with them quite a lot." She smiled at the four she'd brought up front.

"First, we still have Hailey Frost with us as the assistant

camp director." As it stood, Toni wouldn't know up from down without Hailey, and she led the applause for the woman who'd been at her side for the past five years. Hailey smiled, her teeth perfectly straight to go with her curled blonde hair and blue eyes.

Toni had found her to be a bit Barbie-ish the first time they'd met, but Hailey was a hard worker, with a great vision for the camp. She understood budget restraints, and she'd given Toni a lot of help and support over the time they'd worked together.

Not only that, but Toni and Hailey had become good friends. She'd attended Hailey's sister's wedding last spring as her plus-one, and they went to lunch regularly outside of work.

"As you know," she continued. "We had to say good-bye to Isaac last year, as he got married and went on to other things." Toni smiled, because while she'd liked Isaac, he wasn't great at cooking for a crowd. "But we welcome Dalton Walters as our new head chef." She began to clap, pleased when everyone else did. "He comes to us from a beach resort off the coast of South Carolina, so he knows how to serve hot food for a lot of people." And he did too. Toni had asked him to demonstrate a breakfast he'd prepare for a hundred people, and four hours later, she'd fed her entire neighborhood.

She'd asked for feedback, and she'd actually booked two weddings for Dalton from the people on her street who had daughters getting married. He was that good.

Dalton lifted his hand in a wave, his grin spreading from ear to ear. He was a good guy, probably fifteen or so years older than Toni. He'd worked in the restaurant industry for thirty years, and he said he was ready for a change.

He had no biological children of his own, but his wife had three grown children, with grandkids, and they all lived here in Texas. So they'd come here, and it was Toni's blessing to be able to have Dalton at Camp Clear Creek.

"Next we have Annie Lundberg," she said. "I know one of our biggest complaints last year was our activities. Or lack thereof. But Annie is amazing. She worked at the Boys and Girls Club in New Jersey for five years before coming to Texas, where she's been working as an activities coordinator at a charter school. And now we get to have her."

Another round of applause for the brunette who would surely make Camp Clear Creek stand out because of the stellar activities she had planned. "I've upped the budget for activities too," Toni said. "Everyone should be happy this year."

Another introduction, this time to Marco Perez, who would be running their janitorial and groundskeeping staff. "He has thirty people to oversee," Toni said. "They're all part-time, either morning, afternoon, or evening shifts. Marco is only here in the afternoon and evening." She scanned the crowd. "Where's Kiki?"

The strawberry blonde stood up from the back row and waved her hand. "If you need something dire in the morning, Kiki Malone is your gal." She smiled at Kiki. "She reports to Marco. If there's something with the paths, the lake, you find poisonous plants, a toilet backs up, someone spills their root beer, anything maintenance or janitorial or grounds—Marco."

And thank goodness. Last year, Toni had done a lot of the maintenance management, but this year, she'd found room in the budget for a full-time person besides herself.

"And that leaves our head housekeeping supervisor, Marion Whitman. She'll assist with cabin chores, laundry, rec room cleaning, clean-up after meals, as well as run some classes for our campers."

More applause, and Toni was tired already.

"Okay," she said. "I think those are the major players. We're thrilled to have a lot of part-time summer help this year, and we need you all to make Camp Clear Creek the best camp in the Texas Highland Lakes area."

She consulted her clipboard, but really, she was ready to slip out of this huge main building and go down the path a bit to the cabin behind it. Her cabin. The one she lived in from May to December.

Her phone buzzed against her thigh, and she knew who it would be. Her mother. Toni's pulse bounced around a little. Her parents were getting to be elderly. There was no other nice way to say it, and they needed help. Her father had developed pneumonia over the winter, and while he'd been feeling better for a couple of months now, he still struggled.

And Mother struggled to remember to take her medicine, and Toni fielded half a dozen calls from them each day, asking questions about what they should have for lunch to what the nutritional properties of cucumbers were, to where Toni had put their weighted blankets when she'd come to stay with them in March.

"It's time for our getting-to-know-you game," she said. Half the crowd groaned—Griffin was in that group—and the other half perked right up. Toni had learned long ago that she couldn't please everyone, and she'd mostly stopped trying.

"Come on," she said. "Everyone up. You need something to write with and one of these papers." She handed stacks to the four people still up front with her. "We're going to play Bingo with this when we're done, and I have amazing prizes."

"What are they?" someone called out, and Toni turned back to the crowd. Carefully, slowly, she reached under the top paper on her clipboard. "Among other things I will not name at this time, I have two envelopes here." She held them up. Neither had a stitch of writing on them. "One contains a hundred-dollar bill. The other is three paid vacation days."

A roar moved through the crowd, and even the naysayers were arming themselves with something to write with and clamoring for a paper now, Griffin included.

Annoyance ran through Toni that she kept coming back to that cowboy. Yes, he was handsome. Drop-dead gorgeous was a better description. He outshined every other cowboy in the room, that was for dang sure, and her heart bumped out extra beats as she watched him take a paper.

"Write your name at the top," she said. "Someone else will be playing your board."

"Wait, what?" someone asked.

"I don't trust any of you," she yelled with a smile. "So get your board set up. Someone else will mark it. If you win, you'll both get a prize."

The noise with almost a hundred people in the room made Toni want to run for the hills. Her phone buzzed again, ratcheting up her anxiety level. If she didn't answer her parents, they'd eventually call the police, and Sheriff Mittingham didn't need to go find her dad's pills. Or his slippers. Or the television remote—which her father had actually called on the police department to do.

She quickly explained how this game worked, and said, "You have twenty minutes to meet as many people as you can. Get to know them. Put a name next to as many items on your chart as you can." She glanced around at all the eager faces, so glad she'd chosen to do this activity. "Go!"

Chaos erupted, and pencils scribbled, and Toni grinned. As if drawn to shore by a lighthouse beam, her eyes landed on Griffin. He looked at her at the same time, and lightning crackled between them.

She ducked her head, breaking the connection, and stepped over to Hailey. "Nice job," she said. "I think you've properly motivated them to participate."

Toni grinned at her. "I need to make a quick call."

"No problem," Hailey said, watching the sight in front of her with a smile on her face.

"Make sure they don't kill each other." Toni laughed as she left the fray of the big, main room and escaped outside. The tranquility of the Texas landscape surrounded her, and she took a deep breath of it.

She was glad to be able to have so many good people surrounding her, and she pulled her phone from her jeans pocket. Sure enough, her mother had called three times. She probably had three new voicemail messages too, and Toni sighed as she tapped and swiped to get a call connected.

"Mother," she said when her mom answered. "Remember how I'm doing my camp orientation meetings today?"

"Oh, dear," her mother said. "I forgot. It's just that Daddy's lost his puzzle. You know, the one with the buffalo on it?"

Toni pinched the bridge of her nose and took another lungful of oxygen. "Buffalo, Mother?"

"Yeah, and the big mountains. He can't remember the name of them, and heaven knows my memory is like a block of Swiss cheese."

"The Grand Tetons," Toni said. "It's not in the cupboard with the games?"

"The cupboard with the games," her mother said as if she hadn't thought to check there. "Let me look."

Toni waited while her mom's breathing came through the line. She sounded winded, but the house wasn't that big. They didn't go upstairs anymore, and Toni had closed off all the bedrooms up there and told them to stay on the main level. As far as she knew, they obeyed her.

She thought of her father looking for that puzzle. If he hadn't checked the game cupboard, where had he checked? He'd turned eighty-two last winter, and Toni supposed he could've looked in the game cupboard and not seen the puzzle.

"It's here," Mother said, and Toni breathed a sigh of relief.

"Great, Mom," she said. "I have to go. I'll stop by tonight after everything ends, okay?"

"Okay, dear," Mother said. "Have fun at your meetings."

"Love you." Toni ended the call, wondering if the words "fun" and "meeting" could go together in the same sentence.

She turned back to the main building as a cry of delight rose into the air, and she decided that yes, they could. And Toni, who might be crazy for thinking so, couldn't wait to get back inside and join her people.

You just want to see Griffin, she thought, and well, she couldn't argue with herself.

CHAPTER FIVE

G riffin looked around his cabin, a smile infusing into his soul. He loved Camp Clear Creek, and one of the reasons was that he got a place to himself. Maybe he wouldn't be too lonely when Rex moved out of the house they'd bought together.

His fiancée lived across town in a cute little house with their daughter, and Rex would surely move in with her once they got remarried.

Griffin sat down on the bed, grateful for the four-inch mattress topper he'd brought with him. The beds here definitely left something to be desired. His one-room cabin served as a bedroom, living room, dining room, and kitchen, all at the same time.

He loved sleeping in the corner, and he could pull a curtain closed to hide the sleeping area from the rest of the house. He could sit on a single couch, which faced a painting of some people canoeing on the lake. No TV out here, though Griffin had brought his tablet, and counselors had access to the Internet.

Campers didn't though, and Griffin was very careful not to flaunt his ability to watch the streaming services he liked. But the fact was, he wouldn't fall asleep without his favorite sitcom blaring in his face, and he could put in headphones so no one would know.

The kitchen sat in the corner opposite from his bed, and it was just a counter against one wall, a sink, fridge and short counter with a microwave and hot plate along the other. The bathroom was a separate room between the bedroom and kitchen, and a small table with only two chairs served as his "breakfast nook."

He loved the cabins here, and this summer, he'd gotten one of the coveted cabins along the back row, about as far from the main building and epicenter of the camp. All the kids slept in shared cabins closer to the center, and these farther cabins for counselors were preferred for their privacy and sense of silence that could sometimes hardly be found in camp.

He set the last family picture the Johnsons had taken when Travis had gotten married on the shelf next to his bed and looked at his brothers, the three new wives, and his parents. He did love them, and he wondered what it meant that he sure did need a break from them too.

As if summoned by his thoughts, his phone rang, and Rex's name sat on the screen. "Hey," he said, suddenly anxious for a familiar voice.

"Brother," Rex said, his voice already too loud. But Griffin smiled anyway. He and Rex definitely had ups and downs in their relationship, but as the youngest of the brothers, they'd always been thick as thieves too.

"How's camp?"

Griffin's first instinct was to hem and haw, as if he wasn't happy to be there. He pushed against that and said, "It's so great."

"Yeah?"

"Yeah." Griffin leaned back on the bed and looked up into the exposed rafters of the cabin. "We did this getting-to-know-you game, which don't laugh, because I hate them too. But Toni had these awesome prizes."

"What kind of prizes?"

"A hundred dollars," Griffin said. "And three paid vacation days."

"If you need a hundred bucks, bro, I can spot you," Griffin said, laughing in the next moment.

Griffin laughed with him, because it was true he didn't need the money. He didn't need this job in that regard. Out of all the brothers, Griffin had probably spent the least after their parents had given them all billions of dollars from the sale of Momma's part of a cosmetics company her sister apparently ran in New York.

"It was still fun," Griffin said, sitting up and looking at the prize he'd won. "I talked to a lot of people I probably wouldn't have, and I won a water bottle for dogs."

"A what?" Rex laughed again.

"Yeah, Seth's going to love it," he said. "It's a water bottle with a rubber thing on the side, and you pull it out and it makes a bowl for the dogs right on the bottle."

"Sounds amazing."

"I'll send you a picture."

"All right."

Griffin's stomach rumbled, and he got up and went into the kitchen. He'd unpacked his clothes and personal stuff, but his box of food still sat on the counter. Toni had fed them breakfast and lunch today, but dinner was on his own. He thought for a moment about texting her to see what she was doing, but he decided against it, the image of her hard gaze scouring him fresh in his mind.

"Why'd you call?" he asked Rex.

"Just to see how things went," he said. "How's Toni?"

"Great," Griffin said, the lie so obvious to his own ears.

"Is she?"

"She was really busy today." Griffin grabbed a box of cheese-flavored crackers and retreated to the couch. "And do you remember that girl I dated like, five years ago?"

"Dude, five years ago I was barely back in town."

"Oh, that's right," he said. "Anyway, there's this girl I dated a while ago. Lilly Mae Moore. She's apparently a counselor here, and she got all bent out of shape that I didn't remember her. She looked familiar, but yeah."

"How many times did you go out with her?"

"Like maybe five or six times. Five years ago."

"I wouldn't remember that."

"You didn't remember who you'd gone to lunch with," Griffin joked, and Rex half laughed and half scoffed.

"Anyway, she sort of told me off in front of Toni, and I don't know. Toni looked at me weird." Griffin sighed as he opened the box of crackers.

"So you just explain it to her," Rex said. "She's reasonable."

"Yeah."

Scuffling came through the line, and Rex said, "I'm just talkin' to Uncle Griffin. You want to say hello?"

Griffin grinned, because he loved his little niece. He'd been right mad at Rex for not telling him about Holly and Sarah, though even Rex hadn't known about his daughter until March.

"Heya, Uncle Griffin," Sarah said.

"Hey, sweetheart," he said. "What are you up to?"

"Daddy took me for tacos tonight," she said. "Now we're watchin' something on the TV."

He loved how she always said "the" in front of "TV." It was never "we're watching TV." Always, "watching something on *the* TV."

"Whatcha watching?"

"I don't know. Some movie with this guy in it."

"Oh, a movie with a guy in it." Griffin chuckled, and Rex came back on the line.

"Okay, just checkin' on you," he said. "Call Toni. And have fun. You goin' to church up there tomorrow?"

"I haven't decided," he said.

"Well, it's only an hour, and Janelle's girls made that German chocolate cake for tomorrow's lunch."

Griffin's mouth started to water just thinking about the decadent cake. "All right. I'll keep you in the loop." The call ended, and Griffin put his phone on the couch beside him. He warred with himself, part of him wanting to call

Toni and explain. Or ask her to dinner. Was that discreet enough?

The thought of sneaking off the property with her under the cover of darkness set his pulse to pounding.

He knew which cabin she lived in. He could just go knock. It wasn't dark yet, and wouldn't be for hours. A box of crackers wasn't going to sustain him for long, and all he'd brought were snacks to supplement meals.

He had to eat, right?

He got up, a groan coming from his mouth, and picked up his cowboy hat from the table. "Here we go." He left the sanctuary of his cabin, expecting noise and activity beyond it. But there was only green grasses, trees in three directions, a glinting lake down the hill a ways, and a soft, summer breeze.

Griffin paused, his soul on fire as he took a moment to appreciate nature's beauty. He could feel the spirit of the land here, the heart of Texas as it slowly throbbed beneath his feet. He glanced up into the sky and thought he would surely see choirs of angels.

He didn't, but he felt their song way down deep in his roots.

That feeling gave him the courage he needed to walk the distance to Toni's cabin, and he wished it were winter or autumn so he could see if she had lights on in her windows.

She's probably extraordinarily busy, he told himself. With only one day before the campers arrived, she likely had a thousand little things to attend to.

But she still had to eat.

He glanced around as he approached, and her cabin was a little bit different than the others in that it had a back door and a front door. He went to the back one and knocked lightly. If anyone saw him, he could just say he had a question about something. He knew it was a weak excuse, as all the counselors had Toni's number, and he could've easily texted her his question.

Foolishness raced through him. He didn't even know what he was going to say. When she didn't answer, he thought she'd probably gone to dinner with friends. Still, he waited on the steps, feeling like a stalker at the same time indecision raged inside him.

Knock again?

Lick his wounds and go home?

He'd just lifted his hand to knock again when the back door opened. "I know, Mother," Toni said as she came out. "Oh." She nearly ran right into Griffin, who hastened to back up. But the porch wasn't big enough for both of them, and he stepped away again.

There was no porch there, and he nearly fell down the few steps to the ground.

"I'm on my way, okay? Give me twenty minutes. Remember how I'm up at camp?" Toni's eyes shone with frustration, and she couldn't seem to look anywhere but at Griffin. "Okay, Mother. Yes, I'll get them."

She hung up and sighed. "I'm sorry. I didn't see you there." She wasn't quite as cold as she'd been that morning, and Griffin seized onto that information.

"Going to see your parents?"

"Yes," she said. "What are you doing here?" She too

glanced around as if they might be caught on camera doing something they shouldn't be.

"I was hungry," he said, and her eyebrows twitched. Really just the one, as Toni could arch her right over her left—something Griffin really liked and found very sexy. "And I thought maybe you'd be hungry too, and then I thought maybe we could satisfy that hunger in the same place."

Satisfy that hunger.

He wanted to close his eyes and die.

Somehow, he managed to look steadily back at her. "I'd also like to defend myself against what Lilly Mae said, and I think having a lot of cheese and pepperoni there while I do it will help us both."

Toni's lips twitched, and he could've sworn they'd moved upward for a moment as she fought against a smile. She folded her arms and appraised him. "Okay," she said. "But I have to go check on my parents first."

"Sounded like you needed to take them something."

"My father thinks there are two packages for him at the post office." She gave another long sigh. "I'll have to stop there first. Then go to my parents'. You will *not* come in to meet them. You can wait in my car. If it's not midnight by the time I make sure they're not going to call me for the *sixth* time today, *then* we can go to dinner."

Griffin let his smile cross his face. "You've got yourself a deal." He wanted to shake her hand, because then he'd get to touch her skin with his. Instead, he went down the last two steps and waited for her to join him.

"Is pizza really okay?" he asked.

"I would literally kill for a pizza right now," she said.

"I know you're busy," he said. "I can just bring the pizza back."

"I'm not frustrated with the camp things," she said, walking down the path that led back to the main building. She cut him a look out of the corner of her eye. "If I tell you this, which I'm going to have to tell you, because I don't believe for a second you'll wait in my car while I go inside to deal with my parents—"

"I will," he said. He'd do whatever this woman told him to do, and he didn't know if that made him stupid or her dangerous. Probably both.

She looked at him fully then, and Griffin wanted to say so much. He hoped his eyes could broadcast what he was feeling, because he couldn't quite get his voice to work.

"This is something I only tell people I trust," she said.

"You can trust me," he said, a shot of nerves moving through him like a bullet. "Do you not trust me?"

She hesitated for a moment too long, and Griffin couldn't believe it. "Why don't you trust me?" he asked at the same time she said, "Well, you didn't know a woman you dated when you saw her."

"Okay," he said, needing to get this out before the whole thing made him angry. "I dated Lilly Mae five years ago. Five, Toni. Years. Can you tell me who you dated five years ago? Right now. Tell me right now."

Griffin didn't need to get so worked up, he knew. But Lilly Mae had made Toni see him in a bad light, and that wasn't fair.

"No one," she said, once again glancing at him. "Boy, I

would've never agreed that you could come had I known tonight was going to be a confessional for me."

"Confessional?"

"I haven't dated since my divorce," she said bluntly, stopping once they'd reached the asphalt. The parking lot loomed in front of them, with only about a dozen cars. "And that was final nine years ago."

"You haven't dated anyone in nine years?"

"I did not like my first marriage," she said. "I see no reason to do it again." She stepped off the curb, leaving Griffin to wonder what in the world she'd just said.

She didn't want to get married—ever again?

CHAPTER SIX

Toni couldn't believe what was happening. Her boots made angry noises on the asphalt, but she couldn't slow down now. Griffin had not followed her into the parking lot, and she thought maybe it would be best if they ended things now.

Not like there was much that had started, though her lips and her chest and her lungs burned when she thought about that kiss.

And it had been a baby kiss. A ghost of a kiss. A baby ghost kiss, with a man that made her heart wail at her brain for what she'd said.

"Okay," he said, coming up behind her. "We're going to table that for a few minutes."

He could table whatever he wanted. She needed to have a sit-down with her parents and make sure they knew they couldn't call her whenever they wanted now that summer camp season had arrived. They had neighbors and friends who could help. Guilt still twisted inside her, because she was an only child, and she loved her parents. She just didn't love them calling her all day long, especially only to tell her they'd found a new brand of spaghetti sauce.

"I knew Lilly Mae looked familiar," he said. "But she had brown hair when we went out, number one. Number two, she didn't wear glasses. Number three, we went out maybe five times over the course of five or six weeks. Not six months. So I didn't remember her name. It's not like we were engaged, and then I forgot."

He was panting by the time they reached her car, and truth be told, so was Toni.

"Why'd she say six months then?"

"Because *she* forgot too." He reached for her, thought better of it, and fell away from her. "Look, Toni, she was nothing. I didn't remember her, because I didn't feel anything for her. No spark." He stepped toward her again, and Toni's pulse rioted. He touched her hand lightly, and oh yeah. There were some major sparks.

At least for her.

Was she crazy to think there could be some for him too?

"But this?" He looked up into her eyes, his voice barely a whisper. "This is like fireworks, Toni." He gave her a gentle smile, and oh, he wasn't playing fair. Not fair at all. He probably didn't even know what that smile did to women. "Can you feel it too?"

She nodded before she could tell her neck not to move an inch. Her whole body was betraying her today.

Griffin grinned and he stepped away, removing his

rough, callused hand from her skin. "All right. Then I'll sit in the car if you want me to sit in the car. I'll even eat anchovies on my pizza. Whatever you want, Toni."

"Whatever I want?" She cocked her right eyebrow at him, which caused him to chuckle.

"Within reason," he said. "I mean, I have to work here and be able to call my mother on Sundays." His eyes shone from within, and Toni sure did like him.

"So you still call your mother?" she asked, unlocking the car and opening her door.

"Yes, ma'am." He moved around to the passenger seat, getting in and adjusting the seat for his longer legs.

She pulled out of the parking space and turned down the radio, trying to gather her thoughts. "My parents are getting older," she said, feeling the weight she carried starting to lift. "I'm an only child, and a lot of their care falls to me."

"An only child," Griffin said with a bit of wonder in his voice. "Wow, I wonder what meal time would be like without throwing an elbow to get a piece of garlic bread."

Toni glanced at him, realizing he wasn't kidding. She burst out laughing, and just like that, Griffin had taken all of her worries and cares from her.

How he did that, she wasn't sure. She just knew she wanted him to keep doing it.

THIRTY MINUTES LATER—NOT TWENTY—SHE PULLED

into her parents' driveway. "Oh, boy," she said. "Daddy's on the porch. You're going to have to meet them."

"I can meet them, Toni," he said. "It's fine."

Of course it was. He was Griffin Blasted Johnson, and Johnsons were raised winners. Johnsons didn't have to pick up the shattered pieces of their lives, attend therapy for two years before they felt like a normal human again, or deal with aging parents.

Toni hated the vitriol in her thoughts, but it was there nonetheless. The drive from camp to the post office, and then the post office to her parents' house had been fine. Great, even, with easy conversation about the camp, about his ranch, about his brothers and what meal time had really been like.

Intellectually, she knew everyone had problems, even Griffin and his family. He just seemed so perfect on the outside, and Toni had literally just told him she didn't trust men, didn't want to date or get married again, and that her aging parents were a burden to her, all in the space of under an hour.

Frustration filled her, because her parents weren't a burden. She loved them and wanted to help them. She did trust men...mostly. But the other one was true; she wasn't particularly looking to date and get married again, which made the man sitting in her passenger seat all the more troubling.

"Hey, Daddy," she drawled as she got out of the car. "What are you doin' sitting out here?"

"Waiting for you, sweetheart." He stood up from the

rocker, and Toni thought he was going to go right back down.

"Daddy, careful," she said, darting forward and up the steps. She steadied him, and he drew her into a hug.

"How's camp?" he asked.

At least he knew she was there. She felt like she'd told her parents a hundred times. "Good," she said. "Meetings today. Tomorrow is last-minute prep that Hailey and I will do with the counselors. Then we meet the kids on Monday morning." She smiled at him, keeping her hand on his elbow as they turned toward the front door to enter the house.

"Were the packages there?" Daddy asked.

"Oh, yes. The packages." She turned to go get them, only to see Griffin holding both of them and walking toward her. Before she knew it, he'd climbed the steps to the porch, fixing a charming, charismatic smile on his face.

"Daddy," Toni said, her excitement for her dinner with Griffin growing. "This is one of my counselors. I ran into him as I was leaving. Griffin, my father, Craig Beardall."

"Griffin Johnson." He shook Daddy's hand while juggling two packages, and they all went inside together.

"Nina, the packages are here," Daddy called. "And Toni brought home a man."

"Dad," she said, horror pouring through her.

"A man?" Mother appeared in the doorway that led to the kitchen, and Toni was sure she'd thrown out a hip from moving so fast.

"He's not a man."

"I'm not?"

Toni's eyes flew to Griffin's, which sparkled like sunlight off the lake. She shook her head, her smile barely-there. "Fine, he's a man. He's a counselor at camp. Griffin Johnson."

Mother came into the living room, her step more like a prowl. "Griffin Johnson. That's two last names."

"That's right," Griffin said without missing a beat. "I guess by the time Momma got to me, she'd had enough boys." He grinned at her and took her hand in his, lifting it to his lips a moment later. Oh, this guy was so good, and Toni felt like he'd read the playbook on how to handle her parents—and her.

"How many boys did your mother have?" Mother asked.

"Five," he said. "I was almost last."

"What's the last one's name?"

"Rex."

"That's not a last name."

"My parents fell down on the job." He handed her the packages. "It's not to meet you, ma'am." That was his kind way of saying, *Enough talk about my name.*

Toni understood. Heck, she had a man's name, and her parents thought that was perfectly normal. Why was Griffin such a problem for Mother?

Toni met her mother's eye as she tuned to take the packages back into the kitchen. She looked wary. Cautious. Toni couldn't blame her, but she didn't need to do more explaining about the divorce tonight. Then it really would be a confessional for her, and she'd like to save some of her flaws for later.

Much later.

"What are those packages?" she asked, following her mother. She cast a look at Griffin too, but he'd already turned to her father, who'd made it to his favorite recliner.

In the kitchen, Mother sliced open the boxes fairly quickly for someone with a shaky hand. "Daddy got some new seeds," she said. Sure enough, she pulled out a bag of seeds, with an assortment of wildflowers on it.

"You mail order in flower seeds?" she asked.

"Oh, he's crazy about them," Mother said, and Toni thought she'd at least gotten half of that sentence correct.

Her stomach growled, and Toni was ready for dinner. She didn't want to lecture her parents in front of Griffin, but she couldn't leave and have them call her so much while she opened camp.

"Mother," she said slowly. "Tell me where I'm working right now."

"Up at the camp." Her mom looked up from the wildflower seeds. "I know. I call too much."

"Six times today, Mother." Toni didn't want to be exasperated, but she knew the notes of it hung in her voice.

"I won't call that much anymore," she promised.

"Yes, because you can save some things and sum it up for me in one call. I promise I'll call you every night, okay? Every single one until you tell me not to."

"Why would I tell you not to?"

"I'm just saying," Toni said, not wanting to get into a long discussion. "You can tell me you found the puzzle, you got a new brand of spaghetti sauce, you saw a woman walk by with a dog you've never seen before, and that you need a couple of package from the post office all in one phone call." She glanced toward the doorway, but neither Griffin nor Daddy could be seen. "Really, Mother, I only want you to call if it's an emergency. We can talk about everything else at night, or when I'm not working."

"What if I can't find something?"

"I'm not playing what-if," Toni said, probably a little harsher than she needed to. But she hated it, as teenagers were incredibly good at what-if scenarios, and they drove her to the brink of madness. "If it's an emergency, like you can't find your heart medication, call me. But Mom, you know where all that stuff is. I lay out the whole week for you on Sundays."

"I know." She looked up from the second package, which was also a bag of wildflower seeds. "Sometimes I just get lonely."

"Mom, you have Daddy," Toni said. She was going to be the Old Maid, the one with no one to talk to and no one to come visit her when she was eighty years old.

In that moment, she knew keenly that she didn't want to be alone forever. She saw the future flash right in front of her eyes. She was her mother, opening packages of something she was really excited about but that didn't make much sense.

But there wasn't anyone waiting in the living room to talk to. There wasn't anyone she could call. No brothers or sisters. By the time she was eighty her parents would be long gone. Not even a pet, as she couldn't really take care of a dog or cat at her age.

But she'd always been able to keep fish, and she had

taken her bright orange goldfish, Salmon, to the cabin at camp.

And she did not want a solitary life at eighty years old. She wanted someone to share it with, the way Mother had Daddy.

"I know," her mother said. "He's been sleeping a lot lately."

"You need a dog," she said, though Toni knew that if her parents got another dog, she'd be the one to take care of it. And she didn't have time for that. People had goldfish for a reason.

"Toni?" Griffin asked from behind her, and Toni turned toward him. "We should probably bounce. I just looked up that pizza place, and they close the buffet at seven."

"Oh, that pizza buffet is not good," Mother said. "And what does it meant to *bounce*?"

Griffin just looked at Toni, who couldn't help giggling. "Mom, he's saying we need to go." She drew her mom into a tight hug. "I love you. So much."

"I love you too, baby doll," she said, and Toni managed to get Griffin out of the house without further incident.

Back in the safety of the car, she said, "Let's *bounce*, cowboy."

CHAPTER SEVEN

G riffin burst out laughing. "So I spend a little too much time with my youngest brother."

"Rex," Toni supplied.

"Right, Rex." Griffin could see why Toni was overwhelmed with her parents. They were a lot, and she was the only one around to help. They definitely felt very old to him, and he didn't think his parents were nearly as old as hers. "And he says stuff like that all the time. Bro-this, and bounce-that. And 'don't even trip,' which means, 'don't worry about it, Griff.'"

"Oh, he calls you Griff too?" She held a flirtatious tone in her voice that was something serious. "Can I call you Griff?"

"I mean, sure," he said. "It's what my brothers call me sometimes." He shrugged, but he did not want her to call him Griff. He wasn't really a Griff anyway, and literally only Rex called him that when they were teasing each other.

Toni grinned at him. "Don't worry," she said. "I won't call you that."

"Is the pizza buffet really not good?" he asked. "Because the idea of a pizza buffet sounds amazing to me." And not just because he was beyond starving. But a whole buffet of pizza? That was every man's dream, and paired with a beautiful woman, Griffin couldn't imagine a better way to spend an evening.

"Oh, my mother is a little finicky about food," Toni said. "And she doesn't like buffets. Germaphobe." She glanced at him as she came to a stop sign. "But it's not bad. I actually like the spinach and mushroom pizza. With sausage. And it has Alfredo sauce instead of marinara, and it's *divine*."

Griffin liked the sound of her laugh as it filled her car. He liked her driving him around Horseshoe Bay, pointing out the old, red-brick library, the tall flagpole in the downtown park, the festively painted water towers.

"I'll stop talking now," she said. "I mean, you live an hour from here. It's not like you've never been here."

"I like the tour," he said. "When I've come before, it's just for camp or for a day on the lake." Not that his parents had brought the boys on many lake trips. The ranch needed care seven days a week, and if they all left for a day of sunshine and boating, there wasn't anyone to feed the horses, llamas, dogs, chickens, or goats.

And since Daddy had been injured in a horseback riding accident a few years ago, him and Momma hadn't left town at all. Truth be told, Daddy's health problems had prompted Griffin to take a more active role in the ranch as well as move downtown with Rex so they could be closer to their parents should they need help.

The other brothers had lived out at the ranch where they'd all grown up, though only Russ lived there now. Seth still lived next-door with his wife, Jenna, and Travis had built a new house right at the entrance to the ranch, where he lived with his wife, Millie.

So much had changed in the Johnson family in the past ten months, and Griffin fell silent as he thought about all the new additions to their family, from canines to women to houses to three nieces.

"I lost you," Toni said, jolting Griffin out of his thoughts.

"Oh, uh, just thinking about how different things are this summer."

"Different?" Toni asked, killing the engine and reaching for her door handle.

"Yeah." He got out of the car too and met her at the front of the sedan. "Three of my brothers got married in the past seven months." He felt like maybe he was opening a big can of worms, but Toni had brought up the whole never-getting-married thing, and he'd said they'd revisit that.

Might as well be now.

"That is a huge change," she said.

"And Rex is engaged, and he has a five-year-old daughter." They'd talked about his family already, but Griffin hadn't phrased it in such a way that indicated he was frustrated with the changes. He wasn't frustrated with them, only that it seemed like *he* hadn't been swept up in the changes too.

He wondered if he could hold her hand down here in town. Was that discreet? He decided against it when the doors in front of them opened and three counselors spilled out of the pizza restaurant.

"Oh, hey," Clyde said. "You should've said you wanted to come to dinner." He grinned at Griffin and Toni. "You could've come with us."

"I was late unpacking," Griffin said. "I ran into Toni on the way out." Actually, she'd run into him, but Clyde, James, and Serena didn't need to know that.

"And I needed to take care of something with my family," Toni said, a perfectly perched smile on her face. "Is the pizza good tonight?"

"They have barbecue chicken on the buffet," James said. "And the dessert pizza is amazing."

"I think he only ate dessert pizza," Serena said, clearly flirting with him. James burst out laughing and slung his arm around Serena as they walked away. Clyde watched them for a moment and looked back at Toni.

"I'm keeping my eye on them, Boss," he said.

"Someone needs to," Toni remarked, also watching them.

Griffin kept his smile in place, shook Clyde's hand, and held the door for Toni. They'd passed their first test—no one in that group of camp counselors had suspected anything between the two of them.

He sucked in a breath when he joined Toni inside, because it seemed like the entirety of Camp Clear Creek had decided pizza was a good option for dinner that night. Griffin swallowed quickly, trying to remember what he'd just said to Clyde and the others.

Ran into Toni on my way out.

He had. It was true. He didn't want to lie. But the two of them definitely had a few more tests to pass. There would be no hand-holding. No flirtatious laughter. No leaning forward in an intimate booth while she told him why she didn't want to get married again.

Griffin kept the smile on his face, because it was either that or flee the scene.

"Two?" the hostess asked, and Toni and Griffin looked at one another.

"Yes," he ground through his throat. "Just two."

GRIFFIN SIGHED AS JENNA AND SETH'S HOUSE CAME INTO view. He could've easily stayed at camp, as Dalton had prepared a counselor's dinner for that Sunday night before the real work began. Part of Griffin didn't want to miss it. He loved his friendships with the other camp counselors, and he'd be living with them and working with them for the next three months.

But dinner the previous evening hadn't gone exactly the way he'd imagined it would, and he'd walked Toni back to her cabin and stayed at the bottom of the steps while she went inside. Then he'd tucked his hands in his pockets, almost like he was tucking his tail between his legs, and he'd gone on back to his own cabin-for-one.

He'd unpacked his cereals and snacks and texted with his brothers a little bit. Then he'd fallen asleep with the sitcom he loved, waking early as he normally did. He'd run five miles that morning, a circuit around the lake which had refreshed his soul and cleared his mind.

He still wanted Toni. That hadn't changed. He wanted to get to know everything about her. He wanted to know what it had been like growing up as an only child. He wanted to know about her first marriage and why it had ended. He wanted to know what she liked and what she didn't, and what her dreams and goals and aspirations were.

"So be patient," he said again, repeating the thought that had come into his mind that morning as he cooled down after his run. And he'd felt like he should come back for his usual afternoon and evening with his brothers.

He pulled through the gate at Chestnut Ranch, his heart sighing as if he were coming home after a long time away. Which was ridiculous. He'd been gone for just over twenty-four hours, and he'd wanted to go. He craved the solitary nature of his cabin, and his feelings were all jumbled again.

A beam of light shone into his life when he saw Rex waiting for him on the front steps, a harmonica in his mouth. Griffin grinned as he parked and got out of his truck. "I haven't seen you play that for years," he said, laughing as he went up the front walk.

Rex stopped playing, grinned, and stood up to give Griffin a hearty hug. "Sarah found it, and I told her I played."

"Well, you were makin' noise," Griffin said. "I didn't detect a tune."

"Hey," Rex said. "It's been years." He laughed too, and they went up the steps. "It's crazy in there today."

"More so than usual?"

"Definitely."

"Why?" Griffin paused before he opened the door, the energy behind it almost seething against his palm.

"My guess? Millie's pregnant, but neither she nor Travis have said anything yet. But let's just say I've been here for twenty minutes, and they've both laughed, cried, and disappeared."

"Oh, boy," Griffin said. "Exciting." And he was genuinely excited. "Did you bring Sarah and Holly?"

"Yep. They're in the backyard."

Griffin nodded and faced the front door. "Well, here goes nothin'." He opened the door, and someone must've just said something very funny, because everyone was laughing. Griffin loved the spirit here at the ranch, and he smiled his way into the kitchen, which opened up into a large family room and dining room.

"Griffin!" Seth yelled, and Griffin wondered if he'd enter a time warp where he'd really been gone for years for others, but to him, he'd only been gone overnight.

He hugged and laughed and asked everyone how they were. He'd skipped church that morning, but Russ was still wearing his white shirt and tie. Griffin didn't see Momma or Daddy, and surely Travis wouldn't make any huge announcements without them. They didn't normally come to the brotherly afternoons on Sunday, and Griffin wondered if he'd have to hear the news via text on Thursday night.

Probably, as Russ and Janelle weren't here either.

A glorious chocolate cake sat on the kitchen counter, the decorative cake stand beneath it paling in comparison to its beauty. "Kelly," he said. "Did you make that?"

"Yes, sir," she said in her cute ten-year-old Texas twang.

Griffin drew the girl into a hug. "I can't wait to have a piece." He stepped back and looked at her. "How was yesterday without your mom?"

"Good," she said. "My dad is staying in our house, and he took us to the splash pad yesterday." She looked at her younger sister, Kadence.

"Oh, boy," Griffin said. "You got burned, tiny tot." He looked at the shiny, red skin on Kadence's face. "Does it hurt?"

She nodded and looked at Kelly. "But Miss Millie put some cold stuff on it, and it's starting to feel better."

"I'll make sure Daddy puts sunscreen on her next time," Kelly said.

"Time to eat," Millie said, and Griffin turned his attention to her. Seth and Jenna had retreated to the living room area with their dogs, but they all stood up at the announcement of food. Griffin stuck close to the kids, thinking he would've never forgotten to put sunscreen on his kids in a Texas summertime.

He didn't know Janelle's ex husband, but her kids were sweet as apple pie, and Griffin felt quite protective of them.

"Uncle Griffin!" Sarah came running through the back

door, and Griffin swung her up and into his arms, despite Millie trying to explain dinner. But sloppy Joes weren't hard to put together, even if she'd put out Muenster cheese to go on top.

"And sweet potato fries," she said, bending to pull a tray out of the oven. Griffin's taste buds rejoiced, and he hadn't even taken a bite yet.

Sarah stroked her hand down the side of his face. "You got a beard, Uncle Griffin."

"Yeah, I didn't shave this morning."

"And he's the only Johnson brother that can literally grow a beard in a single day," Rex said.

"You sometimes have a beard, Daddy."

"Only after several days," he said, taking his daughter from Griffin. "Come sit down so Aunt Millie can say grace."

Griffin took off his cowboy hat for the prayer, but he didn't close his eyes. He looked around at these people he called family, and his heart swelled. He wanted to bring someone home too and allow them to experience the vibrancy of his family.

So he'd be patient and see if Toni could be that woman. "Amen," he said along with everyone else, and the elbow-throwing began as Seth and Travis both tried to be first in line to get food.

Griffin chuckled to himself, because while his family was loud and sometimes obnoxious, he fit here. He just wanted some*one* to fit with too.

CHAPTER EIGHT

T oni woke before the sun on Monday morning, and that was saying something for June third. The sun came up early and stayed up late, and for the next three months, so would Toni.

She stood in the shower, her eyes closed, taking a moment of peace and quiet for herself. Today was going to be crazy, and she'd be surprised if she was the first one to arrive at the main building.

Of course, Dalton would be there, as there was always an inaugural breakfast at the beginning of every camp session. Parents were invited for that, but by nine, cars and SUVs started pulling out of the parking lot, leaving their kids in the care of Camp Clear Creek.

Hailey would beat Toni to the office as well, and she'd asked all the counselors to be there no later than seven-forty-five. She wanted to be in her jeans, cowgirl boots, and Clear Creek T-shirt and in the office by seven-fifteen.

She almost made her goal, striding through the doors and into the back of the building, where the offices and restrooms were located, at seven-twenty. The air smelled of bacon and maple sausage, and Toni's stomach grumbled at her for leaving her cabin without even pouring herself a cup of coffee.

In her office, she found Hailey bent over one of the six-foot tables they'd set up last week. "Problems?" Toni asked.

Hailey glanced up and tucked her hair behind her ear again. "Coffee on your desk."

Toni moved over to get the liquid caffeine that she needed, telling herself that if she could make it to ten o'clock—when the first activity would start—she could return to this air-conditioned office and sneak a package of M&Ms from her bottom drawer.

"Got an email late last night," Hailey said as Toni picked up the to-go cup of coffee Hailey had brought for her. "Meagan Gardner has chickenpox and can't come."

"Better than someone trying to sneak in someone else when we've been full for three months."

"Right," Hailey said, straightening. "I started at the top of the list, but I haven't found someone to replace her." She sighed and stretched her back. "People make other plans, you know?"

"And teens don't want to show up a day late," Toni said. "It's okay. It's only one person, and there are no refunds." Toni smiled at Hailey. "Thanks for handling all of that."

"And Stephen's mother called again." Hailey ran her hand through her hair, extremely professional, as Toni wanted to roll her eyes.

"Let me guess," he said. "She wants another verbal confirmation that we're going to check with him to make sure he's taking his meds."

"Nailed it," Hailey said. "And I assured her that yes, our on-staff nurse would be checking with her son every day."

"I'll talk to her today," Toni said. "Reassure her again." It was just one more thing to do in a long list of items. She sat in her chair and sipped her coffee, going through her emails quickly as well.

Thankfully, no other parents needed any last-minute fixes, and Toni got back to her feet. "Let's go check on breakfast."

Hailey started to go first, and Toni remembered something suddenly. "Hey," she said. "What about Leon? Didn't you have date number five with him on Saturday?"

Hailey swung back around, her blue eyes dancing now. "Yes," she said, a smile coming to her face.

Toni waited a few moments, expecting Hailey to expound. "And?" she prompted when she didn't.

"And it's probably going to be date number six." Hailey lifted one shoulder in a shrug. "Things were a little chaotic, and he got a call for someone who'd collapsed at the lake."

"You'll kiss him next time." Toni put her arm around Hailey and gave her a squeeze. "If you want to. You do want to, don't you?"

"So bad," Hailey said, and she did roll her eyes this time. "What if he doesn't want to kiss me?"

"Of course he does," Toni said. "He's probably just looking for the right time too." She gave her friend a big smile and nodded. "Want me to talk to him?"

"If you do, you're dead to me," Hailey said under her breath.

Toni laughed and stepped past Hailey. "Let's go see what Dalton's done this morning." She'd given the chef a budget and a company credit card. It was up to him to decide what to buy, what to serve, all of it. She had to approve the credit card purchases, but she didn't know if he was buying muffin mix or pancake mix. She'd given him a little bit of direction by telling him what some of their biggest hits were from past years, but he really could do what he wanted.

So when Toni and Hailey stepped into the large main room where they'd had their staff meeting, she wasn't expecting to see Dalton standing with his crew, all of their arms around each other.

She paused, surprise leaping through her. "Oh."

"He's great with people," Hailey said. "And dinner last night was delicious."

"He's doing an omelet station," Toni said, even more shocked. "For eighty campers and their parents. In an hour."

"If he thinks it's going to work, it'll work," Hailey said.

"We'll see." Toni didn't want to be fatalistic, but...individual omelets?

The long table at the end of the dozen or so skillet stations sat several bowls of fruit, and Toni smiled at his ingenuity.

A cheer rose up from the huddle in front of the omelet stations, and the group broke up. Most of them went into the kitchen only to return moments later with trays full of little bowls that held chopped tomatoes, cheese, green onions, and other omelet fillings.

Dalton came toward Toni, who beamed at him. "Wow," she said. "Omelet stations?"

"They'll be a big hit," he said. "And I've got a couple of guys opening the back doors so people can eat on the patio." On cue, the doors opened, and Toni smiled at the sunshine coming inside. She loved spaces that blended from indoor to outdoor, and she wondered how Dalton had known that.

Counselors started to arrive, and Toni consciously started looking around for Griffin. She almost wished she wouldn't, but she couldn't help it. They'd had a fun time together at dinner on Saturday night, but she hadn't seen him at all on Sunday. He hadn't texted, and after she'd spent the morning finalizing cabin assignments and moving a couple of girls around due to parent requests, she'd gone into Horseshoe Bay to have lunch with her parents.

She'd stayed as long as she could, checking and then double-checking to make sure they both had pill boxes ready for the week. She'd adjusted their air conditioning for them, as Mother kept complaining about the heat, but she hadn't changed the thermostat.

After that, she'd spent a quiet night alone in her cabin. She wasn't bad in the kitchen, and she'd spent most of her life making treats on Sunday afternoon. Her father loved chocolate chip cookies, and Toni had filled her cabin with the scent of freshly baked cookies last night.

She'd wanted to invite Griffin over, but she didn't want to seem desperate. She felt like the two of them were dancing, their hands barely touching, always glancing around to see who was watching.

She knew the moment Griffin entered the building, and she turned toward him. His laugh filled the air as he stood with Ian Traverse and Rob Saunders. The three of them, along with Rex, had gotten along really well last summer too.

Her smile touched her mouth as she watched them laugh and talk, and then an alarm went off on her phone. She startled, hastened to silence it, and Hailey said, "I'll welcome them."

"Thank you," Toni said. "We probably have five minutes." One glance out the window told her that vehicles were already starting to arrive.

"Good morning," Hailey said into a microphone. The chatter and laughter stopped for the most part as everyone focused on the petite blonde that could command a crowd of adults and teens alike. "Doesn't this look amazing?" She beamed around at the counselors and then at Dalton.

"Toni has your packets for assignments, and people will be allowed into the building as soon as I'm done talking. Dalton has an amazing breakfast, and we want you to socialize with anyone and everyone, not just your campers. We'll break into our groups out by the flagpole in about forty-five minutes." She nodded, the speech absolutely perfect.

Toni handed out the counselor packets in record time, taking a moment to meet Griffin's sexy, dark eyes, and nodded to Hailey.

She opened the doors, and camp began.

࣪

THE OMELETS WERE DELICIOUS. TONI CIRCULATED among the parents, not allowing herself to gravitate toward the comfortable people she knew—the returning counselors. When everyone had been fed—which had happened relatively fast for all the people that were there—Hailey moved them all outside to the flagpole.

Her phone buzzed in her pocket, and her heart blasted off toward the stratosphere. Could her mother really be calling already? It wasn't even ten a.m.

She edged through the crowd, inadvertently bumping into someone. "Sorry," she whispered.

A hand landed on her back, and she knew that spark. That touch. She pulled in a breath and looked at Griffin. "You okay?"

"Yeah."

"Hailey's looking for you," he said quietly, nodding.

The buzzing stopped in her pocket, and she focused on the moment. She could call her parents later. She went back over to Hailey and put a smile on her face. They both stepped up on the cement steps next to the flagpole, and Toni called, "Welcome to Camp Clear Creek!"

She wasn't sure who started it, but the cowboy counselors in the group yipped and hollered, and that got everyone else clapping.

She gave her welcome speech, and she smiled through it all, feeling the joy and energy of having eighty new souls to spend the next three weeks with.

"And now," she said. "It's time to say your good-byes.

Campers should have their packets. Counselors have corresponding colors, and our first activity begins in just fifteen minutes. Luggage should be in cabins, not down by the lake."

Movement happened then, as parents hugged their children good-bye, bags were towed over to counselors, and groups began to form.

Toni kept her smile in place until all the groups had started toward the cabins with their various backpacks and roller bags. All the parents left, and Toni still stood next to the flagpole.

"I'll deal with lunch," Hailey said, stepping down and striding back toward the building. She probably wanted to get back into the air conditioning.

Toni did too, and she pulled her phone out of her pocket as she followed her assistant at a slower pace. The call wasn't from her mother or her father, and she frowned. The voicemail icon sat at the top of the screen, and she pulled it down to tap it to get the message.

"Toni, it's Eddie Microneil."

Her pulse shot to the back of her throat. Eddie Microneil was the treasurer for the organization that oversaw Camp Clear Creek, along with some other youth camps in the Texas Hill Country area. Hers was the only one in the Texas Highland Lakes, and most of the others involved horses or other animals as part of the camp.

They only did horseback riding here, but nothing with horse care or handling.

"I was hoping to catch you this morning as I'm heading to the airport," Eddie continued. "I need to talk to you about some things. Could you call me as soon as you can?" He sounded a bit rushed, harried, and probably anxious. Toni knew the feeling, and she hung up without saving or deleting the message and dialed him back.

The phone only rang once before Eddie picked up with, "Toni, sorry to bother you. I know camp starts today."

"Yes," she said. "We just got everyone off to the lake, so I have a moment."

Eddie didn't speak right away, and Toni's nerves split. "I'm afraid I have some bad news for your camp."

"Oh?" She paused just outside the building, but the doors were still open, and the cool air conditioning wafted toward her. She could barely hear him, because her heart was pounding so hard.

So-hard. So-hard.

"The Camden's, who have generously contributed the majority of the money we regulate to Clear Creek, are not donating this year."

Toni heard the words he said but getting them to make sense wasn't happening very fast. "What does that mean?"

"It means Camp Clear Creek will have to close its doors at the end of the summer."

"What?" She gasped, her heart running away inside her body. "There's no other money?"

"Not right now," he said. "Look, I'm about to go through security. I need to come down there and go over everything with you. I'll be in Dallas until Thursday. What does the beginning of next week look like for you?"

"It's wide open," she said, though she didn't know if that was true or not. She'd clear whatever she had to from her schedule to meet with Eddie. Camp Clear Creek simply couldn't close.

"Let's set up something for Monday," he said.

"Okay," Toni said.

"I'll email you."

"Thank you," Toni said. The call ended, and she turned around as if someone would be standing there that she could tell. She needed someone to confide in. Someone to reason through things with. Someone to tell her that everything was going to be okay.

But the truth was, if Camp Clear Creek closed, Toni would lose her job of the past eight years.

Tears sprang to her eyes. This camp had saved her after the failure of her marriage. It had given her back the confidence she'd lost completely. The things she'd learned here had driven away her ex's demeaning and damaging messages, and the therapy she'd done for two years after escaping Jackson's verbal, mental, and emotional abuse.

Her therapist had used terms like "gaslighting," and "reinvention."

Toni had fought her way back to a normal life, clawing at times to get where she was.

And she could lose it all in just three short months.

"Toni?" Hailey asked. "Let's debrief with Dalton."

She nodded and went inside, pulling the doors closed behind her. No sense in cooling the Texas countryside when she didn't have to. She also didn't say a word to Hailey about the possible loss of funding, or the closure of the camp, or anything even remotely close to it.

She'd bear this burden on her own for now.

CHAPTER NINE

G riffin whooped as one of the boys in his group—
Mike—ran toward the rope, leapt, grabbed it, and
swung out over the lake. He dropped into the water while
the other boys in the group cheered for him.

Griffin went down to the water's edge and pulled the
boy into a hug, forgetting that he was still wearing his T-
shirt, and now it was wet. "You did it, man." He pounded
the boy on the back and stepped back. "How did it feel?"

Mike grinned from ear to ear, and dripping wet, he
high-fived the other boys in the group. He was definitely
the scrawniest. The geekiest. And a couple of the other
boys were clearly athletes, with no qualms whatsoever
about throwing themselves at a very skinny rope and then
dropping into a lake.

"Felt great," he said, still smiling like he'd won the
lottery.

"That's what this camp is about," Griffin said to his

group of six boys. "Doing things you might not have done before. Forming friendships with people you might not back home. And food." He grinned as Toni appeared on the path with a cooler in a wagon. "We're having lunch here at the lake, and then we'll go back to the cabin and unpack."

He went up to the path and gathered an armful of sandwiches and sodas. "Haws, come help."

The boy with plenty of muscles joined him, taking the stuff back down to the beach.

"Hey," Griffin said, noticing something in Toni's eyes. What, he wasn't sure. "How are things going?"

"Great," she said falsely. "How are your boys?"

"Amazing," he said, glancing over his shoulder and smiling at them as Haws started passing out the sandwiches. "Do we have chips?"

"Dalton's coming with all the snacks," she said. She started walking again, and Griffin didn't want her to go. Jumping to follow her would be way too obvious though, so he watched her go, his mind racing.

When he finally figured out he couldn't stand there staring longingly at her either, he ducked his head and walked back to his group. They were silent as they ate, and Griffin seized the moment to text Toni.

Something seemed off just now. Hope you're okay.

He had no idea what any of that even meant, but he sent the text.

Maybe it's just the first day?

He sent that one too, hoping Toni wouldn't find him overeager to talk to her or help her, even if he was both.

He sat down in his advisor's chair and accepted a hoagie from Haws. "What do you guys want to do this afternoon?" he asked. They'd had a water safety lesson as a big group first, then a canoeing lesson, and then the counselors had split up and taken their groups where they wanted.

"We could go see if there's another group who wants to play volleyball," he said. "Stay here. Go check out the canoes." He picked up the can of sunscreen he'd taken from the main building. "George, put more of this on. You're starting to look a little red in the ears."

The last thing Griffin wanted was one of his boys to get sunburnt on the first day. He thought of Kadence, and he didn't want to see that shiny, burnt flesh on his campers.

His phone buzzed, and he deliberately didn't take it out. The campers weren't allowed their devices, and he'd never felt the need to have his phone out to see who'd texted. The buzz nagged at him, though, and he turned away from the boys and checked it.

First day, Toni had said. *I'll talk to you tonight.*

Hope filled his heart, and he smiled as he tucked his phone away again.

"Volleyball?" Ian held the ball, his eyebrows raised with all of his boys behind him.

"Boys?"

"Let's do it," TJ said, and Griffin grinned as they all got up and left their beach items right where they were. The sand court wasn't far away, and Ian gave a quick lesson on the rules of the game.

Griffin couldn't believe he got paid to eat sandwiches,

swim in a lake, throw a Frisbee, and play beach volleyball. But he did. And if he needed the money, he'd be even more thankful. As it was, he did have extreme feelings of gratitude, because while he loved the ranch in Chestnut Springs, he sometimes wondered if he was cut out to do it full-time.

He loved wearing the cowboy hat. The boots. The big belt buckles. Those things were all fine. But he knew better than most that there was a big difference between dressing like a cowboy and actually being one.

Russ and Travis and Seth, they were real cowboys. Half the time, Griffin thought he and Rex were playing at it. Though now that Rex had bought six miniature horses and was teaching his daughter how to ride them, train them, and show them, even he was more of cowboy than Griffin felt like.

He was a jack-of-all-trades. If there was something that needed doing around the ranch, Griffin had been the one to take a class and figure it out. He loved learning, but he'd never gone to college. So the accounting course for small businesses had appealed to him even if Seth hadn't asked him to take over the finances after Daddy's injuries.

He bent down, trying to focus on the volleyball game, especially since Ian was now serving. The cowboy had a wicked hit, and Griffin knew the ball was coming straight to him. Ian yelled as he jumped and served, and just like Griffin predicted, the ball came right at him.

He had to move his feet to get to it, and he managed to get it back in the air for one of the boys to hit over. Griffin couldn't care less who won the game, but Ian had a couple of competitive boys, as did Griffin.

TJ set, and Miles spiked, and they roared as if they'd won a million dollars when the opposing team couldn't dig the ball out of the sand.

Griffin couldn't help smiling at them as they high-fived each other and then everyone else on the team. That spike had earned them a side-out, and it was Mike's turn to serve.

"You've got this," Griffin said, picking up the ball and handing it to him.

He took it, his eyes past Griffin on TJ and Miles, both still positioned at the net.

"Don't worry about them," Griffin said. "They're giants anyway. Just get it over, and they'll stop it from coming back to us." He grinned at Mike and put his hand on his shoulder. "Okay?"

Mike finally moved his eyes to Griffin's, and he could see all the anxiety of a non-jock trying to perform in front of athletes. "Okay."

"Okay." Griffin hadn't been particularly into sports in high school, but he could play them. He could pick up a basketball and shoot it, getting the majority of the shots to drop. He could throw a football, and heaven knew he'd spent plenty of time in his life tackling his brothers. He could catch a baseball, and hit one, and he liked to run.

So volleyball wasn't particularly hard for him, but he *did* have things that were hard for him. Sitting down in front of a computer and knowing what to do was one. He was a

pro with his phone, but he didn't do a lot of Internet surf-
ing, writing, researching, or anything else on the computer.

He did have to force himself to use the office at the
homestead once a month to take care of the finances, but
he'd even let that fall a bit behind since Momma had sold her
cosmetics shares. Because not only did the boys have plenty
of money since that had happened, but so did the ranch.

Mike called out the score and served the ball under-
hand. Griffin prayed with everything in him that the Lord
would reach down and guide it over the net with His hands
if He had to.

Miraculously, the ball went over. It was a soft serve,
easy for the other team to set up. But TJ and Miles
crouched in wait, and they both seemed to know the exact
moment to explode up, their arms up, hands together.

They roared again, the block successful. Griffin laughed
and slapped hands while Mike grinned and grinned and
grinned.

Five minutes later, his team won the game, and TJ and
Miles ran around their side of the court, spraying sand into
the air, before they finally lifted Mike onto their shoulders
and proclaimed him their lucky charm.

Griffin hadn't had to tell them to do it. Somehow they'd
sensed the same need in Mike that he had, and they'd
responded to it. Mike's face shone red, but thankfully it
wasn't from a sunburn.

George, on the other hand, looked about like a cooked
lobster, and Griffin said, "Time to go unpack, boys. Ian will
have to see if his team can beat us another time."

"Oh, it's on," Ian said with a wide grin. He told his boys the same thing about going to unpack, and they vacated the volleyball court.

"Let's see," Griffin said, bending to pick up his folder. "Yep, nothing until dinner tonight, men. So we have from now until five to shower, unpack, and get settled in." He closed the folder with that day's itinerary in it, and looked up at his boys.

They definitely weren't men, as he'd been assigned the fifteen and sixteen-year-olds. None of them had to shave, though the athletes definitely had muscles that said they spent time lifting weights.

They'd been to their cabin before, and Griffin picked up his T-shirt and towel and went with them to the teen cabins. The girls stayed closer to the main building, and the boys spread out in the woods. His team had a cabin right along the edge of the trees, and when they arrived, Griffin found Toni herself hanging two hammocks between two tree trunks.

Another woman helped her, and Griffin recognized her as the woman over maintenance and groundskeeping in the morning, if Marco wasn't available.

"Hey," he said easily, changing his course to go see if they needed help. "I didn't know we'd get hammocks." He dropped his shirt and towel. "Need some help?"

Toni and Kiki turned toward him, and both of their eyes widened. He wasn't sure why, and he glanced over to his boys to see them going up the steps and into the cabin. They'd work out who would sleep where in the three sets of bunk beds inside. He'd be surprised if they hadn't already assigned beds and bathrooms.

The cabin had two, with a small set of cupboards for snacks too. There was a kitchen sink and a mini fridge, but no way to heat anything up. Griffin had heard all the horror stories about what teenagers put in microwaves, and after the third fire, the administration at Camp Clear Creek had removed anything like that from the teen cabins.

He looked back at Toni, whose whole face was bright red. "I've got a few minutes. They're going to unpack."

"We're fine," she said.

"I'm Kiki Malone," the other woman said, dropping her rope and coming toward Griffin. He'd been dating a lot more over the past ten months, and he recognized the look of interest on Kiki's face.

"Griffin Johnson," he said.

"That's two last names." She giggled like that was the funniest thing in the world, and Griffin could only gape at her. Why was everyone fixating on the fact that he had two last names? Did they think he didn't know? Had never heard someone tell him that before? Did they think he'd named himself?

A soft snuffle came from Toni, and his eyes shot to her. She was smiling and obviously trying to hide it.

"Let me help." He didn't doubt Toni's abilities around the camp. She could probably start a fire faster than anyone, including him, and he'd seen her tie knots before. She definitely knew what she was doing.

He picked up Kiki's rope and pulled it, bringing the

hammock higher, the lines more taut. He swung it around the tree trunk and adjusted it so it was level with Toni's. "Right here?"

"Yep," she said, her voice slightly higher than normal. "Looks good."

He tied the line in place and stood back. "Want me to try it out?"

"Oh, yeah," Kiki said suggestively, and it was in that moment that Griffin realized he wasn't wearing a shirt.

Instant embarrassment hit him, and he almost dove for the T lying on the grass several feet behind Toni. But he didn't. Her eyes hadn't left his, and a powerful, crackling sensation moved between them.

Wow, he hoped Kiki hadn't been able to feel that. And he hoped Toni had. He stepped over to the hammock and sat down in it, bouncing it a little to test his weight. "I think it's great."

He lay down and clasped his hands behind his head with a big sigh. "I know where I'm going to be while the boys are off at their activities." A smile filled his face, especially when Toni leaned over him.

"Yeah," she said. "With them. No unsupervised groups, remember?"

He wanted to grab her hand and pull her into the hammock with him. But that was about as *in*discreet as he could be, so he simply grinned up at her. "Yes, Boss." Calling her *boss* made everything in him flare with heat. Could she feel that too?

The sparkling glint in her eyes said yes. She glanced

over her shoulder to Kiki, and said, "Okay, as long as we're clear," before backing up quickly.

"Dinner's not till five, right?" He closed his eyes, imagining Toni to be looking at his bare chest. "I think I'll take a little nap before then." He wouldn't really, and Toni knew it.

"See you later, Griffin," she said.

"Bye." He opened his eyes, startling when he got an eyeful of Kiki and not the gorgeous brunette he'd been dreaming about for a couple of months now. Maybe longer.

"I should get your number," she said. "In case I need to get in touch with you."

"I'm a counselor," he said. "Don't you already have my number?"

"Oh, right." She giggled again and tucked her hair behind her ear. She flounced around, turned, looked back at him, and said, "See ya, Griff."

He just stared at her, in a state of complete and total shock. Griff?

Yeah, she's a hard pass, he thought as he relaxed again. He only stayed in the hammock for another five minutes, but it was long enough to imaging Toni cuddling with him in a hammock just like this one. Only theirs would be concealed in the woods, and he'd kiss her under the cover of darkness, whisper how beautiful she was, and ask her if they could see each other once camp ended.

And wow, what a good daydream.

CHAPTER TEN

Toni could've stared at Griffin's bronze body for days and not been bored once. The man clearly worked plenty of days without his shirt on, because there wasn't a farmer's tan or tan line in sight.

And he worked out. Oh, boy, did he work out.

She was just glad she hadn't embarrassed herself the way Kiki had. However, it didn't seem like Kiki even knew or cared that she'd made a fool of herself.

Toni finished setting up the hammocks she'd bought that year, each one reminding her of how much she'd given to this place. And now, each one also told her what a waste it was to buy them. She'd purchased the hammocks as hammocking had become more and more popular over the past few years, thinking it would be a good long-term investment. They could reuse the hammocks from year to year.

Except now there was no next year, and Toni's breath caught in her throat. She must've made a gasp or a sound, because Kiki looked at her. "You okay?"

"Yeah," she said. "Just a hiccup or something." She took off her cowgirl hat and wiped her hair back. It was hot and sunny today, which was perfect for the first day of camp. Hammocks could be hung, the lake was cool and brilliant against the heat, and no one had to drag suitcases through the rain.

Texas weather could change in the blink of an eye, but today, the sky was only blue for miles and miles.

With an hour left until dinner, Toni thought a little shut-eye sounded like a good idea. Her parents hadn't called once, and she might actually get to take a nap. She parted ways with Kiki at the main building and continued out the back doors to her cabin.

The air conditioner had been hard at work staving off the heat and humidity, and Toni sighed as she closed the door behind her.

But her phone call with Eddie wouldn't leave her mind. She lay down on the couch, an alarm set on her phone, but she never did fall asleep. Worry ate at her until she felt chewed through, and only then did she remember she'd told Griffin she'd tell him what was going on that night.

She just needed someone she could trust, and if that wasn't Griffin Johnson, she didn't know who it was. She didn't want Hailey to worry. She'd just hired a lot of her other senior or supervisory staff. She didn't want the campers to know, or the parents. Not yet. Not until decisions had to be made—hard decisions.

Just a few minutes before her alarm would've woken her anyway, she got out her phone to send Griffin a text.

After lights out tonight? I have something I need to tell you.

Sounds serious, he said. *Are you sure you're okay?*

I just need a friend. She stared at the words, knowing with every cell in her body she wanted Griffin to be more than a friend. Heck, the man had already kissed her once, and the mere memory of it had her lips buzzing in anticipation.

And someone I trust. And maybe if you come after lights out tonight, you can hold my hand and tell me everything will be okay.

She sent that longer follow-up text so he'd know she wasn't thinking of him as a friend. To her surprise, her phone rang, and Griffin's name sat on the screen.

"Toni," he said, his voice almost sharp. "You're scaring me a little. Tell me everything is okay."

"With my family?" she asked. "Yeah, everything is okay with my family."

He paused, clearly trying to figure out the rules to this game. "What about with you?" he asked. "Your health?"

"All fine," she said, smiling at the air around her.

"With the camp?"

"Ah, there's the problem."

"So this is a camp problem? A serious camp problem?"

"Very serious."

"Oh, boy." He pushed his breath out. "And we have to wait until lights out? Maybe you could just tell me now."

Toni thought about it for about five seconds before she said, "I got a call this morning, and it was from the treasurer of the organization that funds Clear Creek. He said we lost our major donor, and we'll have to close at the end of August."

"No," Griffin said, plenty of shock and horror in his voice. "That can't be. What about the September and October camps? Those were filling up."

"There's no money," she said. "Apparently. I'm not sure. I have to wait until next Monday to talk to him, as he's already traveling somewhere else this week."

"After lights out," he said, almost under his breath. "Your cabin. I'll be there." The line went dead, and Toni checked it just to make sure. Yep. Disconnected.

She sighed heavily, then took a long time to breathe in again. When she finally did, she got to her feet. Time to get over to the building and see what Dalton needed help with. Knowing the man, probably nothing. Already in one day he'd done a better job with the food than Isaac had in an entire summer, and Toni thanked her lucky stars that she'd found him, even if it was only for one summer.

Half an hour later, she stood out at the flagpole again, the campers arriving in a steady stream. Griffin brought his boys right over next to her, and he was wearing jeans and a T-shirt. But, oh, she'd seen what that T-shirt concealed, and she couldn't un-see it. Didn't even want to.

Warmth filled her, but she refused to acknowledge him with more than a nod before she turned back to the steps where Hailey stood with Dalton and Annie.

"Ladies and gentlemen," Hailey called, and most of the noise quieted. "We're going to have dinner in just a few minutes. Dalton will explain it all to you. After that, Annie has our first camp-wide activity, and I'm going to let her explain that. There will be sodas, cider, and hot chocolate, along with s'mores at the fire pits tonight at eight-thirty. Attendance is optional, and if counselors have some kids that want to come and not others, please combine into groups and make sure there's at least one adult for every ten kids. We just don't want to lose anyone between there and their cabin, and we're quite spread out this year."

A hand touched Toni's, and she startled away from it before realizing it was Griffin. He didn't look at her, but as she let her arm settle down naturally again, he threaded his fingers through hers.

She had told him, *you can hold my hand and tell me everything will be okay,* but she hadn't meant for him to do it at a general session, where anyone could see them.

Her eyes met Hailey's, and it felt like the entire world narrowed to the two of them—and Griffin's hand in Toni's.

Hailey's eyes widened; Toni stepped away from Griffin; Hailey moved down the stairs; Dalton started explaining dinner, which apparently was a Dutch oven affair down at the fire pits.

"That way, everyone will know where they are tonight," he said with a wide grin. "And don't let Hailey fool you. The s'mores tonight are so much more than regular chocolate and graham crackers. I have saltines, Oreos, peanut butter cups, and more. Anything is good with a roasted marshmallow, right?"

Toni's hand burned, and she wasn't even touching Griffin anymore. When she looked to her right to find him, he'd blended into the crowd. Gone. Away.

Hailey appeared in front of her, her expression

demanding an answer. But Annie started talking about the activity that night, which was a co-ed bicycle ride. "But," she said into the mic. "Here's the catch. You can only ride a bike with someone of the opposite sex. And the bicycles are built for two."

"No way!" someone nearby said. Laughter filled the sky, as did a general sense of excitement. Toni loved the four-teen to sixteen camps, as the kids were a bit more mature than the younger camps, but most of them weren't super experienced with the opposite gender. Fun things like a bicycle-built-for-two would help break that ice and get them talking to each other.

Toni didn't disapprove of summer camp romances that operated within the rules at Clear Creek—unless it was Griffin and Kiki.

But he'd seemed pretty surprised at the way she'd acted toward him, and Toni had felt the Earth move when he looked at her. That couldn't be one-sided, even if a twinge of jealousy swam inside her.

Annie finished talking, and the crowd broke up as they started their walk down to the fire pits, which sat directly in the middle of the cabins. On the east lay the main build-ing, parking lot, and girl's cabins. On the right were all of the boy's cabins. Counselor cabins lined the back of the camp, and the lake sat in front of it all.

She started to go with the flow, but Hailey said, "Toni."

She turned back to her assistant, already knowing what Hailey was going to say. "I know," she said. "Okay? I know."

"What do you know?" Hailey asked, folding her arms. She'd make a very good mother one day, that was for sure.

"What were you going to say?"

Hailey glanced around, but almost everyone had left. Those that hadn't were on their way, and none of them were within earshot. "You and Griffin Johnson?"

"No." Toni scoffed, but everything about the word and the noise was false. "I mean..."

A smile spread across Hailey's face, and a tiny squeal came out of her mouth. "Toni." She made her two-syllable name into three, and she gripped Toni by the forearms. "He is very good-looking."

"He's younger than me," Toni said. "And I told him we couldn't broadcast our relationship here." She frowned, a smattering of annoyance moving through her. "And what's literally the first thing he does? Holds my hand in front of everyone?"

"So you'll set him straight," Hailey said. "And girl, you couldn't see his face. He doesn't care about the age difference, and you shouldn't either."

"What did he look like?" Toni couldn't believe she was gossiping about a man like a teenager.

"That he'll do anything you tell him," Hailey said with a laugh. They linked elbows and started down the path that would take them to the fire pits. "So you tell him, no more hand-holding, Mister. But kiss me with the doors closed."

"Hailey," Toni chastised, but not an hour had passed since Friday night where Toni hadn't thought of his kiss.

They laughed together, arriving at the fire pits to find four well-organized lines and all of Dalton's helpers hard at work getting everyone served. Toni sighed happily at the sight of them, and her resolve hardened.

She would not let Camp Clear Creek close. She didn't know how she'd find the money they needed to operate, but she had to try. She had to do something. She couldn't just let the past eight years of her life be for nothing.

&.

TONI BARELY MADE IT TO LIGHTS OUT WITHOUT collapsing. She didn't have to walk the whole camp every night, but the first night, she did. She'd sent a group message to all of the counselors to let them know that if they had concerns, she'd be around to every counselor cabin between ten and ten-thirty.

She got several waves and a couple of questions, but nothing too major. She texted Stephen's mom after checking with his counselor, and she smiled at the gratitude in the response she got.

Toni had never been a mother, so she didn't quite understand the worry and concern of his mother, but she knew she could alleviate it with a simple conversation with Wade Monroe and sending a text.

Griffin had been standing on his porch when she passed, and he'd touched two fingers to the brim of his cowboy hat in a sexy salute that had left her breathless for several more cabins.

She reached her cabin with barely enough energy to climb the few back steps to the door. A long sigh moved through her whole body, and she'd barely set a teapot on her stove when a light rap landed on her back door.

"Griffin," she whispered, and she suddenly found her second wind.

CHAPTER ELEVEN

G riffin stood on Toni's back porch, feeling completely exposed. He glanced left and right like a burglar, but her back porch wasn't in the direct sightline of anything. The only way someone would know he'd gone to Toni's was if they walked by or they followed him.

The door opened with a whoosh, and Toni stood there, wearing the same jeans and camp polo she'd had on all day. "Come in," she said.

Griffin didn't waste time with words. He stepped into her house, pressing right into her personal space. "Hi."

"Hi." She smiled and reached up to pull her hair from its ponytail. "What a crazy day, right?"

"It hasn't been bad for me."

"Yeah, you get to play volleyball and lounge by the lake," she said, throwing him a dry look.

"And you pay me to do it." He grinned at her and looked around her cabin. "Making tea?"

"Trust me, I need it." She moved past him, and Griffin took a deep breath of her shampoo or hairspray.

"I'll bet. It only gets easier, though, right?"

"Yeah," she said. "It will get easier." She busied herself with the tea by pulling down a cup and turning to him. "I don't suppose you drink tea?"

"Sure," he said. "I'll take some tea." He didn't normally drink tea—he preferred coffee—but he could do it. Especially if she had honey, as Griffin was a sucker for anything with honey in it or on it.

"I've got a nice spiced orange," she said. "And some honey from the wildflower farm down in Fredericksburg."

"Sold," he said, glancing around for somewhere to sit. She had a small dining table for two as well, and Griffin took one of those seats. But his knees barely fit underneath the table, and he wondered if they could sip tea on the couch.

"I'm not super happy with you," she said.

Griffin's heart flopped like a fish out of water. "Why's that?"

The tea kettle whistled, and Toni removed it from the burner. She poured the water over the bags she'd set in the teacups, her eyes completely focused on her task. "You held my hand during dinner announcements."

"No one saw."

Toni looked up at him, her expression full of challenge. "My assistant saw. Hailey saw."

Griffin's chest turned cold. He'd screwed up with a ten-second touch. In his opinion, it was worth it, but at the same time, he wouldn't choose a ten-second hand-hold over being able to hold her, run his hands through her hair, or kiss her.

"I'm sorry," he said, because he was. "It won't happen again."

"I told you after lights out."

"I know." Griffin sighed and removed his cowboy hat. "I just...you seemed so stressed, and I just wanted you to know you aren't alone." Griffin had been stewing about what she'd said about the funding for Camp Clear Creek for hours now.

He had plenty of money, just sitting in the bank.

Toni set his cup of tea on the table in front of him. "I know, and I appreciate that." She sighed as she sank into the other seat at the table and lifted her teacup to her lips. She continued to relax while he stirred honey into his tea.

"How much does the camp need to stay open?" he asked.

"Our budget is quite large," she said. "I mean, we're feeding over a hundred people two meals a day. We have full-time staff, part-time staff, facilities."

Griffin couldn't comprehend all the moving parts of this place that cost money. "I do something similar on the ranch," he said. "Electricity, water, salaries. But there's only a dozen of us."

Toni looked tired as she smiled. Beautiful, but tired. He reached across the table and covered her hands with his. "I'm sorry about earlier. I won't do it again."

She nodded, relaxing even further.

"So how much?" he asked, thinking about salaries, benefits, repairs. His head began to spin.

"The Camden's were our main benefactor," she said. "When someone donates to the Youth Camps of Texas, they can specify which camp they want to fund. The Camden's are from this region, and they've kept our camp open for years."

She still hadn't said how much it would take, and Griffin wondered if he could fund something like this for even a year. Seth was paying for the Edible Neighborhood on Victory Street where their parents lived, but that was nothing to running a camp for youth. And not just one. Multiple camps of different lengths and types.

Griffin sipped his tea, the hot liquid delicious and soothing. "Mm, this is great."

Toni gave him another sleepy smile.

He wanted to ask if he could come to her meeting with the treasurer of the Texas Youth Camp Program. He wanted to ask how much it took to fund a camp like this—again. He wanted her to tell him more.

But she seemed so tired, with barely enough strength to keep her hand in his. She did do that, and Griffin said, "Can we sit on the couch for a bit?"

"Sure." Toni got up, and they moved over to the couch.

"Ah, yes, this is better." Griffin put his arm around her, and she snuggled into his side. "So, Toni Beardall, tell me something about yourself. I feel like I've been talking a lot about me the past couple of times we've been together."

"Something about myself," she said. "I eat dark chocolate every day."

"Ah, smart and beautiful." Griffin chuckled, glad when

Toni gave a light laugh too. He felt sure she'd forgive him for his slip at dinner.

"I've worked out every day for the past three hundred and forty-seven days," she said.

Griffin looked at her, at that coy little smile on her face, and he burst out laughing. Toni did too, shaking her head, her dark hair swinging with the movement.

"Wow, that's a good one." Griffin finished his tea. "Do you run?"

"Mostly hiking," she said. "Some yoga. I'm too old to run."

"Oh, you are not." Griffin wasn't even sure how old she was. Older than him, he knew that.

"How old do you think I am?" she asked, plenty of teasing in her voice.

"I'm not playing this game." He smiled at her. "Number one, my momma would be horrified. Number two, I don't really care how old you are."

She took the last drink from her teacup and handed it to Griffin. "Thirty-six," she said.

"Thirty-three," he said, putting her cup next to his on the end table. "That's not a terrible difference. It's nothing, really."

Toni said nothing, and Griffin's brain was starting to soften with the lateness of the hour. His eyes dropped to her mouth, and Griffin knew it was time to leave. He'd kissed her once—randomly—and he wasn't going to do that again.

He stood up and yawned, making it a little bigger than he really needed to. "I should go."

"Okay," she said, tucking her legs up under her body and looking up at him from the couch. He wanted to take her in his arms and kiss her until he couldn't see straight.

He backed up a step instead. "Listen," he said, clearing his throat. "If you need anything. You know, with your parents, or around camp, let me know. My guys are pretty easy-going."

"I'll let you know."

Griffin hesitated, toying with the idea of telling her about the numbers in his bank account. He quickly decided against it and lifted his hand in an awkward wave. "Okay, well, I'll see you bright and early in the morning."

"Bye, Griffin," she said, and Griffin really wanted her to say his name again. Perhaps while she kissed him.

He strode away from her and practically burst out of her back door. His momentum carried him down the steps and away from the halo of light spilling from her cabin. He moved quickly, unafraid of the darkness surrounding him. But he was completely freaked out by his fantasies.

If he and Toni lived in Chestnut Springs, he wouldn't feel this way. But since he was here, and trying to start a relationship with his boss, he couldn't take their relationship too fast.

"Two years isn't fast," he muttered to himself, though he knew he hadn't been dating Toni for two years. Over the course of those years, he'd spent six months with her. So he could be patient.

By the time he returned to his cabin, his pulse beat in a normal rhythm. He grabbed a bag of popcorn and stuck it in the microwave. While it popped, he got his sitcom queued up and changed into a pair of basketball shorts and a T-shirt.

His cabin didn't have central air conditioning like Toni's, but the window unit was doing a pretty decent job of keeping the single room cool. Before he went to bed, he snacked on the popcorn and went through tomorrow's activities. His boys were doing archery this week, one of Griffin's favorite activities.

Breakfast at seven-fifteen. He had to be over to his teens' cabin by seven. So if he wanted to run... "That's a five a.m. wake-up call," he muttered. He set the alarm on his phone, crawled beneath the covers, put in his earbuds, and closed his eyes.

While the sitcom blared, he usually fell right to sleep. But tonight, his mind went round and round, imagining situations where he and Toni interacted. They had lunch together and then snuck away for a kiss.

Or he managed to leave camp with her to check on her parents, and then they shared a kiss in his truck.

No matter how the conversations or situations went, Griffin couldn't stop thinking about kissing Toni. And it was absolute torture.

૭৯

THE FOLLOWING MORNING, GRIFFIN WOKE TWO MINUTES before his alarm went off. A groan pulled through his throat, and he collapsed back onto the pillow. But he was up now, and he wasn't going to go back to sleep.

So he got up, got dressed, and stretched through the

stiffness in his calves. Then he set off on a jog, deciding not to go all the way around the lake. He didn't have time anyway, and he had a full day ahead of him again.

He loved Texas as the sun colored it with its rays, and a smile filled his soul with every step he took. He went down past the beach where he'd hung out yesterday. Past the canoe docks. Past the water trikes.

About a quarter of the way around the lake, he stopped and turned around to go back. He'd probably been going for about a mile, and he'd just hit his stride. He started back toward his cabin, passing a group of four girls that were jogging the same path as he was.

They didn't have a counselor with them, and Griffin said, "Are you guys alone?"

"No," one said without stopping. "Our counselor is with a couple others behind us."

Griffin wasn't going to enforce the rule anyway, but he'd like to be able to tell Toni he'd asked if it came down to it. There were four girls together, and they'd be okay. Thirty seconds later, he passed the counselor and two other girls, and he nodded at her. She was new, and Griffin couldn't remember her name.

Someone stood on the docks where the canoes were kept, and Griffin wondered how many more people he'd encounter. Most of the campers had to be dragged out of bed at seven to make the seven-fifteen wake-up call at the flagpole.

The woman worked with a canoe, and Griffin knew the movement. He immediately veered off the path and sprinted toward the woods. He could get back to his cabin by following the tree line.

But he couldn't handle another encounter with Lilly Mae. Not this early in the morning. He ran all the way until he could see his cabin, and then he slowed, eventually walking the last hundred yards as he cooled down.

It took him a moment as he tried to make out the shape on his front porch, but when the woman stood, he knew it was Toni.

And she was crying.

He broke into a jog again, his pulse sprinting as it had when he'd seen Lilly Mae, but this time for an entirely different reason. "Hey," he said, taking her right into his arms, despite the sweatiness of his body. "What is it? What's wrong?"

She sniffed and gave him a quick hug. "My mother just called." She swiped at her eyes and drew in a deep breath. "She said she woke up and Daddy was gone."

Griffin's heart plummeted to his running shoes. "Okay," he said, wiping his hands through his hair. "Let's go find him."

CHAPTER TWELVE

Toni paced away from Griffin. "We both can't go." Why had she come running to him? Why hadn't she just gotten in her car and gone?

"Let's call the police," Griffin said.

"I already did," she said. "I was hoping maybe you could stand in for me today." She looked at him, pure anxiety streaming through her. "I'll split your boys and give them to a couple of other counselors on your circuit, and—"

"Ian will take them all," Griffin said. "I'll call him now." He walked with her as they started back toward the epicenter of the camp.

She didn't know what to do, as her mind ran in a million directions. She didn't trust herself to drive herself safely to her mother's, but she couldn't stay here and do nothing. Griffin couldn't come with her. What would everyone think?

Her phone rang again, and Toni was starting to hate the

sound of it. But Hailey's name sat on the screen, and Toni swiped on the call.

"I saw you called," Hailey said, her voice bright and chipper. "I was going through that dead zone at the mouth of the park. What's up?"

"Can you manage without me today?" she asked at the same time Griffin lowered his phone. He nodded, which meant he'd gotten Ian to take his campers that day.

"I guess," Hailey said. "I'm confused. What's going on?"

Toni quickly explained the situation, and then she said, "I'm taking Griffin Johnson with me. He's gotten Ian Traverse to take his boys."

"Yes, go," Hailey said. "Everything will be fine here. I'll be there in five."

"Thank you," Toni said, and she had a feeling she'd be saying those two words a lot today.

"I'm in the upper lot," Griffin said. "It's closer."

"Do you have your keys?"

"Yep."

They changed direction, and only a minute or two passed before she climbed into his truck. She was so glad he'd come with her even though she'd said he couldn't. She never would've been able to drive the windy roads down into Horseshoe Bay and her parents' place.

Two police cars sat in the driveway, and Toni's need to get out of the car and find out what was happening increased to an unbearable level.

Griffin finally stopped the truck, and Toni slid to the ground. She couldn't see any officers, and her mother hadn't come out onto the front porch. "Mother?" She ran toward the front door, yanking it open as she called for her mom again.

"I'm right here," she said, coming out of the kitchen.

Toni's pulse ricocheted around inside her chest. She scanned the house. "Where's Daddy? Where are the officers?"

"One's in here," she said at the same time the young man appeared behind her. "We had to stay here in case Daddy comes back."

Toni stepped into her mother and gathered her into a hug. "Tell me everything, Mother."

Griffin came to her side, slipping his hand into hers. She wasn't embarrassed or frustrated this time, as he had just become her lifeline.

"I got up, like I always do," Mother said. "It was just after six, and Daddy wasn't in bed. That's not that big of a deal. He's always gotten up a lot earlier than me."

"When did you know he wasn't here?" Griffin asked.

Mother looked at him, and Toni reached out with her free hand. Mother shook slightly, but those tremors had started a year or so ago. "I came into the kitchen for coffee, but there was no coffee. Craig always makes the coffee." Her bottom lip trembled, and Toni's eyes teared too. This was too much. Just too much right now.

"So I searched the house and yard for him, and when I couldn't find him, I called you."

"You did the right thing, Mother." Toni hugged her tight and stepped back to Griffin's side. "They'll find him." In her worried mind, she couldn't quite piece together how long Daddy had been missing.

The radio on the officer's shoulder chirped, and Toni's eyes flew to him. "Yancey, come back."

"Here," he said into his radio.

"Be advised that we've located the subject, and we're on the way back to the house."

"They found him?" Toni asked, more hysterical than she liked.

"That's right," the officer said, a smile touching his mouth. He clicked his radio on. "Copy that. ETA?"

"No more than ten minutes."

"Where was he?" she asked.

"They'll fill us in when they get here," Yancey said.

Toni wanted to fly at him and say that wasn't good enough. She needed all of the answers, and she needed them now.

Griffin touched her arm, and she found her center again when she looked at him. He didn't smile, but she could feel his positive energy at her side. And she was so grateful he was at her side right now. She hoped he knew, but she made a mental note to tell him in no uncertain terms.

"I'm going to go outside," Toni said, taking Griffin's hand and moving through the front door. Her emotions were all over the place. Up one moment, down the next. She walked over to the porch railing and leaned against it, exhaling heavily. "Well, I feel stupid."

"Why?" Griffin came up beside her, sliding his hand along her waist. She leaned into him, trying to find the right words.

"I was trying so hard not to panic. I didn't need to drag you away from camp."

"It's my pleasure," he said. "My boys are going to archery this morning, and they won't even miss me. I just sit in the shade while they do their thing."

Toni took strength from him, feeling comfortable in his presence. Humiliation flowed through her though, because she'd wept in front of him. She reached up and wiped her hand down her face just to make sure she didn't have things leaking where they shouldn't be.

It's my pleasure.

He wanted to be with her.

Toni couldn't quite believe it, but all signs seemed to point to the fact that Griffin did like her, and she wondered what he saw in her. She tried to shake those thoughts out of her head, because they were her ex-husband talking.

She couldn't believe Jackson still had sway over her, all these years later.

She pushed, shoved, the negative thoughts out of her mind and looked up at Griffin. He was so close, and if he just leaned his head down, he could kiss her again. Her pulse went erratic, and Toni quickly looked away.

She wanted to kiss him, but not on her parents' front porch while waiting for her father to be brought home by police.

His arm tightened, and he said, "I'd love to take you to breakfast after this."

"Breakfast?"

"Yeah," he said. "We missed breakfast at camp, and there's no way I'm making it to lunch without something to eat. We're already in town..." He let his words hang there, giving Toni a moment to think about what he'd said.

"I suppose we are already in town," she said. "A lot of French toast and bacon sounds great."

"Bacon and French toast, huh?" He chuckled, his breath tickling her ear. He leaned closer, his lips catching on her ear as he said, "I'm more of a steak and egg guy myself."

Toni shivered despite the bright sun in the sky, and Griffin chuckled again. Excitement built inside her, and she said, "That doesn't surprise me."

"No?" he asked. "What would surprise you?"

"I'm a little surprised you don't have a girlfriend in Chestnut Springs," she said. "I'm surprised you were wearing your T-shirt while running this morning." She looked at him, feeling flirty and playful. "What would surprise you about me?"

"Oh, you're an open book, Miss Beardall." He grinned at her and nodded toward the road. "They're here."

Toni swung her attention to the two police vehicles pulling into the driveway. She stepped away from Griffin and opened the door. "Mother, he's back." She waited for her mom to shuffle her way outside, and together, they went down the front steps.

Toni let Mother hug her husband first, and then Toni embraced her father. "What happened? Why did you leave like that?"

"I ran to get doughnuts and coffee," he said. "And when I came out of the coffee shop, my car was gone."

Toni looked at the nearest police officer. "Was it stolen?"

"The car was on the other side of the street," the officer said. He reached out and shook Toni's hand. "I'm Officer Myers."

"I'm Craig's daughter, Toni."

"Near as we can tell, he got disoriented and confused, and he walked down the street looking for the car."

"I didn't park it across the street," her dad said. "I would remember doing that."

"Okay, Craig," Mother said. "Come inside. It's so hot today."

Another officer followed the two of them with the doughnuts and coffee her father had gone to get.

Toni watched them until they disappeared through the front door. Then she sighed and turned back to Officer Myers. "Okay, so do we need to go get the car?"

He glanced at Griffin and back to Toni. "Yeah. He had the keys and everything." He handed them back to her. "I wouldn't let him drive anymore, ma'am."

Another big sigh escaped her lips. "Yeah, I know. I need to talk to them about that." She wasn't looking forward to that conversation, and she didn't have to have it this morning. "Is that it? Do I owe you guys anything?"

"Just doin' our jobs." He nodded at her and turned to go back to his SUV. The other officers followed, and Toni stood on the front sidewalk while they loaded up and drove away

She looked at Griffin. "I need a few minutes to talk to them. Can you wait for me in your truck?"

"Take your time," he said, leaning toward her. His lips

brushed her cheek, and then he walked down the sidewalk too.

Toni held very still for a few moments, enjoying the zing of energy that ran down her neck from where he'd touched her.

And she was suddenly starving—and not just for bacon and French toast.

She put a stern look on her face and went into the house. "Daddy," she said when she found the pair of them sitting at the kitchen table.

"I know," he said, more agitated than usual. "I won't go get coffee and doughnuts again."

"It's not just that," Toni said. "You forgot where you parked the car. But it's okay." She hugged him again. "I'm just glad you're back, and that you're okay."

Her father patted her back, and pure love flowed through Toni. She did need to talk about their driving, and she hoped she wouldn't have to forcibly take their car keys. "I'll go get the car," she said. "You two are okay?"

"We're fine," Mother said, giving her a smile. "Thanks for coming Toni."

She nodded, turned, and left. She had so much more to say, but she didn't want to say it. Her parents knew they were getting older. She didn't need to tell them that.

But the fact that her father thought he hadn't parked the car where he had... That concerned Toni.

She climbed into Griffin's truck, and said, "Ready."

"All right." Griffin backed out of the driveway and added, "You know, my father hurt himself a few years ago, and nothing's been easy with them since then."

Toni looked at him, surprise entering her emotions. "I'm sorry about that."

"He can't drive. We've told my mother not to drive too, but sometimes she runs to the grocery story. Seth—my oldest brother—does a ton for them. Rex and I live in town, and we help with grocery items or anything else they need."

Toni didn't know what to say, so she just nodded. He understood. That was all that mattered. "Thank you for coming with me," she said. "Even if it wasn't an emergency, and I didn't really need you."

"You did need me," he said. "And I'm happy to be needed." He reached for her hand, and Toni smiled as his fingers clasped hers.

She didn't argue with him, because it was okay to need someone. And he was a good someone to need.

Her mood lightened as Griffin made turns to get to a diner near the library. "Is this one good?" he asked, peering up at it. "Doesn't seem terribly busy."

"I think we're in between the rush times," Toni said. "People either come really early, or after the regular folk go to work."

"Does that make us irregular?" He shot a grin in her direction and got out of the truck. Toni stayed where she was when he indicated she should, and she watched him round the hood of his truck to open her door for her.

"Wow, a real gentleman," she said as she slid out of the truck and practically into his arms.

His dark eyes filled with electricity. "I don't have a girlfriend in Chestnut Springs," he said. "In case that wasn't crystal clear."

"Why's that?" Toni asked, sobering slightly. "No pretty girls there?"

"No amazing *women*," he said, his voice dropping. He hadn't stepped back, and Toni felt a bit trapped between him and the truck, the door still open and creating a third side on her left. "At least no one like you."

"I'm not all that special," she said, her voice full of air.

"Yes, you are," he said, and he wasn't kidding.

Toni wanted to believe him, so she started working on that.

"I ran with a shirt on this morning, because I knew I'd probably see a lot of teenage girls. Or worse, Lilly Mae." He gave a theatrical shiver, and Toni giggled.

She hated that she giggled, but it seemed to light an additional fire in Griffin. He brought Toni's hand to his lips, his eyes never leaving hers. "You asked what would surprise me about you, and honestly, I'd love to know why you haven't dated in nine years."

Unadulterated terror gripped her heart and squeezed.

CHAPTER THIRTEEN

G riffin backed up, the panic streaming from Toni's entire being. "You don't have to tell me right now," he said. "But I'm sure there are some pretty decent men up here in Horseshoe Bay."

If he'd had any doubts about Toni's feelings for him, they'd been eradicated that morning. When she was in trouble, she came straight to him. That meant something. She'd held his hand, leaned right into his touch along her back and waist, and flirted with him. She'd shivered in his arms—in a good way—when he whispered in her ear.

And Griffin himself was about to combust. He'd thought about kissing her right there in the parking lot, but that wasn't terribly romantic. But if he didn't kiss her again soon—really kiss her—he felt sure he'd lose his mind.

They walked into the diner, and Griffin said, "Two, please," to the woman standing at the hostess station. She plucked two menus from the holder and led them to a booth around the corner.

"There are some decent men here in Horseshoe Bay," Toni said as the hostess walked away. She pulled her wrapped package of silverware toward her. "I'm just not interested in any of them."

"Why's that?" he asked, unwrapping his knife and fork.

"Drinks?" a woman chirped, and Griffin put in an order for Diet Coke. Toni opted for water.

She kept her eyes on the waitress until she was truly gone, and then she looked at Griffin again. "My first husband was not a nice man," she said, lifting her chin as if daring him to contradict her. "I stayed with him too long, and I believed the horrible lies he told me about myself."

Griffin's heart wailed for her. He frowned and looked down at the table. "I'm so sorry." He reached for her hands, glad when she gave them to him.

"I spent some time in therapy, and I started working at Camp Clear Creek." She pulled her hands away when the waitress reappeared and set down their drinks. "Thanks."

"Thank you," Griffin said. "We need a minute."

"Do we?" Toni asked. "I know what I want, and I bet I can order for you too."

A smile popped onto Griffin's face. "Do it, then."

Toni looked at the waitress, but Griffin only had eyes for her. She seemed confident and charming as she said, "I want the French toast breakfast, with hash browns and bacon."

"How do you want your eggs?"

"Scrambled."

"Okay."

"And he wants chicken fried steak and eggs." Toni flicked her eyes toward him. "Country potatoes."

"How do you want your eggs?"

Griffin nodded to Toni, his eyebrows lifting.

"Over easy," she said, and Griffin was impressed.

"Pancakes or toast?"

"Pancakes."

"Comin' up." The woman picked up the menus and walked away.

Toni leaned her elbows on the table and said, "How'd I do?"

"Flawless," he said, and he didn't just mean the ordering.

"Really? Or are you just saying that?"

"I never just say stuff," Griffin said, unwrapping a straw and putting it in his cola. He took a long drink while Toni did the same with her straw and water. He didn't know how to prompt her to keep talking about her ex, and maybe he didn't need to know.

"Anyway," she said. "I started retraining my mind to focus on positive things. I learned that I do have worth, and that I was very good at my job."

"You didn't know those things before?"

"Jackson was abusive," she said. "My therapist actually said I'd been gaslighted, and it takes a very long time to re-route those neuro-pathways."

Griffin wanted to find this Jackson and wrap his fingers around his throat. But anger was more of Rex's personality, and Griffin relaxed a moment later. "How long were you married?"

"Just a couple of years," she said.

"And you don't want to get married again." He wasn't asking, and he watched her closely.

She shrugged one shoulder and stirred her straw in her cup, making the ice clink against the sides of the glass. "I mean, I didn't."

"Am I the first man you've dated?"

"Are we dating?" She lifted her eyes to his, that familiar sparkle residing there again. He much preferred it to the heavy desperation or pure panic.

"Yes," he said, this time the one to lift his chin, totally daring her to contradict him. "I mean, I snuck out after hours last night. That's a fire-able offense."

She pealed out a delightful laugh. "It is not," she said. "Not for a counselor."

He chuckled too and readjusted his cowboy hat. "Still. It was late, and I'm going to be paying for that for a while. I'm not as young as I once was."

She scoffed and looked at him again. "Don't talk to me about being young."

Griffin wanted to talk to her about everything. "Do you want children, Toni?"

"Oh, we're going for the gold this morning," she said, clearly surprised.

"Yep," he said, because if he got the gold, that meant he'd have kissed her before the clock struck noon. And that was so happening if there was anything about it he could control. Which, of course, there wasn't.

"Yeah," she said. "Maybe more than one and less than five."

He laughed, making room on the table when the waitress appeared with plates in her hands. She set down the pancakes and the French toast, the steak and eggs, the bacon and eggs.

Once she'd gone, Griffin said, "I think that's probably a good number." Then he picked up his knife and fork and cut into his chicken fried steak.

The conversation after that was easy, and Griffin kept it focused around Camp Clear Creek. Toni obviously loved the camp, and the idea of funding the camp loitered in the back of his mind.

He wanted her to be happy, and he had plenty of money. She still hadn't told him how much it cost to run a camp like Clear Creek, and he hadn't had time to do any independent research. She'd literally told him about the camp's possibly closure last night.

He thought of Seth and Rex, the two brothers he'd reach out to and ask for advice before he spent a dime. What would they do?

Rex was a bit more hot-headed and quick to make decisions, and he'd probably offer to fund the camp before asking a single question. Seth would move slower, examine things from every side, and ask a ton of questions.

Both of them would get Griffin to think about all sides of the question, Rex would be more emotional, and Seth more practical.

And when it came to Toni, Griffin needed all the help he could get.

"Finished, cowboy?" she asked, and he looked up from his nearly-gone pancakes.

He took one more bite, with the delicious blackberry syrup, and nodded. He pulled his wallet out and tossed some money on the table while Toni scooted to the edge of the booth.

He got up and took her hand in his, his heartbeat accelerating with every step he took.

"Sir?" the waitress called behind him.

He turned around, surprised. "Yeah?"

"You left way too much." She extended some cash toward him.

Griffin glanced at Toni. "No, I didn't. Have a great day." He reached up to tip his hat, only to realize he wasn't wearing one. Of course he wasn't. He'd been running when he'd come upon Toni, and he hadn't gone inside to shower or change either.

He suddenly felt naked, and he ran his hand through his hair, wondering why he hadn't given it a second thought. He suddenly didn't want to kiss Toni, not with blackberry syrup-scented breath and no cowboy hat to hide behind afterward, and without fresh deodorant and cologne.

"You really left a lot," Toni said once they were free of the diner.

"Yeah, well, she looked like she could use it," Griffin said easily. For some reason, he didn't want to talk about his money right now. His black truck loomed ahead, and Griffin felt his opportunity slipping away from him.

He led Toni to the passenger door, but he didn't open

it. She paused and looked at him, and Griffin decided on the spot to go for it. He hadn't asked to kiss her after Russ's wedding, but today, he said, "Toni." He cleared his throat, and his hand automatically went up to remove the cowboy hat that wasn't there.

"Are you going to kiss me?" she asked.

His eyes widened. "Uh, yeah. Is that okay?" He felt like a complete idiot, and Toni wasn't tipping up on her toes to make herself more available.

Toni looked at him, and he found fear, flirtatiousness, and lots of desire. He leaned down, and that got her to move too. He breathed only a moment before her lips met his, and his pulse began to sprint.

Last time, he'd barely experienced kissing Toni before his senses had taken over. But this time, he gave into those senses, fed them, and thoroughly enjoyed kissing his boss.

§❧

GRIFFIN RETURNED TO CAMP, SHOWERED, AND FIRED UP his tablet. He had a laptop in Chestnut Springs, but he hadn't brought it with him. His boys would be in their archery workshop until lunchtime, and he had about an hour before he had to meet his campers and Ian for lunch.

He began searching the Internet for summer camps for youth, administrative costs, how much tuition was, and how much part-time people made.

He made a ton of notes, circling numbers as he counted the number of people who currently worked at Clear Creek—at least to the best of his abilities. After forty minutes, he pulled out his phone and started adding every-thing up.

For the three months in the summer—the bulk of the camps here at Clear Creek—Toni spent over three-quar-ters of a million dollars to keep this place running. And that didn't include the fall or holiday camps.

He leaned away from the notepad, math not necessarily his strong suit. But he'd inherited just over two billion dollars from his mother, and his father had advised the boys not to spend a dime for a year.

Griffin, for the most part, had taken that advice and not bought anything. If he donated a million dollars a year to fund Camp Clear Creek, he could do it for a hundred years and only have donated a hundred million dollars.

And he had two hundred, three hundred, four hundred, five hundred, all the way to one thousand million dollars.

"That's a billion," he said to himself. And that was only half of what he had in the bank. So he could fund the camp for a thousand years and only spend half of what he'd been given.

His phone buzzed, and he jolted away from the note-book, instinctively covering it with his tablet. Why, he wasn't sure. No one was going to come barging into his cabin and demand to know what he'd been looking at.

Rex had texted, and the message said, *I'm having this feeling that I need to talk to you. Call me when you get a chance?*

Tonight, Griffin said, leaving the punctuation off so Rex would think he was busy. He *was* busy. He grabbed his cowboy hat and positioned it on his head just-so. He stuffed the notebook and tablet in one of the drawers in the kitchen.

And he left his cabin to go meet his boys and his friend for lunch, the idea of proposing his ability to fund the camp to Toni that evening, during their after-lights-out rendezvous revolving through his mind.

CHAPTER FOURTEEN

Toni paced in her office, her cute high heels pinching her pinky toe on her left foot. But she couldn't meet with the treasurer of the Texas Youth Camp Program wearing cowgirl boots and jeans.

She'd gone to her cottage in Horseshoe Bay yesterday afternoon, while the campers were doing their skits and tin foil dinners, and retrieved some more professional clothing for today's meeting with Eddie Microneil.

A meeting for which the man was late.

Toni had offered to meet him down in town, but he claimed to want to tour the camp anyway. "Just to see how things are going," he'd said.

She knew what that meant. He was going to be making an assessment on the camp to decide if he should shuffle funds around to keep Clear Creek in operation. She should've told Hailey why she'd been a basket case this past week, but Toni's nervous and curt behavior could've been attributed to the situation with her parents.

Or her secret relationship with one of her counselors.

Her heartbeat bounced strangely in her chest, because she should've warned Griffin too. "He knows you're meeting with Eddie today," she muttered to herself. She hadn't mentioned a tour to anyone, and she wondered if he'd want to mingle during lunchtime or see the teens as they did their afternoon classes.

Meeting first? Tour second?

Toni didn't know, and she wished Eddie would arrive so she could move on with her life.

"Toni?" Someone knocked on the door at the same time they said her name, and she spun toward the man she'd been waiting for.

"Eddie." She put a wide smile on her face and strode toward him, all thoughts of her smashed pinky toe gone. "Good to see you." She extended her hand and shook his, noting his black slacks and white shirt. He wore a tie too, and he'd absolutely melt on a tour. His shiny shoes wouldn't allow him to go traipsing around much either and that was just fine with Toni.

She couldn't really navigate the camp in high heels either.

He carried a briefcase, and he glanced around her office. She'd never been happier that she'd cleaned up her coffee cups and mugs, cleared the files off her desk, and opened the blinds. "Come and sit," she said. "Or do you want to take the tour first? The campers will be finishing up their morning workshop in about a half an hour."

"Let's talk first," he said, moving over to the only other chair in her office. Hailey usually sat there, though Toni had conducted all of her interviews here too. A flash of the countless hours she'd dedicated to this camp entered her mind, and she didn't want to lose Clear Creek. She couldn't.

She pressed against the depression and anxiety as she rounded her desk and sat down. She waited for Eddie to say something else, show her a piece of paper, something.

He sat down too, setting his briefcase on the ground without removing anything from it. He steepled his fingers and looked at her. "Tell me how things are going here."

"Things are great here," she said, taking care not to speak too quickly. She knew Eddie and had for the past eight years. He'd sat on the board when she'd been hired. She drew in a deep breath. "Our waiting list is longer than ever. Our facilities are immaculate. The kids love coming here, and Hailey and I are very good at public relations and handling parents."

Eddie started nodding as she spoke, as if he agreed with her. "Do you know why the Camden's stopped donating?" he asked.

"I assume it's because Verona died," she said, her heart skipping a beat.

A sympathetic look crossed his face. "That's what her daughter said. The siblings have to agree on how to split the estate, and only one of them wanted to keep donating to the camp fund at the level they were."

"Perhaps they could donate something smaller," she suggested.

"I told her that, but she said they simply couldn't."

"This is one of your top-rated camps," Toni said. "Perhaps there is money that could be moved from somewhere else." She folded her arms on the desk. "I want to be reasonable, but I know our enrollment is one of the highest, and our expenses are lower than other camps, especially the equine ones." She reached for a paper she'd prepared and slid it across her desk. "This is our annual budget right now from all of our camps. Summer, fall, winter, holiday."

Eddie picked up the paper and looked at it. He was an accomplished man, and while he didn't look at the sheet for long, Toni knew he'd seen what she wanted him to.

"And this one is what I'd need to simply do summer camps, in that first column there." She handed him a light blue paper. "In the second column is what I'd need to just do summer and holiday, which as I'm sure you're aware, our holiday camps fill the same day we release them, and they're wildly popular."

Eddie looked at the second paper.

"And the third column is what it would take to run all the seasonal camps I do now, but with a reduced budget. Less counselors. Higher tuition from the attendees." She swallowed. "A part-time chef and assistant instead of full-time, benefitted positions."

She didn't want to do that. She couldn't even *imagine* calling Hailey in and telling her she had to cut her pay and hours, and oh, *no more benefits either. Sorry.*

She swallowed when Eddie still said nothing. "As you

can see, I'm committed to Camp Clear Creek. I do *not* want this camp to close."

"I can see that," Eddie said. He bent and tucked both papers in his briefcase. "I'll take everything to our board meeting at the end of the month."

"You're on my side here, right?" she asked as he stood. She got to her feet too. "We've always gotten along just fine, Eddie. I don't need sugar-coating. Just tell me the truth."

Eddie gazed at her, his dark eyes hard as steel. "The truth is, Toni, I don't know. It's not all up to me."

"But you're great with numbers," she said. "You can make it work. Present the case to the board in the right light."

He nodded. "I'll do my best. There's a lot to consider."

"I understand that," she said. "Would you do me a favor?" She didn't normally have to be so professional and have such hard conversations, and her hands shook.

"Sure."

She pressed her palms against her thighs. "Let me know as soon as you can," she said. "Don't wait until the last minute. My people deserve a chance to find another job without a major delay in their income stream."

"I'll definitely do that," he said. He drew in a breath too, and everything about him softened. Toni realized that he didn't enjoy conversations like this any more than she did. "Now, would you mind showing me around camp for a few minutes?"

"Absolutely," she said. "Let's start here in the main

building, where our full-time, on-site chef is doing a cooking class for our fourteen-year-olds."

🐚

A WEEK HAD PASSED SINCE EDDIE'S TOUR AROUND CAMP Clear Creek. Toni hadn't heard from him yet, but it was only halfway through June, and she knew the board for the Texas Youth Camp Program met the last Thursday of every month.

The TYCP was a good organization Toni believed in. Perhaps if Clear Creek did close, she could find a position within their infrastructure.

She and Griffin saw each other around camp, but he didn't try to hold her hand again. Everything between them where other people were around remained strictly professional. But the way he kissed her pressed up against her back door only a few moments before he left her cabin late at night sure wasn't strictly professional.

Toni found herself falling for him, and fast. He was kind. He was good-looking. Hard-working. Brilliant. He liked to have fun, but he knew when he was getting close to the line. He loved his family, and he was willing to help Toni with whatever she needed.

Thankfully, she'd had no more personal drama flare-ups. She still hadn't told anyone else about the possible funding issue, nor had she had the hard talk with her parents about their driving habits and that maybe it was time to hang up the car keys permanently.

She had every Thursday off while Hailey took every

Tuesday. They swapped days on the weekends, and Toni almost always gave Hailey Saturday while she took Sunday. Then she could go to church with her parents and enjoy a leisurely day without the stress of getting everything done that seemed to permeate Saturdays.

For her counselors, she allowed them to pair up and give each other breaks throughout the week. They each got a full day off on one weekend day, and then two half-days throughout the week.

Griffin had quickly chosen Sunday as his day off, as well as Tuesday mornings and Thursday afternoons. That way, he could hang out in her office on Tuesday morning while everyone was at their AM workshop and Hailey wouldn't walk in on them kissing.

And they'd been exploring the other natural wonders of the Texas Highland Lakes area on Thursday afternoons as they got off the ranch together. He still came to her cabin every evening too, after he'd checked on his boys and made sure they were following camp rules. He didn't stay long, because his hours as a counselor were long, and he claimed not to bounce back as easily from not getting enough sleep.

Kayaking at Lady Bird Lake next Sunday?

Toni grinned at Griffin's text. They'd had a great conversation about paddling and what a great form of exercise it was. She'd teased him that he'd cut into her exercise streak, and he said he'd just take her to do things she could count as such.

Yes, she sent back. It was a bit of a drive to get to Austin, but that was prime conversation and hand-holding time. And Griffin drove the nicest truck Toni had ever been in, and she loved riding with him as she could relax and let someone else do the hard work.

Pick you up at ten, he sent back, and she loved that he planned their dates almost a week in advance.

"What are you smiling at?" Hailey asked, and Toni scrambled to pick up her phone as if her best friend would beat her to it.

"Nothing," Toni said.

"Yeah, totally looks like nothing." Hailey grinned as she sat in the chair across from Toni's desk. "Are you kissing nothing yet?"

Toni's face heated, because she'd been kissing Griffin for a couple of weeks now.

Hailey giggled, but she sobered quickly. "If I wasn't blissfully happy kissing Leon, I'd be so jealous."

"So you're still in blissfully happy." Toni was thrilled for Hailey, as she hadn't always had the best luck with men. And Leon Landers seemed like a great guy. A bit reserved when she'd first met him, but strong, and capable, and pretty much a hero around Horseshoe Bay, as he was a paramedic and literally saved people for a living.

"So much so," Hailey said with a smile. "So what are you and Nothing doing?"

"Nothing," Toni said, giving Hailey a look. They'd agreed that Toni wouldn't tell her much. That way, if something happened, Hailey could say she didn't know and not be lying.

Toni didn't want to lie. It wasn't against the rules for camp counselors to see each other, so it wasn't technically against the rules for her to have a relationship with Griffin. She just didn't want the news to get around.

"There you are," a woman said, and Toni looked to the doorway.

"Lilly Mae," she said, rising from her seat and shooting Hailey a look at the same time. This was exactly why they didn't talk about Griffin at work. Or ever. "What can I do for you?"

"I cannot partner with Jericho. Or Jennika. Or whatever her name is." She stomped into the office like a petulant child and put her hands on her hips. "I need to take Thursday morning off for a hair appointment. It's literally the only time my stylist has, and she said she can't switch me."

Toni exchanged a glance with Hailey. "Why can't she?"

"Her boyfriend is getting out of the hospital or something." Lilly Mae rolled her eyes, and Toni couldn't believe this woman. Worse, what had Griffin ever seen in her?

Everyone makes mistakes, she told herself, also reminding herself that their relationship was five years old, and surely Griffin had learned a thing or two in the past few years.

"Oh yes," Toni said. "She spoke to me about that already. She's taking the whole day that day." She picked up her phone and started tapping. She didn't want to give into Lilly Mae's demands, but with personalities like hers, sometimes it was better to avoid a conflict than have to wade through one for any length of time.

"I assigned her afternoon to Reggie. Could you talk to her about taking them all day? Hailey or I can help too."

"It's Thursday," Hailey said, and Toni thought of her

day off camp campus with Griffin—at least in the afternoon.

"I could at least help in the morning," Toni said.

"But—"

"It's okay, Hailey," Toni said. "If Lilly Mae will talk to Reggie, then we can cover it." She looked back at Lilly Mae. "But Lilly Mae, if Reggie can't—I don't know what her girls are assigned to this week—you have to accept that. Not everyone has to bend their will to yours."

Lilly Mae opened her mouth to say something, but it just hung there like a fish out of water. She sputtered the same too, her brain obviously catching up to what Toni had said.

"Thursdays are *my* days off," Toni explained, her voice gentle but firm. "So you going to get your hair done affects me. And your partner's name is JenniLynn, and she's a fantastic counselor who's worked here for four years. She's flexible, and she's kind, and I think a boyfriend *getting out of the hospital* is more important than your cut and color."

"Well, I—"

"We're done here, Lilly Mae," Toni said with a smile. "Talk to Reggie about it. Be kind. *Ask* her. If she can, great. If she can't, you might need to call your stylist and see what else she can do for you." She folded her arms and leaned against her desk. Guess she wasn't going to let Lilly Mae run the show.

No, that was Toni's job, and she was extraordinarily good at it.

"I'll talk to Reggie," Lilly Mae said, a flush moving through her face.

"Thank you."

She nodded and left the office. Hailey and Toni looked at one another, only silence between them.

"Did that just happen?" Hailey said. "Why didn't I record it?"

Toni tipped her head back and laughed. Truly laughed, as she was happier in that moment than she'd been in a while. She had a thoughtful, handsome boyfriend. A great job. Amazing friends. And she'd put Lilly Mae Moore in her place.

Now, if she could just figure out a way to *keep* her great job—and this camp open—Toni would be holding the world in the palm of her hand.

CHAPTER FIFTEEN

G riffin heard Toni's laughter, and it caused him to turn his head toward the sound. He caught sight of her walking with a group of girls younger than his campers. She tossed her dark hair over her shoulder and leaned forward to see one of the girls in the line.

She said something he couldn't hear from where he stood on the edge of the patio on the west side of the main building. His boys were doing a cooking class this morning, but he'd had to escape the room when Miles had burned something that had sent noxious fumes into the air.

It was hot outside, but in the shade, it wasn't melt-your-skin hot, and Griffin hadn't gone back inside yet.

Toni wore a short skirt that barely reached mid-thigh, and a flowing blouse she hadn't buttoned. All at once, he realized she was dressed to go to the beach, and he wondered if he could sneak away from the cooking class to watch her.

You're not a stalker, he coached himself. But Toni was oh-so-beautiful, and he wanted to see her in a swimming suit.

Then he remembered it was Thursday, and she shouldn't be on the grounds at all. They had plans to meet at the golf course outside of town later today. He quickly sent her a text, asking her about it, but she didn't reply right away.

He watched her disappear down the hill toward the lake, and he knew he was in very real danger of falling in love with her. He wondered if he already was, and how he would know if it did happen.

His phone rang, and his heart leapt. But it was only Russ, and he quickly swiped on the call. "Hey," he said, a smile filling the word and his face.

"Griffin," Russ said. "I know you can't talk much up there, but I wondered if you'd be coming home on the weekend any time soon."

"Not this week," he said. "But next Sunday, yes. It's the hard break between camps, and I have Saturday and Sunday off."

"So the twenty-third?" Russ asked, as if he had a calendar in front of him.

"Yes," Griffin said, going with it. "And that next camp is only ten days. I'll have the Fourth of July weekend off too. Thursday through Sunday."

"Awesome. Seth and Jenna are hosting a huge barbecue on the Fourth. I'm sure he'll talk to you about coming."

Griffin looked toward the hill where Toni had just been. "Could I bring someone?"

"Bring...someone?" Russ repeated as if he didn't know what Griffin meant.

"I'm seeing someone up here," he said, trying not to be so proud about it. But he couldn't keep the smile off his face, and he knew then that he really liked Toni. Really, really liked her.

"I'm sure you can bring her," Russ said. "So the twenty-third, and the fourth of July."

"Yep."

"See you then."

The call ended before Griffin could think that he should ask why Russ cared when he was going to be coming home. It had to be some sort of announcement, as the brothers tried to do big things in the presence of everyone, and he was the only one unavailable right now.

"Griffin," George said, and he turned toward his camper.

"Yep."

"Mike wants you to come try his brownies."

"Oh, boy," Griffin said, smiling. "Am I going to like them?"

"He's the only one that got them to look like normal brownies," George said as he ducked back inside the building, Griffin right behind him. "So maybe?"

"Is there ice cream?"

"Did someone say ice cream?" The chef, Dalton, joined them in the hall, an ice cream container in his hand. "Can you eat brownies without ice cream?"

"I don't recommend it," Griffin said.

"Neither do I." They all entered the room where the

boys had been working, and Griffin was happy to see the smoke had cleared out. The scent of burnt chocolate still hung in the air, but it was a lot less potent than before.

He walked over to Mike, who indeed had a pan of brownies in front of him. "Wow," Griffin said. "These look amazing." He beamed at the boy, and they knocked knuckles. The other boys came over to Mike's station, and the shy boy who'd come out of his shell a little bit more every day started serving brownies.

"I don't know how you did this," Miles said, taking a bite of the brownie without ice cream. "But it's awesome." They high-fived, and Griffin's heart and soul warmed. They were from opposite ends of the universe, and yet they got along great. Not only that, but they were genuine friends.

Haws moaned with his first bite, and Griffin turned to find a bowl. He wasn't one to pass up sweets, that was for sure, and the combination of warm brownie and cold vanilla ice cream was one of his favorites.

He thought of Toni and her dark chocolate bite every day, and he put the rich dessert in his mouth. A moan came from his mouth too, and it was completely involuntary. His body had just done it, because the brownies were that good.

"Do you cook at home?" he asked Mike.

"Yeah," he admitted. "My dad isn't around, and my mom...works a lot." He ducked his head as if he was embarrassed about his mother having a job. Griffin sensed there was something else there, and he glanced at the other boys.

They looked at Mike and then Griffin, and George wore a look of surprise on his face.

"What am I missing?" Griffin asked.

"Nothing," TJ said, stepping to Mike's side.

"Oh, it's something." He looked at all of his boys. They slept in the cabin together, and just because the lights went out at ten-thirty didn't mean they had to be silent after that. "Who's going to tell me?"

"It's not a camp thing," Haws said.

"Mike?" Griffin asked. "It's obviously your thing. If you want me to know, that's great. If not, I understand."

"Just tell him," Adam said, and since he didn't say a whole lot, what he did say carried a lot of weight.

Mike looked around at his fellow campers. His friends. "It's just my mom drinks a lot," he said. "So I have to take care of a lot of things around the house." He focused on the brownies still in the pan. "That's all."

But Griffin thought there was more. What he was supposed to do about it, he wasn't sure. Adults could drink. "Does she...?" He didn't even know what to ask.

"She doesn't hit him," Miles said. "She's not abusive."

"She's *neglecting* him," TJ said. "That's totally abusive, dude." They'd clearly had this conversation before. The quieter boys—George, Adam, and Mike—listened to the other three as they argued about what was abuse and what wasn't.

"Guys," Griffin finally said, holding up one hand. "Enough."

They felt silent, and the tension between them tightened. "Mike," he said. "Do we need to talk privately?" If he had to report abuse, he'd need to do so through the official camp procedures.

"No," he mumbled. "I'm fine."

"You're *not* fine, dude," TJ said. "Stand up for yourself." He shook his head and walked away.

Miles said, "Don't worry about him, Mike. He's just passionate about some things."

Griffin had the afternoon off, but he could get Ian to take the other five while he had a private lunch with Mike. "Me and you for lunch," he said to Mike. "Outside my cabin. The rest of you will go with Ian for lunch, okay?"

"Yes, sir," Adam said, and he wasn't giving Griffin an ounce of sass. He just had good Texas manners.

His phone buzzed, and Toni's name appeared at the top. He quickly shoved the phone in his back pocket, as teenagers had the eyes of eagles. He didn't want his boys to know about his relationship with the camp administrator, and his own face grew hot in the silence.

"Let's talk kitchen clean-up," Dalton said, and he made the chore sound like an amazing rock concert the boys would like. Then he turned on the music, and it was every song from his childhood. Surprisingly, with the sixties and seventies tunes blasting, cleaning up wasn't as bad as it could've been.

Griffin peeked at his phone while they took dishes into the kitchen, and he saw that Toni had said she was just covering for someone for the morning, but she'd be ready for their lunch.

His heart stuck between his ribs for a moment, struggling to beat against the cage. Their lunch.

I have a boy who needs me for lunch, he said. *Can we go after?*

Of course, she responded. *I'll be in my cabin whenever you're ready.*

🙞

GRIFFIN WAITED DOWN THE BLOCK AND AROUND THE corner from Toni's parents' house. She'd passed him ten minutes ago, so she should be showing up soon. He half-hated the secrecy of their relationship, and half-loved it. That half liked sneaking around in the dark to kiss her, and hiding under his blankets at night to text her, as if he were one of the fifteen-year-old boys he mentored at camp.

He'd told her about Mike's mom after the boy had opened up at lunch on Thursday. His side of the story did make the mother seem neglectful, especially when Griffin asked about food in the house and Mike had said they barely had any.

He'd wanted to ask Mike how he'd paid for the three week camp, which was the most expensive one. He'd wanted to give him ten thousand dollars and tell him to order his groceries and put it on Griffin's debit card.

But he'd learned his first year at Camp Clear Creek that he couldn't save anyone. Money fixed a lot of things though...

"Hey," Toni said, interrupting his thoughts as she opened the passenger door and climbed into the cab of the truck. She wore a smile and the same clothes he'd seen her in on Thursday. Short swim skirt, with a flowy cover-up she now had buttoned.

"Ready for this?" he asked. He'd put two kayaks from the camp in the back of his truck that morning, after properly checking them out.

"So ready." She buckled her seatbelt, and added, "My parents are doing pretty good today."

"That's great, sweetheart," he said.

"How's Mike?"

Griffin exhaled heavily as he got the truck in gear and back on the road. "I think he's dreading going home."

"I called his mother on Friday, but she didn't answer."

Griffin glanced over at her, unsurprised to catch a look of concern on Toni's face. "What's the next step, then?"

"I'll call again," she said. "And those are not fun phone calls to make."

"I'm sure they aren't." And he hated putting her in that position.

"If I can't get in touch with her, I'll call child services," she said. "I'll have to report it anyway, but I'd like to say I was able to speak to her and get some sort of promise that she'd pay the bills and make sure there was food in the house."

"He's only fifteen," Griffin said. "When I was fifteen, I was fishing and riding motorcycles down ravines."

"Motorcycles, huh?" Toni grinned at him, that flirtatious glint in her eye. "Sounds about right."

"I worked plenty, too," he said. "Four or five hours every day, sometimes before the sun was up." He'd hated drawing the early morning feedings, and as he'd gotten older, he realized his father was always up then too—and he stayed out until the last chore on the ranch was done too. How he'd done it, Griffin didn't know.

"Do you like the ranch?" Toni asked, pretty much the same question running through Griffin's own mind.

"Yeah, sure," he said lightly. "I like it just fine."

"But you're not passionate about it." This time, she wasn't asking.

"Is it that obvious?"

"Yes," she said. "You're a counselor up here during what I would assume is one of the busiest times on the ranch."

He nodded, his thoughts moving quickly and then getting stuck in honey and barely flowing. "It's a love-hate relationship, I guess," he said. "Sort of how I feel about running. I love it while I'm doing it. I feel good after, like I accomplished something. And it allows me to eat whatever I want."

She giggled and shook her head.

"But the thought of doing it...I don't like that. I don't want to do it. I force myself to do it. Ranching is like that."

Toni remained quiet for a moment. "Sounds like you might like something else better. I mean, if you can afford to leave the ranch." She sighed and ran her hand through her hair, quickly gathering it all into a ponytail. "I love doing what I do, and I might not be able to keep doing it."

Griffin's throat closed. He wanted only the best for Toni too. But was he trying to save her, the way he'd initially thought he could save Mike from his drunk mother?

"I hate dealing with money," she said.

"Me too," he agreed, simply because he could. He'd never really worried all that much about money, even before the inheritance that had made him and his brothers billionaires. There was always a job waiting for him at Chestnut Ranch, and he had family he could ask for help.

But he could see that not everyone had the resources and support system he did. His heart tore a little, and thankfully Toni moved the conversation to something else. That didn't stop Griffin's mind from whirring though, and he thought about her plight—and Mike's—and now his own with regards to the ranch all the way to Lady Bird Park.

Determined to enjoy his day with his girlfriend, he pushed the circular thoughts away. "Okay," he said, yanking on one kayak to get it out of the truck. "Do you want the blue one or the yellow one?"

"I'm definitely the yellow one in this pairing," she said, smiling at him.

"What does that mean?" He laughed, because a kayak was a kayak, and he'd never given himself a color before.

"I have no idea," she said, laughing too.

Griffin looked at her, and his feelings for her turned to marshmallow. So soft, and gooey, and he knew he was definitely falling in love with her. He wasn't sure if he should be scared about it or not.

As he put on his life jacket and handed one to Toni, as they checked their packs for food and water, and as they pushed the kayaks into the lake, Griffin thought he should call Rex and ask him.

His gruffest, loudest, and youngest brother had fallen in

love before, and he seemed okay. But Griffin wondered if he'd been scared the woman of his dreams might leave town with his heart.

And with Toni's job up in the air, anything was possible.

So Griffin pulled back on the reins and got his heart to go a little slower. If they were heading for a fall, they didn't have to hit the edge of the cliff at breakneck speeds.

"This is the perfect day," Toni said later, after they'd paddled around, talked, laughed, and pulled their kayaks out of the water to eat a picnic lunch. She currently lay on her back, her eyes closed behind her sunglasses, a wide smile on her pretty face.

Griffin chuckled as he lay down beside her. He easily took her into his arms, not caring that they were in a public place. They weren't going to get terribly frisky—it was too hot for that anyway.

"Pretty perfect," he agreed just before kissing her. Yes, things in Griffin's life were pretty darn near perfect in that moment, and he wanted to hold onto that feeling for as long as he could.

CHAPTER SIXTEEN

Toni woke on Monday morning, her skin a little bit tight from the amount of sun she'd taken in on Lady Bird Lake yesterday. "Worth it," she said to her reflection as she got a washcloth wet with cool water and dabbed at her face.

She applied plenty of moisturizer after that and covered all of her exhaustion and stress with makeup and lip gloss—and a smile.

She showed up to the morning devotional on time, and she praised Dalton for his egg muffins, bagel cream cheese bites, and platters of bacon for breakfast. The kids went off to their last week of activities, and Toni exhaled as she faced Hailey.

"Camp one almost done," she said with a smile.

"Yep." Hailey started back toward the main building. "Let's go get the packets ready for next week's group." Her tenacity and willingness to jump right into the next big project was one of the reasons Toni loved her so much, and she smiled as she followed her friend.

She waited until they'd arrived in her office, and then Toni pushed the door closed behind her. That got Hailey to turn around, surprised etched clearing in her face.

"I have something to tell you," Toni said.

"Sounds serious," Hailey said.

"It is." Toni pressed her palms together and wished she had the stomach for difficult conversations. "We might lose our funding after the summer camps," she said. "Nothing's for sure yet, but the Camden's aren't donating anymore."

Toni exhaled and tried to find something else to focus on. Nothing in the office caught her eye and she ended up looking back at Hailey. She wore concern on her face, and her eyes kept getting wider and wider. "Will we—I mean. We can't operate without funding."

"No, we can't," Toni said. "We'll lose our jobs." She moved past Hailey and took a seat at her desk. "It's why I didn't tell you until now. I don't want everyone to worry."

"They should know, though," she said. "So they can start looking for new jobs. I mean, I need this job. *A* job."

Toni nodded. "I know you do. I met with Eddie last week, and he said he'd let me know as soon as possible. He's not going to let us go all the way to August."

Hailey pushed out her breath as she sank into the chair opposite from Toni. "I'm just stunned. Camp Clear Creek has been open for decades."

"Eddie said he'd do everything he could," she said. "His meeting isn't until next week though."

"I hate waiting for news like this." Hailey lifted her

hand to her mouth and chewed on her nails for a moment. Just as quickly, she pulled her hand away.

"I know," Toni said. "I told Griffin—" Her voice froze in her throat.

Hailey just looked at her though, and Toni reminded herself she'd told her friend about Griffin. Maybe not everything—*actually, nothing*, her mind whispered—and the way they sat in silence, staring at one another, spoke volumes.

"Griffin," Hailey said, her eyes widening again. "Of course. Griffin!"

Toni cocked her head. "What do you mean?"

"He's super rich, right? Maybe he could donate."

Toni felt like she'd had a gallon of ice-cold water poured over her head. She blinked several times in quick succession. "He's super rich?"

"He's not?"

"Why would you think he was?"

"I heard...or assumed...I don't know."

Toni had no idea why Hailey would've assumed that. Nor how she would've heard anything about Griffin Johnson, whose family lived an hour from here, down in Chestnut Springs.

She narrowed her eyes at Hailey. "Why would you think that, though?"

"He drives a nice truck."

"So do a lot of cowboys," Toni said, but something zinged around inside her head. Was Griffin in a position to donate to Camp Clear Creek? And if so, why hadn't he ever said so?

Humiliation and embarrassment squirreled through her at all the times she'd talked to him over the past couple of weeks, complaining about the camp's financial problems. He'd said nothing. At least nothing beyond supporting her and commiserating with her.

"So what are we doing to do?" Hailey asked.

"I'm going to wait to hear from Eddie," she said. "And if we need to get our own donors, I'm going to dedicate every spare moment I have to finding them."

"Maybe we should start on that right now," Hailey suggested. "It can't hurt, can it?"

The thought of fundraising made Toni's heart shrivel up and turn a little blacker. She'd do it if she had to. But right now, she didn't have to. Eddie's meeting wasn't for another week and a half, and maybe she just wanted to keep enjoying her Tuesday mornings and Thursday afternoons with Griffin.

"I'll start making a list," Hailey said, nodding like that was that. And with Hailey, it was. "Now, tell me about you and Griffin."

"Oh, well." Toni ducked her head and reached for the folders for next week's campers. They'd only be on-site for ten days instead of this nineteen-day camp they'd started the summer with, and the shorter resident camps were some of the most popular. For the price, they couldn't be beat.

She handed half of the folders to Hailey and said, "We're getting along fine."

"Mm hm." Hailey flicked her eyes up, the message Toni had tried to convey without using many words clearly getting received. "Same number of counselors for next session?" She reached for the post-it notes, and soon the whole table behind her would be covered with the colorful squares.

"No," Toni said, waking her computer by jiggling the mouse. "We're losing Steve for this session on the male side, and Nicole and Pam on the female side."

"Same number of campers?"

"Similar," Toni said. She didn't have the numbers for every session memorized. Registrations for each camp opened on the first of March, and she set the numbers for campers the third week of February. She didn't have to think about it again after that.

She clicked while Hailey made the counselor squares on blue paper for the men and pink for the women. "We have twelve on the waiting list," Toni said. "I'll send our final confirmation email to the registered campers right now. We might get a few drop-outs."

Her phone buzzed on the desk next to her, and her eyes moved to it. Griffin's name sat there, and Toni swiped to open the message.

Going home for the weekend, he'd said. *Want to join me on Sunday? Meet my brothers? See the ranch? Hang out in Chestnut Springs?*

Her heart pumped until it was beating double-time. Her fingers hovered above the screen while her brain tried to figure out how to respond. Meeting his family. All of them. At once.

Her stomach flipped over, and she didn't know if she was ready for that. "You already know Janelle," she whis-

pered, and thankfully, it was quiet enough that Hailey
didn't turn toward her. The marker scratching on the post-
it notes was louder than Toni's whisper.

It'll be low-key, Griffin said next. *I should've led with that.
Haha.*

How can meeting all of your brothers at once be low-key? she
asked him.

They all have wives and girlfriends, he said. *And it'll be
crowded, and honestly, no one will even notice if I'm there or not.
That's how it usually is, at least.*

Toni detected some bitterness in the words, and if she'd
been in the same room as him and heard him say them,
she'd for-sure know he was a little bitter about his position
in the family.

Okay, Toni said. If she and Hailey could get everything
set up for next week, she could afford to take the weekend
off. She'd spend Saturday with her parents, and she'd make
the drive to Chestnut Springs on Sunday.

Yeah? Great. Griffin sent a smiley emoji with the words,
and Toni flipped her phone over so she could focus on her
work. The campers couldn't assign themselves to their
counselors.

※

TONI ONCE AGAIN ATTENDED THE FLAG-RAISING
ceremony and morning devotional, but she didn't partake
of the pancake buffet Dalton had whipped up for breakfast. Tuesday mornings took her and Griffin off campus,

and he could eat two breakfasts without a problem. Toni, however, couldn't.

She didn't run halfway around the lake every morning as the sun rose, and she could only stomach one meal in the morning. Even then, she usually only had coffee and a bite of two of what Dalton put out.

She didn't check to see when Griffin left. They had their meeting schedule down pretty well by now, and she arrived at the parking lot where he parked, along with some other counselors, and waited on the bench there.

He arrived several minutes later, reached for her hand, and laughed when she jumped up and went with him to his truck. "Morning, beautiful," he said, pressing his lips to her temple. "I didn't freak you out with the meet-my-family thing, did I?"

"A little," Toni said truthfully.

"It really won't be a big deal," he said.

Toni decided she could be honest with him. If not him, then who? "It's a big deal for me," she said. "Remember how I haven't dated in nine years?" She nudged him with her elbow. "You may have brought home a lot of women for your brothers to meet, but I haven't met anyone's family in a long time."

"They already met you at the wedding," he said. "And I do not bring home a lot of women."

She laughed at the slightly wounded tone in his voice. "No? How many have you taken to meet them?"

"None," he said almost instantly.

"Really?" Toni looked at him as he reached to open her door for her. "None?"

"I dated," he said. "But nothing too serious."

Toni's chest tightened. "Are we serious?"

"Oh, I'm serious about you, Miss Beardall." He gave her a sexy, little grin and bent down to kiss her.

Toni enjoyed that, but she'd rather they be away from camp before all the kissing started, and she pulled back after only a few seconds. He chuckled, opened her door, and she climbed in. He rounded the truck and got behind the wheel.

"I wanted to ask you something," she said, her nerves starting to shout at her. But she hadn't been able to shake what Hailey had said yesterday about Griffin having a lot of money.

"All right," he said easily.

Toni couldn't get herself to ask. Wasn't it rude to ask someone how much they made? She looked at him and back out the front windshield. "Hailey and I were talking about trying to keep the camp open. You don't have to, at all, and we're talking to everyone. But maybe, if you have the money, you could donate to Clear Creek."

Her throat felt so dry, and she hated that she'd basically just made the idea up twenty seconds ago.

"Oh." Griffin held plenty of surprise in his voice.

"It's fine," she said, her voice too high and full of air. "I was just—" She cut off as Griffin pulled to the side of the road unexpectedly. "Whoa, okay."

He exhaled and looked out his window. "Okay, I have to tell you something."

"Okay." She watched him carefully, because it felt like

the two of them were at the top of a hill, and one of them was about to step off. Or get pushed.

"I wanted to talk to my brothers first," he said. "And I haven't done that yet. I can't commit to anything."

Toni wasn't sure what he was talking about. Or why he'd had to pull over to say it. They'd had plenty of conversations while he drove them somewhere.

She waited, because Griffin seemed to be having an internal war that kept his tongue silent.

"I have a lot of money," he finally blurted. His eyes flew to hers and latched on.

"A lot of money," she repeated, the words soaking into her brain and making it numb. That same foolishness that had bled through her yesterday did the same thing today. She'd worried about the camp and it's funding so many times over the past couple of weeks.

And he'd said nothing.

"I've been thinking about donating to Camp Clear Creek," he said. "But like I said, I want to talk to my brothers first."

She wasn't sure why they would have anything to do with it, and she squinted at him, trying to see some of the answers he hadn't given.

He exhaled, his shoulders sinking. "I guess you need the whole story."

"Maybe just a few more details," she said. Her hopes were rising, no matter how she tried to tether them.

"My mother is a cosmetics heiress," he said. "She sold her shares in the company a year or so ago, and all of us boys got an inheritance. I haven't spent very much, and I don't know. I want to talk to my brothers about what to invest my money in." He reached up and removed his cowboy hat from his head, resettling it a moment later.

Toni could only blink at him. "How much money?" she asked, a frog in her throat.

"A lot," he said, swallowing. "Enough to fund your camp for years and years." He cleared his throat now, a loud, grinding sound that made Toni flinch. "And years." He put the truck in drive and pulled back onto the road.

Another passenger rode in the truck with them now, and it was a huge, invisible elephant holding an *awkward* sign.

They reached town several minutes later, and Toni couldn't stand this tension between them. "I feel like a fool," she blurted out.

"Why?"

"I've been whining about the financial situation at the camp for weeks." She shook her head and pressed her lips together. "That wasn't to make you feel guilty."

"I know that."

"And all that crap about asking all the counselors to donate. That wasn't true." Tears pricked her eyes. "I don't know why I said that. I just…Hailey said you were rich, and I don't know. I wanted to see if you were."

"Why would she think I had money?" Griffin asked, alarm on his face as he glanced at her.

"I don't know," Toni said. "She said she thought she'd heard it somewhere."

"Where?"

"I don't know."

Griffin did not look happy as he pulled into the restaurant where they ate breakfast every Tuesday morning. He got out of the truck without saying anything else, and he looked like a tornado ready to touch down as he went around the hood.

Toni slid out of the truck before he could open her door, and she came face-to-face with Griffin-the-stormcloud.

She opened her mouth to say something, but she didn't know what.

CHAPTER SEVENTEEN

G riffin wasn't sure why other people knowing about his wealth bothered him. Only that it did. A lot.

The fact that Toni had known but had made up some flimsy thing about asking all the counselors to donate also threw fuel onto an already simmering fire. He really needed to talk to Seth and Rex before he said anything else about this to Toni.

"It's fine," he said, though his own feelings still bubbled inside him. He'd had plenty of practice pushing down the feelings of being left out, abandoned, and angry though, and that was what he did now too.

"Are you still hungry?" he asked. He'd eaten at camp, and he didn't need to eat again. He would, of course, and he sure did like spending time with Toni. At least he had in the past. He didn't care what they did together, as long as they were together.

And he didn't want his money to keep them apart. It

should have no sway on his relationship with Toni, and yet, deep down, he knew it did. He could fund the camp, he knew that. And now she did too.

If he did that, though, would she only like him because of it? And if he didn't fund Clear Creek, would the relationship end? He did know how important to her the camp was. It was her *job*, and if he funded Clear Creek, he'd be paying her too.

"Griffin?"

He blinked and looked a Toni. "Sorry. Yeah?"

"I said let's just get something to drink and go for a drive."

"Okay."

They got back in the truck, and Griffin navigated over to a convenience store, where they went inside and got snacks and drinks. Then he just drove. She didn't say anything, and he didn't either, and eventually, he just went back up to camp.

"I'm sorry," Toni said as they sat in the parking lot. "I didn't mean to make today awkward."

"I didn't either," he said. "I just...I'm not sure what to do here, is all, and I don't want anything to come between us."

"I'm sure Eddie will find us the money," she said with a smile. He scooted across the seat, kissed him in the same passionate way she always had, and things started to settle inside Griffin.

Not completely, but enough for him to smile and get out of the truck, steal one last kiss from Toni, and ask, "Thursday okay for lunch, sweetheart?"

"Mm," she said, melting into him for another kiss. Griffin sure did like that, but he also knew there were things between them now that hadn't been there a few hours ago.

§

"ALL RIGHT," GRIFFIN SAID, GESTURING FOR HIS SIX BOYS to come in for a huddle. "Get in here. All y'all." He put his arm around Mike on the right and Adam on the left. "You boys are good boys. Don't forget that out there, okay? You all have my number, and if you need anything—anything—you call me. Text me. Whatever. Y'all hear?"

"Yes, sir," most of them murmured. Mike said nothing, and Griffin didn't dare look at him in case his emotions would overwhelm him.

The bell rang above the flag pole, and that meant it was time to go. Griffin straightened, and the boys stepped back. They'd had an amazing nineteen days together, and Griffin didn't want to see them leave.

"Thanks, cowboy," TJ said, grabbing Griffin in a tight hug. He pounded him on the back. "When I'm down in the Hill Country, I'm calling you for a place to stay."

Griffin laughed as he hugged TJ back. "I hope so."

He hugged Miles, and Adam, and Haws, and George. They grinned and shook hands and picked up their bags to go. Finally, it was just Griffin and Mike, who toed the ground with his sneaker.

"Get over here," Griffin said, grabbing the kid and pulling him into his chest. Mike cried against Griffin's shoulder, and Griffin fought against his own emotions. He couldn't save this kid, but he'd done what he could.

"Toni called your mom," he said, his voice rough around the edges. "She's going to do better, she said. And we called child protective services, and they're going to make *sure* she does better."

Mike didn't say anything. He just clung to Griffin as if the moment he let go, he'd collapse. After another minute, he stepped back. "What if she doesn't, Griffin?"

"Then you call me," he said as if that would be an easy call for the fifteen-year-old to make. "And I'll come help you." He knocked knuckles with the boy. "Whatever it takes, right? Isn't that what we learned these past few weeks?"

"Whatever it takes," Mike repeated, nodding. "Okay."

"And dude, don't forget: you can talk to your mother too. Tell her how you feel and what you need."

"I'll...try," he said.

And Griffin couldn't ask for more than that. He nodded, and Mike stepped away to get his bag. He walked among the other teens heading down the slight hill to the parking lot, where their parents were supposed to be waiting.

Griffin watched him go, wishing with everything in him that he could take Mike back to the ranch with him. He'd make sure the boy was never hungry again, and that he got to ride as many horses as he wanted.

He felt a powerful sense of gratitude for his own parents in that moment, and he finally looked away when he couldn't see Mike anymore.

"You ready?"

He swung his gaze toward Ian, who wore his own cowboy hat and a big smile on his face.

"So ready." Griffin and Ian had agreed to get an early dinner together, then return to camp to get their cabins cleaned up enough to leave for the weekend. Ian was headed to San Antonio, where he lived, after dinner, but Griffin was coming back here until Sunday, when he and Toni would head to Chestnut Ranch together.

"I'll drive," Ian said, and Griffin didn't argue. It was Ian who'd have to come back up here before heading home for the weekend. "Oh, I got a text from my sister, and she wondered if you'd let me give her your number."

Griffin looked at his friend, trying to get his words to make sense. "Your sister wants my number?"

"Yeah, I posted a couple pictures of us, and I guess she thought you were cute." Ian grinned as his gaze slid down Griffin's body and back to his face. "I don't get it, but whatever."

Griffin didn't know what to say. No, he didn't want to give Ian's sister his number. But he needed a reason why.

"Uh...I'm not really dating right now," Griffin said.

"She just wants to text you," Ian said. "There's a difference."

Somehow, Griffin didn't think Toni would think so. "I'm pretty busy this summer."

"You want to see a picture of her?" Ian paused and started swiping on his phone. "She's pretty, man."

"I'm sure she is." Griffin kept moving, his stride actually getting longer, as if he could avoid this conversation just by walking faster.

Ian caught up to him, saying, "Look."

Griffin did not look. His heart pulsed, and he had no idea what to say next.

"Do you not like women?" Ian asked.

"I like women," Griffin said, glaring at his friend.

He smiled and shook his head. "Okay, then, what's the big deal?"

Griffin came to a full stop and met Ian's eye. "I'm seeing someone."

Confusion crossed Ian's face. "But you just said you're not dating right now."

"Because I'm seeing this other woman."

"Who?"

"It's—no one."

"How long have you been seeing her?"

"It's recent."

Ian looked like Griffin had just spilled a whole bucket full of secrets. Glee crossed his face while Griffin tried to figure out what he'd said that had given too much away.

"So it's someone here." Ian looked around, like the woman in question would appear. Thankfully, Griffin knew Toni was meeting with Hailey and her other supervisory staff that afternoon, and then they'd all take the weekend off too.

"No." Griffin practically shouted the word, and that brought Ian's attention back to him.

"Oh, I think so," Ian said through a hearty chuckle. "Okay, so it's just a matter of deduction."

"Oh, boy." Griffin rolled his eyes and continued toward the upper parking lot. "Let's just go get something to eat. I'm starving."

"Who has Griffin been chatting with? Let's see...Tammy?"

"I'm not going to say yes or no to anyone you say," Griffin said.

"So not Tammy." Ian continued to speculate who Griffin had started a summer romance with, tossing out a couple more names before they reached the truck. Griffin said nothing, hoping that if Ian said Toni, he could keep the same straight face.

Ian didn't guess another name until they got to the steakhouse in Horseshoe Bay. He put the truck in park and snapped his fingers. "I know who it is."

"I'm getting out now."

"Toni." Ian snapped again, his smile widening. "Yeah, it has to be. You're always talking to her at dinner, and I'm pretty sure you two have the same mornings and afternoons off."

Griffin felt like he'd been backed into a corner. No matter how hard he searched for a way out, he couldn't find one. "Fine," he said. "It's Toni."

"Wow." Ian shook his head now, some of his joviality gone. He got out of the truck, and Griffin did too.

"What does that mean?" he asked. "Wow?"

"It's nothing." Ian clearly had something to say, but he didn't want to say it. Which meant Griffin probably wouldn't want to hear it. At the same time, he did.

"It's something," he said as they went inside. Ian said

nothing until they had a table and had ordered drinks. Then he looked at Griffin and leaned his weight into his elbows.

"She's our *boss*, man."

"I know who she is," Griffin said, but hearing the words in someone else's voice somehow made it worse. "And we're consenting adults." He lifted his water glass to his lips, almost desperate for something stronger, with a lot of carbonation.

"I'm just saying, you must like to complicate things," Ian said. "My sister would be totally uncomplicated."

"I'll keep that in mind," Griffin said, though he had no intention of doing any such thing.

❧

A FEW HOURS LATER, HE LAY IN THE HAMMOCK OUTSIDE the cabin where his boys had lived for the past nineteen days, the phone in his hand ringing as he dialed Rex.

"Bro," Rex practically bellowed into the phone. "You made it through your first camp."

"Sure did," Griffin said. And he didn't want Rex to know that he was glad he'd come alone this year. Though Rex was younger than him, Griffin had lived in his brother's shadow for a lot of years.

"And you're staying on your day off?"

"Well, Toni and I are hanging out tonight."

"Ah, I shoulda known we'd lose to *Toni*." He laughed after sing-songing Toni's name.

"Hey, you've ditched me a ton of times for Holly."

"I just didn't think you even knew Toni *existed*," Rex said, really laying the sarcasm on thick.

"Okay," Griffin said, though he'd expected the teasing. "She's coming with me on Sunday, as I'm sure Russ told you."

"He didn't mention it, actually," Rex said. "But wow. Good for you, Griffin. Things must be going well then?"

"Well enough," Griffin said. "Listen, I wanted to ask you something."

"Okay," Rex said, quieting as if he could sense that Griffin wanted a serious conversation now. "Is it going to make me think? It's been a long week already."

"It has? Why's that?"

"I'll tell you after you ask me something."

"Okay," Griffin said. "But I'm fine going second."

"You go first."

"Okay, so it has to do with Toni," he said.

"I figured."

"And the camp. See, their funding is probably going to be cut, and I was thinking of becoming their next donor..." He explained the situation to Rex, who did him the courtesy of listening all the way to the end.

"And now I feel stuck between a rock and a hard place," Griffin said, his frustration rearing right back into existence. "If I don't contribute, she loses her job. If I do, then will she feel like she owes me something?"

"Wow," Rex said. "I think this might be more compli cated than my ex-wife showing up after five years with a little girl that she says is mine."

Griffin laughed, and that did get some of the tension

out of his shoulders. "I don't think so, Rex," he said. "But what would you do?"

Rex heaved a big sigh. "Honestly, Griff? I don't know. You like Toni a lot, I know that. And you haven't spent a dime on anything in nine months. I know that too. If you fund the camp, and then break-up with Toni, you'll have to ask yourself what that looks like for you. And if you don't fund the camp, and you're with Toni, what does that look like?"

Griffin thought for a few seconds. "It's crazy how much I like her," he practically whispered.

"I understand that, brother," Rex said. "On a deep level. And honestly, Griff, what's it going to cost you? Money? You have plenty of that."

"I just don't want her to stay with me because I funded her camp."

"Then do it anonymously."

"She'll know it was me."

"Will she, though? How?"

"Suddenly, her financial manager or whatever calls her and says they have an anonymous donor?"

"Yeah, sure," Rex said. "It happens all the time."

"And then what? When she tells me about it, I lie? I act all happy and like I don't know who it is?" He did not see that ending well for him. Not even a little bit.

"I mean, when you put it like that."

Griffin could just see Rex shrugging, and he didn't say anything else.

"Okay, why'd you have a bad week?" Griffin asked.

"Oh, Holly doesn't think we need a big wedding, and I definitely want to throw a huge party."

"Of course you do," Griffin said with a chuckle. Everything about Rex was big, from his personality to his collection of cowboy hats.

"I couldn't give her anything last time," Rex said. "And now I can give her anything she wants, and she doesn't want it."

"I see your conundrum."

"Is it so bad that I want her to have the wedding of her dreams?"

"It's not, Rex," Griffin said, trying to find a tactful way to say this. "But Rex, maybe this isn't about you giving her a huge wedding, but you know, *what she wants*. Maybe a big, huge elaborate wedding *isn't* what she wants."

"How could—? Oh."

"There it is," Griffin said.

"Crap," Rex said. "Well, my week just got worse."

Griffin laughed, glad for the happiness streaming through him. Not only that, but he didn't always get the opportunity to get one leg up on Rex. "Because now you know you were wrong too?"

"I have to go talk to Holly," he said. "Listen, Griffin, you have a ton of money."

"So you're saying I should donate to the camp fund."

"I'm not saying that," Rex said. "I'm just saying, if you do, will you even miss the money?"

"No," Griffin said.

"So it mattereth not to you, but to her...it would mean a lot."

"Mattereth not?" Griffin burst out laughing again.

"I'm hanging up," Rex said over the laughter, and the line went dead.

Griffin let the phone fall to his chest, and he gazed up into the treetops and the blue sky beyond that.

He knew what he wanted to do—fund the camp.

But he did not want that to be the reason Toni stayed with him should she ever want to leave.

CHAPTER EIGHTEEN

Toni's heart beat harder and harder with every mile that passed. Griffin made easy conversation about the camp, her parents, and his brothers. He'd told her all about all of them, as well as their wives. Rex still had the fiancée, though he and Holly had apparently been married before.

That had been a very interesting story, and Toni had realized that the truth was often stranger than fiction.

"So they're getting married when?" Toni asked.

"September," he said. "They were waiting for me to get home, and my parents should be back by then too."

"How are your parents doing?"

"You know," Griffin said, making a turn. The ranch was just down the road and around a curve, and Toni almost opened the door while the truck was still moving. She could jump and roll, then make a mad dash for the tree line.

She told herself she'd driven this road before. She'd met his brothers at Russ's wedding. Janelle would be there, and that was at least one familiar face.

She told herself that she met hundreds of parents and adults as part of her job. She could meet a few Johnson brothers as Griffin's girlfriend.

She told herself she was *Griffin's girlfriend*, and that got her to smile and relax.

"Here we are," he said, pulling under the arch that labeled the ranch. "There's Trav's new place."

"It's nice," she said. "He built it himself, didn't he?"

"That's right."

"Would you ever live out here?" Toni asked.

"No," Griffin said. "I have a house in town. Rex is going to move into Holly's house, and I'll just...have the house."

He didn't sound happy about it, but Toni didn't question him further. Mostly because he'd just eased the truck to a stop behind several more equally large and expensive trucks. In that moment, she realized that all of the Johnson brothers were billionaires, not just Griffin.

"Ready?" he asked.

"Yes." Toni slid out of the truck, her black maxi skirt billowing around her legs. Griffin secured her hand in his, gave her a broad smile, and said, "Let's do this."

They entered the house, and Toni almost got blown backward by the amount of noise inside the house. But the air conditioning felt like heaven, and Toni resisted the urge to wipe her forehead.

No wonder Griffin faded into the background in this

family, though Toni believed Griffin was a shining star among the other men she knew.

He took her through a doorway into the back of the house that contained the kitchen, a large dining room, and a huge living room. Millie stood at the stove, though she didn't live here, and it was Janelle who first turned toward her and Griffin.

"They're here," she called, and the game at the table that had all the men roaring broke up.

"Griffin's here," someone said, and they all mobbed him. He hugged them all, laughing and patting them on the back as they said hello. He'd been gone for three weeks, and Toni couldn't believe this welcome home.

"Hey, Toni," Janelle said, pulling her into a hug. She didn't say anything suggestive about Toni and Griffin, thankfully, and finally the chaos quieted.

"This is Toni," Griffin said, migrating back to her side. "You might remember her from Russ's wedding. She's a friend of Janelle's."

"And your boss," Rex said, his smile ridiculously wide.

"And my girlfriend," Griffin said, smiling at her. "Seth's the oldest. Then Russ. Then Travis. Then me. Then Rex."

Toni said hello to all of them, feeling herself slipping into the professional persona she used with the parents. She didn't want to do that, but she'd just met seven strangers—for the second time.

Three little girls came skipping into the homestead, and one drawled, "Momma, when are we eating?"

"Right now," Janelle said. "Go wash up. Uncle Griffin just got here."

The girls cheered and ducked into the bathroom to wash their hands.

"Okay," Millie said. "The meat is ready."

"And we have an announcement," Travis added. He glanced at Seth and then Russ. "Millie and I are expecting a baby in January."

The wall of noise swelled again, this time higher than before. Toni couldn't help getting swept up in the celebration of it all, and she marveled at how this family supported each other and loved each other.

She didn't have any siblings, and she'd never seen a family quite like this before. And it was absolutely wonderful. Amazing. Everything she wanted her family to be. She watched Griffin talk to Travis and Millie, and she fell a little further in love with him in that moment.

"Okay, okay," Millie finally said, lifting her hands. She wiped her eyes and added, "The French dip is getting cold, and I know y'all don't like cold food."

They all surged toward the island where Millie had set out the food, and Toni got a bird's eye view of what Griffin meant about throwing elbows and being loud in order to get fed.

And she loved it.

CHAPTER NINETEEN

Darren Dumond woke the day after his birthday, wondering if his thirty-ninth year on Earth would bring him anything new. He knew it wouldn't. If he wanted something different in his life, he'd have to make it happen.

"Today is going to be a great day," he said to the ceiling. The sun rose so early in the summer, he couldn't beat it awake like he did in the autumn and winter. "You're going to work around the ranch, and you're going to get lunch at the homestead."

He was a very routined man, and he liked knowing what every hour of the day would hold for him. Working at Chestnut Ranch had provided that routine and stability that Darren hadn't had on the ranch he'd once owned.

Sometimes, he thought he'd like to buy another ranch, be his own boss, and live in a house bigger than a postage stamp. But he could keep his one-bedroom, one-loft-no-one-used cabin clean in an hour a week, and that left him plenty of time for other things.

Not that he did other things, unless playing cards with Brian, Tomas, and Aaron counted. And he was pretty sure they didn't.

The fact was, he worked a lot, and he liked it. The work kept him busy, and when he didn't have anything to do, Darren focused on the past. And the past was not a pleasant place to be. Not for him.

Diana's face filled his mind, and he launched himself out of bed. He had to get going, or everything would derail, and the day had barely begun.

He showered, mentally going over his to-do list for the day so his late wife wouldn't take over for the day. He hated that he didn't want to think about the woman he'd once loved. But honestly, his life was easier if he didn't fall into wallowing. And he was still in the phase of grief where he definitely wallowed sometimes.

Other times, he missed her so much he regretted selling the house and ranch they'd been building and where they'd been working together. She'd originally come to Dovetail Ranch as a cowgirl, and his father had hired her. But when Darren and Diana had gotten married, they'd bought a place of their own.

Lantern Hollow had been a fixer-upper of a ranch, and Darren had worked right alongside his wife to get the work done. She'd gotten sick and died within the first five years of their life together, and though she'd been gone for five now, Darren hadn't figured out how to move on yet.

He wondered if he ever would.

He'd been working at Chestnut Ranch ever since, and when Lantern Hollow had been identified as the exact parcel of land where oil could be found, he'd sold it for a heckuva a lot more than he'd bought it for.

Short story was he didn't need to work at all. And the long version of that story had him crippled sometimes, when he thought of the memories he'd sold and how he'd never be able to get them back.

He left his cabin and got on the four-wheeler he drove all over the ranch. Today, he and Aaron would get behind the wheel of harvesters and balers and get the mowing done in the north sector.

Aaron had coffee in the equipment shed, and he handed a thermos to Darren. Aaron had only been working the ranch for a few months, but he and Darren had become fast friends.

"Thanks," Darren said, taking his first sip. "Do you want to mow or bale?"

"Bale," Aaron said immediately, just as Darren predicted he would.

He grinned at his friend and said, "All right, give me a thirty-minute head start." He climbed into the harvester while Aaron opened the huge cargo bay doors on the back of the shed. He set out for the trip out to the north sector, glad he'd been able to tame his thoughts of Diana this morning.

Part of him thought about putting himself out there again. There were plenty of ways to meet women in Chestnut Springs, but Darren hadn't taken advantage of any of them. For so long, he didn't want anyone else. He couldn't even fathom being with a different woman.

But the past several months, watching Seth, Russ, Travis, and Rex find people to settle down with, to love, had reminded Darren of just how wonderful having a partner in life could be.

"Maybe you want that for yourself," he muttered to the horizon. It, of course, did not answer back. And he wasn't sure if he really wanted to try to find a new girlfriend.

He mowed, and Aaron baled, and the sun arced through the sky. He pulled over to eat lunch, and he and Aaron relaxed in the shade by the fence line that separated Chestnut Ranch from Fox Hollow.

Aaron said, "Okay, I'm getting back to it."

"I'll be right behind you," Darren said, but he lay down on his back and closed his eyes, positioning his cowboy hat over his face. He just needed a twenty minute nap, something he always did in the middle of the day if he could.

His thoughts turned soft, and he wasn't exactly sure when he fell asleep.

A scream jolted him awake again, his adrenaline spiking and his heartbeat racing. He sat straight up, his first thought that he'd simply dreamed the terror-filled sound.

Then it came again—only this time, Darren knew the screech was borne of frustration and anger, and not pain.

He stood up, calling, "Hello?" He saw Aaron's baler moving down the field a bit, and he turned as another sound met his ears.

It came from the other side of the fence, and this time, it was the gut-wrenching sound of someone sobbing. Hard.

"Hello?" he called again, walking cautiously toward the fence. "Is anyone there?" He reached the fence and leaned his hands against the top rung, peering around. Fox Hollow Ranch was run and kept by the Adams family, and Darren knew them. Well, as well as anyone could know a reclusive family.

The Adams' kept to themselves most of the time, and the rumor around Chestnut Springs was that Will Adams hadn't been to town in seventeen years. He had three daughters who lived at the ranch, but Darren had heard that only the oldest actually did any actual work.

"Hello?" he tried one more time. That was a good effort, and if no one said anything, he'd go get in his harvester and get back to cutting hay.

A woman poked her head out from behind a tree, and she quickly got to her feet. She faced him, and Darren didn't know what to do. She'd clearly been crying, and though he stood probably fifty feet from her, he could sense her anguish easily.

"Are you okay?" he asked, feeling stupid. She obviously wasn't okay. "Are you hurt? Do you need help?"

She just looked at him, and she seemed wild and untameable with her dark hair blowing around her face in the Texas breeze. She wore jeans and a T-shirt, with a pair of boots, so she wasn't ill-prepared to be out this far.

Finally, after several long seconds where they just watched each other, she asked, "Can you bring back the dead?"

Darren's heart stopped. Just quit working, becoming a lump of ash in his chest.

Was this some cruel trick? He glanced around, even behind him, and saw no one else.

"No," he said.

"Then you can't help me," the woman said. With that, she spun on her toe and marched away from him, disappearing into a thicket of trees before long.

Bring back the dead.

If Darren had been able to do that, he would've done it five years ago when Diana had died. He'd have kept his ranch, and they'd still be living on it, enjoying their lives together. Maybe with a child or two.

Bitterness coated his throat, and his stomach lurched. This was not how today was supposed to go. He wasn't supposed to spend all day thinking about Diana, or what might have been had she not died.

He turned away from the land that belonged to Fox Hollow and braced his elbows against his knees. *Breathe*, he told himself. *Just breathe.*

He did, but there didn't seem to be enough oxygen. Never enough.

And in the next moment, he himself felt the primal urge to bellow his pain and hurt and missing and desperation to just see his wife one more time into the atmosphere.

And in that moment, he knew Will Adams had died. That could be the only explanation for one of his daughters being out this far and screaming in such a way.

With that thought firmly anchored in his mind, he straightened, breathed, and reached for his phone.

CHAPTER TWENTY

S arena Adams couldn't believe an ambulance waited in the front driveway. "Did you call nine-one-one?" she asked Sorrell, who'd retreated to the back porch after Daddy's death. She hadn't said a single word since, and she didn't speak now.

"Where's Seren?"

Again, no answer.

So Sarena did what she'd been doing for years now: She handled everything. She spoke to the paramedics on the doorstep. She learned someone had called emergency services and said they though there'd been a death at Fox Hollow.

And they'd be right.

Sarena instantly knew it was the cowboy she'd tangled with a half an hour ago. Tangling wasn't quite the right word either. He'd actually been kind, asking her if she was okay or if she were hurt.

She wasn't okay. She was hurt.

But not in a way the paramedics could fix.

"My father passed away," she said. "He's in the bedroom."

"Mind if we take a look?" one of the paramedics asked.

"No." Sarena stepped back to allow them room to come inside. Numbness moved through her, and she couldn't really feel her feet. So her movement was stilted and stumbling, and she kept a tight grip on the doorknob for support. The last thing she needed was to fall and break something.

Or break down in front of someone.

Sarena Adams was the tough sister. The one no one messed with. She knew how to brand cattle and deal with diva-minded horses. She'd been working Fox Hollow alongside her father for the past thirty years.

But if there was one thing she didn't know how to deal with, it was the death of her father. True, Daddy had been on a steady and steep decline these past few weeks, but Sarena had never once doubted that he'd pull through.

As the medical examiner arrived, she had to admit to herself that Daddy wasn't going to pull through. He hadn't pulled through.

He was dead. Gone.

A fresh wave of panic and desperation and sadness coiled together into one terrifying tornado that threatened to suck her right into the vortex.

Everything around her happened with a din of white noise around it. Sometimes the paramedic would have to explain something more than once before Sarena caught on to what they were telling her to do.

There was *so much* to do.

Daddy had only been diagnosed with lung failure in January. And only six months later, he was gone.

Six months.

Not nearly long enough.

Though they'd known this day was coming, none of them had anticipated it happening so soon. They didn't have a whole lot of plans for the funeral. Nothing scheduled or paid for, and as the paramedics returned with her father on the stretcher, Sarena stepped over to him.

She took his hand and squeezed it. "Love you, Daddy."

He was wheeled out, and Sarena was the only one there to say good-bye. She turned her attention to his bedroom, and she leaned into the doorjamb as she surveyed the room her parents had once shared.

It looked like a bomb of towels, orange prescription bottles, and bedding had gone off. The TV still flickered and everything. The channel was set to four—Daddy's favorite nightly news.

Sarena suspected it had something to do with the very pretty anchorwoman, but Daddy had never admitted to such a thing.

But the channel and the fact that the TV was still on signaled to Sarena that her father had died sometime in the night, before the news had ended. He'd never slept with the TV on before, and had he been alive at the conclusion of the news, he'd have turned off the TV.

She'd know for sure once the medical examiner did his thing, but deep down, Sarena already knew her father had been dead for hours before she'd found him.

Are you okay?

Are you hurt?

She pressed her eyes closed against a flood of tears. "Yes," she whispered, because it answered both questions. She was okay—for now—for this one minute—but she was definitely hurt. She wrapped her arms around herself, as if she could keep the emotions contained that way. It didn't really work, and she turned away from the bedroom.

There were a little million details to see to, and neither Sorrell nor Serendipity would do any of them. They never had, and Sarena felt the weight of the world settle on her shoulders.

But she could do whatever needed to be done.

She had to, otherwise it wouldn't *get* done. And Daddy deserved a nice memorial service of him and his life—and Sarena was going to give it to him.

§

SEVERAL DAYS LATER, SARENA WASN'T QUITE SURE HOW the sun could shine so merrily. Didn't Texas know that her daddy was being buried today?

She kept her head held high through the service. She wept quietly at the cemetery, but nothing that called overt attention to her. Everyone was watching anyway, and Sorrell had to be comforted and led away by their grandmother.

Sarena stuck close to her aunt, and when most of those who'd come to the gravesite dedication had gone, they left too. The pastor's wife had gotten some ladies together, and they'd planned a meal for the family.

Sarena didn't want to attend the lunch, as none of those ladies had known her father. Heck, Sarena had barely known her father. He hadn't left the house, except for the back porch and the barn in the backyard, in almost five years. He hadn't left the property in almost two decades.

Very few visitors came to the ranch. Only those that Sarena invited in order to sell the cattle or crops, or anyone who needed to work on the equipment or repair something Sarena couldn't do herself.

Her sisters lived in the homestead with her, and while they didn't do much around the ranch, they kept the house clean and in good repair, and they both had jobs in Chestnut Springs

Sarena felt the weight of the ranch descend on her, though she'd been doing most of the work for years now.

"Hello, dear," Leisha Hamilton said. The pastor's wife leaned into her and hugged her tight. "Your daddy was such a good man."

"Thank you," Sarena said, hugging the woman back. She didn't know her, but she could feel the woman's generous spirit, and she truly had compassion for Sarena and her sisters.

"Come, and sit," Leisha said, leading Sarena and her aunt to a table near the front. A few minutes later, Sorrell and Serendipity arrived. Sarena put a brave smile on her face and took Serendipity's hand.

"This is so nice," her youngest sister said, glancing around. "And it smells great."

"These church ladies are the best," Aunt Scottie agreed. She got up and socialized with those at the table next to them, and Sarena realized why they'd put this lunch together—Aunt Scottie.

She came to this church, and these ladies had put together this meal out of their love for her.

Sarena felt the welcome warmth of that love, and she let the ladies pamper her and serve her delicious smoked turkey and mashed potatoes. There were homemade rolls and cinnamon butter, along with barbecue baked beans and a rich chocolate cake.

Sorrell managed to keep her emotions in check, and they all thanked everyone for their service and hospitality. Sarena linked her arms through her sisters' and said, "Well, it's just us now, guys."

That got Sorrell sniffling again, but Serendipity just said, "Yep. Can we go now, do you think? These shoes are killing me."

"Let's go ladies," Aunt Scottie said, returning to them. Her dark eyes watered, but she looked sophisticated and regal as ever, with silver in her dark hair.

Sarena wondered where they would go, and as she let her aunt drive her back to the ranch, she wondered where her life was going.

What's the point of all this? she wondered.

She couldn't stand to be in the house, as the roof seemed to have trapped so much sadness underneath it. Aunt Scottie bustled around the kitchen, making coffee and tea, but she'd eventually leave to return to her house in town. Her husband was disabled, so he'd only come to the funeral before one of Sarena's cousins had taken him home.

Sarena changed out of her dress and sandals, and put on a pair of denim shorts and a purple tank top. She laced on her hiking boots and joined Aunt Scottie in the kitchen. "We just ate," she said, taking in the spread on the kitchen counter.

"The neighbors brought this," Aunt Scottie said.

"Which neighbors?" Fox Hollow Ranch sat in the middle of several pieces of land. Chestnut Ranch lay to the south, while the Wright's land also touched the southwest edge of Fox Hollow. The Merry Meiser was on the east, and to the north, the horse breeding farm of Stallions & Stables was run by the Fernandez brothers.

"The Johnson boys," Aunt Scottie said.

Chestnut Ranch.

Sarena nodded. "I'll send them a card," she said. "I'm going to go for a walk."

"It's hot outside, baby," Aunt Scottie said, her concern right there in her eyes.

"I know." Sarena took her cowgirl hat from the peg by the door. "I'll stay in the shade." She left the house then, walking south through the backyard. The ranch had clear roads, and Daddy had laid everything out on a grid, so it was almost impossible to get lost.

She let her thoughts roam as she kept her feet moving, and soon enough, she reached the fence separating Fox Hollow from Chestnut.

The cowboy she'd seen a week or so ago wasn't there

today. Of course he wasn't. He'd only come out to mow the field, and Sarena would probably never see him again.

She hadn't dated anyone in a while, as she didn't get to town as often as she needed to in order to meet a nice man. Daddy had a few ranch hands that worked at Fox Hollow, but they didn't offer room and board, and four of the five cowboys they employed were married. The other was twenty years older than Sarena.

She almost scoffed at the path her thoughts were on. She could barely keep her head above water with the work around the ranch. She had no room for a man in her life. At the same time, she knew she was desperately lonely.

"And something in your life needs to change," she whispered to the beautiful land on the other side of the fence.

The buzzing sound of an engine met her ears, and she saw someone on a four-wheeler coming toward her. She wanted to move, but she didn't at the same time. Maybe she could have a conversation with someone that didn't include their condolences.

It was the same man as the previous week, and this time, Sarena lifted her hand in an acknowledging wave.

"Hey," the man said as he swung off the ATV. He was tall and good-looking, with a strong jaw that had plenty of stubble on it. He wore a cowboy hat with his long-sleeved shirt and blue jeans, and Sarena couldn't quite get a read on his eyes.

He flashed her a smile, and Sarena's heart did a weird bobbling thing inside her chest. She watched him look around on the ground, and she finally got her voice to work enough to ask, "Did you lose something?"

"Yeah," he said, barely glancing up. "I haven't been able to find my wallet since I was out here last week." He looked at her. "I fear it might be gone for good." An accompanying sigh followed the words.

"That's the worst," Sarena said.

"Yeah." He came a little closer to her, apparently giving up on the wallet search. "Do you hang out back here often?"

"Probably not as often as it seems." She smiled at him, thrilled when he returned it. "I'm Sarena Adams."

"Darren Dumond." He reached up and touched the brim of his cowboy hat.

"My ranch isn't as big as Chestnut," she said. "I can walk from here to the homestead in about a half an hour."

"I can get from our center to here in thirty minutes on an ATV."

She leaned against the fence. "Yep, your ranch is definitely much bigger than mine."

"Oh, it's not my ranch, ma'am."

Handsome and polite. Sarena's pulse went wild, and she practically leaned over the fence.

"Well, I best be gettin' back," he said. "I've got to get a signal so I can call and cancel my credit cards." He gave her another smile, tipped his hat, and turned around.

Sarena didn't want him to go, but her attempts at flirting had obviously failed. Miserably. She sighed as the engine roared to life and Darren swung the machine around. He drove away, and Sarena felt like the action summed up her life pretty well.

Always left behind.

Embarrassed of her behavior, and more lonely now than ever, Sarena turned to start the thirty-minute walk back to the ranch. At least now she had the handsome image of Darren's bearded face in her mind to keep her company.

CHAPTER TWENTY-ONE

Toni pulled on the blouse she'd bought especially for the Fourth of July. It was a navy blue silk with bright white stars covering it. She smiled at her patriotism, pulled on a pair of white jeans, and completed the red-white-and-blue look with her blood-red fingernails and a bright shade of red lipstick.

She normally wouldn't have gone to such great lengths for a picnic, but today, she and Griffin were once again going to Chestnut Ranch to celebrate the holiday with his family.

Since they'd had their little money talk, there had been a new divide between them Toni hadn't known hot to bridge. And sometimes, it wasn't there at all—like when he caught her eye through all the other campers and grinned. He'd touch two fingers to the brim of his cowboy hat and duck his head, and Toni would imagine the way he'd kissed her the night before.

Sometimes, when they snuck away from camp on Tuesday mornings or Thursday afternoons, it was almost like she didn't know he had a lot of money and he didn't know the camp could be closed at the end of the summer.

Other times, there seemed to be that invisible gorilla between them, making the silence uncomfortable as he drove them somewhere for breakfast, lunch, or dinner.

She'd learned that he could cook, he just didn't like it all that much. He would always take a turkey sandwich if there was one on the menu, and he loved the one at a specialty shop that served it with all the Thanksgiving trimmings, including cranberry sauce, gravy, and mashed potatoes.

He loved spending time outside, and he took his boys waterskiing, hiking, horseback riding, and boating. And seeing him pilot a boat...Toni got hot just thinking about it.

A knock sounded on the door, and she startled away from the mirror. How long had she been standing there, thinking about Griffin?

"Too long," she whispered to herself, though the man deserved a lot of thought. He wasn't infallible, she knew that. He kept things to himself she wished they could talk about. He didn't text her back all the time, and later he'd say, "Yeah, sorry, I didn't answer." No other explanation, no reason for why he didn't answer.

Which was fine. Toni didn't need him to respond two seconds after she texted. She was fine keeping their relationship under wraps, and Griffin treated her like a queen when they were together.

"Hey," he called as she left her bedroom.

"I'm coming," she said, flying down the hall toward him.

"We're not in a hurry," he said, grinning at her. She smiled back, and today seemed like it would be one of those days where there was no divide between them. Toni hated the walking-on-eggshell feeling before she saw him though, as she wasn't sure what would happen when she finally saw him.

"I was just finishing up," she said, reaching for her shoes. "We're just hanging out today, right?"

Griffin took her into his arms and gazed down at her. "Look at you, all patriotic." He grinned at her, and Toni basked in the warmth of his whole being.

"And you're not even wearing a stitch of red, white, or blue."

"I must not have gotten the memo."

"You didn't get the memo? From the huge country we live in? You know, the United States of America? Literally everyone in the country knows to wear red, white, and blue for their family picnics."

He tipped his head back and laughed, and Toni was glad there were no eggshells today. She snuggled into his embrace, enjoying the sound of his laugh in her house.

"I just need to grab the pie," she said, stepping out of his arms. "Wait. Should I even bring it? I mean, Millie is such a good cook, and "

"Is it that apple-cheddar one Dalton made yesterday?"

"Yes, he saved me two of them, and I baked them last night."

"Oh, bring them," he said. "Or don't, and we can hoard them to ourselves. In fact, let's have one for before we go."

"Be serious," she said, giggling as she pulled out a roll of aluminum foil to cover the pies.

"I am serious," he said, stepping beside her. But he took the roll from her and ripped another piece of foil from it to cover the second pie.

Her phone rang, and Toni crinkled her foil over her pie and pulled her device out of her back pocket. Eddie's name sat on the screen, and she squeaked.

"Get it," Griffin said. "Before it goes to voicemail."

Toni's fingers felt like she'd rubbed butter on them, and she fumbled her phone. Her heart beat wildly fast in her chest as she swiped the call open. "Eddie," she practically yelled. "Hey."

"Toni," he said, clearly surprised. "I wasn't expecting to get you."

"You called me, not expecting to get me?" Toni turned and looked at Griffin, but he still had his head down over the pies.

"Well, it's a holiday."

"Yeah," she said. "But my cell phone travels with me."

Eddie chuckled, but Toni couldn't quite put a smile on her face too. "I guess it does," he said.

"I was expecting to hear from you last week," Toni said, hoping she didn't sound accusatory. But the board meeting for the Texas Youth Camp Program was last Thursday, and she'd waited patiently for seven days.

And he'd called on a holiday, not expecting to get her.

Her heart fell all the way to the bottom of her cute,

festive sandals. "There's no money, is there?" she asked, letting her chin drop to her chest.

"Toni," Eddie said. "I tried. I really did. But our other donations have already been earmarked, and any excess isn't enough for Clear Creek. Without the Camden's—"

"Could Hailey and I work on some fundraising?"

She'd clearly caught him off-guard, because he didn't say anything for a few seconds. "Well," he said slowly. "Any funds have to go through TYCP...so if you could send them there, and they marked it as specifically for Clear Creek...I suppose you could."

"Okay," Toni said, feeling the fight rise within her. She was not going to let Camp Clear Creek go without a fight.

"We're not talking about an insignificant amount," Eddie said.

"I know exactly what it takes to run this camp," Toni said, perhaps a bit icily. "I've been doing it for eight years, and I've never employed an accountant." She drew in a deep breath. "I'll let you know."

"Toni, we can put a button on our page," he said.

"Okay."

"We can put flyers at our other camps."

"Okay," she said. "Whatever you can do, Eddie, I'd appreciate it. I just...I just can't let this camp die. It's a great place, with good people, and we're always fully booked. I just don't see how—" She cut herself off, because she didn't want to tell him how to do his job. She didn't want to have negative thoughts about the program that had employed her for almost a decade.

"I understand," Eddie said. "I'm really sorry, Toni."

"I know you are. Thanks, Eddie." She hung up and kept her back to Griffin, because now there were a whole herd of gorillas in the room with them.

Another deep breath later, she faced him. "Okay, let's go." She picked up one pie, and Griffin the other. They didn't talk as they walked up to the parking lot where he parked.

"No funding, huh?" he asked once they'd gotten in.

She focused on buckling her seatbelt as she said, "Nope. But it's okay. Hailey and I have been brainstorming some fundraising options for the past couple of weeks."

He nodded and pulled out of the lot. She didn't know what else to say, so she just looked out the window at the beautiful summer day.

It seemed to take a year to get to Chestnut Ranch, not just an hour, and by the time they arrived, Toni already wanted to leave. But she took a cheddar apple pie while Griffin took the other one. They walked into the home-stead, and Toni braced herself for the noise.

It was deathly silent, and she looked at Griffin.

"This is weird," he said, walking ahead of her. The kitchen was empty. Backyard, empty. "I wonder where they are." He pulled out his phone and called someone, smiling at her. "I must've missed a text or something."

She simply smiled at him, because missed texts happened. *Especially for Griffin*, she thought, and she was surprised by the somewhat poisoned thought. She didn't welcome the annoyance, but it was there nonetheless.

While he frowned when one brother didn't pick up, she

wandered out onto the back patio, expecting it to be hot. But air conditioning gently blew down from the ceiling above, and Toni looked up at it.

These brothers all had a lot of money, and Toni wished her throat wasn't so tight because of it.

It's not their job to fund your camp, she told herself. *It's not Griffin's responsibility to help you keep your job.*

She'd told herself that a couple of times before Griffin came outside and said, "They're next door."

"Okay." She put a smile on her face, but it was harder than it should be. She went, though, because she saw no other option at the moment.

The grand plantation-style house next door had plenty of trucks parked in front of it, and the moment Griffin led her through the double-wide doors, the noise hit her. This time, it was music, and the scent of sugar and grilled meats hung in the air.

All the brothers and wives welcomed Griffin and Toni, as they were once again the last to arrive. Toni stepped away from Griffin this time, as it was easier to chat with those she'd met before—and she didn't want her annoyance to be known to anyone.

Several minutes later, she practically collapsed onto a loveseat on the back patio. This one too was air conditioned, and she gazed up at the marvel of cooling the outdoors.

Janelle sat next to her with a heavy sigh.

"You too?" Toni asked.

"Me too—what?" Janelle asked.

"Oh, uh, nothing," she said, quickly stabbing another piece of watermelon and putting it in her mouth.

Janelle released a peal of laughter, only adding to the noise coming from inside the house. "They're loud, aren't they?"

"I live alone," Toni said. "That's all."

"And you're an only child." Janelle linked her arm through Toni's for a moment. "But you seem to really like Griffin."

"I do," Toni said, her voice only a touch false.

Of course, Janelle was a lawyer, and she was trained to hear things no one else did.

"You don't?"

"Of course I do," Toni said, scooping up a bite of potato salad.

"What's going on?" Janelle asked. "And trust me, Toni, I have all day to listen. My girls are with their dad, and I've literally got nothing else to do."

Toni didn't want to talk about her insecurities and irritations when it came to Griffin. So she just shrugged. "No one's perfect, right?" She looked at Janelle. "I mean, surely there are some things about Russ you don't like."

"Uh, you shouldn't get me started." Janelle laughed and finished all of her apple pie before taking a bite of real food.

"Do you always eat the dessert first?" Toni asked.

"Always," Janelle said. "Then I always have room for it."

"Brilliant." Toni liked sitting with Janelle, a woman she'd known for many years now, and she finally relaxed.

She didn't see Griffin much or talk to him much until it was time to leave. Then she had to face another hour-long drive of uncomfortable silence. And she hated that. Hated that she didn't know how to break it, and hated that Griffin said nothing too.

CHAPTER TWENTY-TWO

G riffin welcomed another group of boys. He walked through the darkness of the hot, summer nights and found respite in Toni's air-conditioned house and the comfort of her arms.

He knew things between them weren't quite right, but he wasn't sure what to do about it. In the back of his mind, he wanted to test her. See if her attitude toward him would change if he donated to keep the camp open.

But he couldn't bring himself to do it. If she warmed toward him after that, his heart would crack right down the middle. And if she didn't, their relationship was already broken. And he didn't want to acknowledge that either.

He felt absolutely stuck. Trapped. He couldn't break-up with her without a reason—and the reason he had, he absolutely hated. If he'd have known his money would cause such a problem for him, he would've refused it.

Griffin said good-bye to another group of boys. He

went home for the weekend alone, as Toni said she had a lot of work to do for the new batch of campers. She'd become busier and busier over the past few weeks, as she worked with Hailey to find more funding for the camp.

Griffin felt stalled. He laughed and smiled and counseled his boys. But none of the groups were as special as that first one of the summer, and early morning often found him texting TJ or Mike, Haws or Adam, George or Miles, just to see how their jobs were going. How their classes were. If they were ready for the tryouts and auditions that were coming up.

He got a new group of boys the last week of July, and one of them looked beyond rough. Griffin didn't have it in him to be the tough disciplinarian he needed to be, and he just glared at the boy.

Lars Grundy glared right back, wiping his hand through his long, greasy hair every once in a while. He didn't change into his swimming trunks to come to the lake with everyone else, but he came. He didn't swim. He didn't play volleyball. He just sat in a camp chair and glared at everyone.

Griffin usually did an activity on the first night to help the boys get to know one another, and while Lars sat in the circle with them, he refused to speak. Griffin was impressed by the boy's ability to go all day long and not say one word. Even some of his quietest boys over the past three summers hadn't managed that.

"Can I talk to you for a sec?" he asked the boy once the unpacking, the eating, and all the activities were done for the day. Thankfully, this was only a two-week camp, but

Griffin couldn't fathom going through eleven more days like this one—for both him and Lars.

Outside, the sun had set, but God had decided to make sure Texas never cooled off during the month of July. Griffin exhaled as he took off his cowboy hat and put it back on. "Did your mother make you come?"

Lars didn't answer, and Griffin looked at him. Slowly, he shook his head.

"Are you going to say anything while you're here?" he asked.

Lars's eyes widened for a flash, and then a general sense of annoyance filled his expression. Griffin was well-acquainted with the look, as Toni had been wearing it more and more lately.

"It's okay," Griffin said. "If you don't talk. I was just wondering if I should be concerned about it. If you say I don't need to be, I won't be."

Lars opened his mouth, and a low sound came out. "Y-y-you don't-t need to be," he said, the last few words rushing out without a stutter.

Griffin understood him at once. He leaned his elbows against the railing and bent over. He took his time choosing his next words, because he didn't want Lars to think he didn't consider all things.

"You could trust the other boys," he said. "And you don't need to hide behind a scowl and the long hair."

"I'm n-not hiding," Lars said, and his voice almost sounded rusty from how little he used it.

"Okay," Griffin said. "But the other boys won't make fun of you, and you might need them up here at camp."

"I—I—" He didn't finish, and Griffin didn't try to force him to. The door behind them opened, and another one of the boys said, "Griffin?"

"Yep." He turned around and looked at the boy standing there. A skinny kid who looked a couple of years younger than the fifteen he was, Jacob gestured for Griffin to come inside.

He did, immediately seeing the problem. Or rather, smelling it. "Okay," he said. "Who has the lighter? Matches? Hand 'em over." He'd already given them the speech about why the cabins didn't have microwaves, and one of them had started playing with a lighter?

Sam, the boy with trouble in his eyes, handed over a blue lighter than was still warm to the touch. Griffin gave him a hard look, and said, "If you burn down this cabin or this camp, Sam, you'll feel so bad."

He had the manners to hang his head in shame, and Griffin looked around at the other boys. "All right, it's lights out, day one. We're up and ready by seven for the morning devotional, flag raising, and breakfast."

He waited for all the boys to nod, and then he gave them one final nod before stepping back outside. He looked east and west, trying to decide which way to go. Toni's cabin lay to the east, and his to the west.

"Griffin," someone called, and he looked out toward the lake. A group of counselors walked together, and one woman had stopped.

Kiki Malone, the woman who'd flirted with him weeks ago as she and Toni had hung the hammocks outside this very cabin.

"A bunch of us are going to West Lake for a drink and a dessert. Do you want to come?" She'd invited him along to such group outings a time or two in the past. He'd never gone, and she'd never asked why.

Tonight, he looked east one more time, and then he stepped off the steps. "Sure," he said. "I could really use one of those chocolate mousse pops tonight."

Kiki smiled at him, extending her hand toward him as he drew nearer. He didn't take it, but she tucked her arm in his. "How are your new boys?" she asked.

"Oh, they're gonna be just fine," he said. "What about you?"

"I got an extra girl," she said. "And six is already a lot, and now there's an extra." She sighed like this was the end of the world. "It'll be a rough couple of weeks."

"You always say that," another counselor said.

"I do not, Pearla," Kiki said, but Griffin got the idea that yes, she did always say it was going to be a rough camp. She'd been called on to be a counselor the past couple of times as others left for specific camps. And this time, Griffin thought camp would be a bit rough too, but only because he was going to get a treat with a group of other counselors instead of prowling the other way to kiss his girlfriend.

ANOTHER WEEK PASSED, AND GRIFFIN DIDN'T GO ON ANY more group dessert runs. Kiki, however, had been texting him more and more. She wanted to meet up at West Lake just the two of them, and Griffin severely regretted his decision to go with her last week instead of heading to Toni's as normal. He'd told Toni that he'd been tired after a hard first day of camp, which wasn't entirely a lie.

Their relationship had cooled considerably since the Fourth, when she'd basically spent the entirety of the day with Janelle and Millie instead of him. No one had said anything to him about it, but their division was a scent that hung in the air.

While his campers went to their first aid class, Griffin pulled out his phone and navigated to the Texas Youth Camp website. One, two, three taps later, and Camp Clear Creek filled the screen. Everything looked perfect, from the bluest of blue skies to the brightest green grass. All the campers wore smiles only champions did.

The red *DONATE* button sat on the top of the screen, the same as it had for the last few weeks.

He'd looked at it so many times. Today, he tapped on it. Just to see what would happen, he told himself. But it took him to a place where he could easily put in his financial information—bank account or credit card number—and donate.

Just like that.

He'd talked to Rex about it, but he'd never discussed anything with Seth. And he found he didn't need to. He had a mind of his own, and it was his money. He used the screenshot he had of his bank account, and he put in the information required.

He paused on the donation amount, unsure about what to do. The seconds ticked by, and he didn't complete the transaction. His heart pulsed in rapid succession. Just as quickly, he tapped out of the donation screen and instead, tapped on the phone number there.

The line rang, and Griffin seriously considered hanging up before a man said, "Eddie Microneil."

Griffin couldn't get himself to say anything. He hated this indecision inside him. But he had to do something. He couldn't go to Toni's tonight without taking a step. Whatever direction it took him, he needed to go. He couldn't stand still any longer.

"Hello?" Eddie asked.

"Yes, hello," Griffin said. "I'd like to make a donation to the youth camp program." He watched as Lars, in the distance, bent over the dummy and administered CPR. "I want it to be an anonymous donation. What does that look like?"

"Only you and I will know," he said. "Did you want to make a one-time donation or a recurring donation?"

"Recurring," Griffin said without ever having decided. "And I want the money to go to Camp Clear Creek. That's the one with the donate button, right?"

"Yes," Eddie said smoothly, never giving away a single thing. He was good, Griffin would give him that. "So an annually recurring donation, Mister...?"

"Yes," he said without giving his last name. "And I want to fund the camp in its entirety so it doesn't close."

That got Eddie to leave some silence on the line. He exhaled in a burst. "Mister...uh, that's a lot of money every year."

"How much?" Griffin asked.

"Six hundred thousand dollars," Eddie said. "With what the camp gets from our foundation, that donation would keep them open and operating at the capacity that they have for the past eighty years."

"So the foundation does give them some money?" he asked.

"A small amount," he said. "Enough to pay for some administrative things and general upkeep of the land. Your money would fund everything else." He launched into what the camp did, and how many people they employed, and the various activities Clear Creek provided, and to how many kids.

"And they eat better than any of our other campers," Eddie said with a laugh. "I was just up there a few weeks ago, and it's a fantastic camp."

Griffin could agree, but he didn't. He didn't need a rundown on what Clear Creek did either. He knew how amazing everything was here, and he knew who the credit belonged to.

Toni.

His heart simultaneously sang and cinched at the thought of her. But he also knew who Eddie's next call would be to, and selfishly, he wanted to be at Toni's side when she got that call.

"If the camp is so great," Griffin said. "Why is it not being funded through your foundation anymore?"

"We lost one of our major donors," Eddie said without missing a beat. He was almost too smooth. "And they happened to directly fund Clear Creek."

"I see."

"You can withdraw your donation at any time," Eddie said. "But we'll take your donation on September first for the next year, and once that's done, we can't return the funds. But you could call me on August thirty-first and say you don't want to donate, and I won't put it through. It's entirely up to you."

"Okay," Griffin said. "Let's do it."

"Okay." Eddie seemed to breathe in a new kind of energy Griffin could practically feel through the telephone line. "I'll just need your name and bank account number. We can use the routing number and all of that."

"I don't see why you need my name," Griffin said. "I think the transaction will go through without it."

"Oh, uh, well, possibly."

"Let's try it," Griffin said. "Take a dollar or some small amount. See if it goes through." He pulled up the screenshot of his check, which had the bank account number and routing number, and he gave them all to Eddie, who repeated them back to him in a slow, annoying way.

Several moments passed, and he said, "Yes, that worked."

"Perfect," Griffin said. "So we're set?"

"Yes, Mister—yes, we're set," Eddie said. "I've got your number here, and I'll just call you Mister Smith, if that's all right."

"Who would you need to tell my name?" he asked.

"Our camp administrator will no doubt ask who donated," he said. "And the board of directors. But Mister Smith is fine, I assure you."

"Great," Griffin said. He might as well have a third last

name to go with the two he already had. He ended the call and leaned back in the chair where he sat in the shade.

It was done.

Now, Griffin could only pray that Toni would never find out that he was Mister Smith.

He also closed his eyes and tipped his head back, offering up a plea that things between them could go back to normal.

CHAPTER TWENTY-THREE

Toni wept at her kitchen table, her head cradled in her arms. This was too hard. Trying to find people to give her camp money was too hard. Even Hailey, who was very good on the phone, had only managed to get one business to give them a few thousand dollars.

And that wasn't going to keep the doors open.

It was Tuesday morning, and while she and Griffin had been spending Tuesday mornings together for the past couple of months, he hadn't texted her yet this week.

She knew his number, yes.

But she couldn't bring herself to ask him if he still wanted to see her. At least with the silence, they hadn't broken up yet.

Her phone rang beside her, but she didn't bother to pick it up. If Hailey had a true emergency, she'd hang up after the third ring and immediately call again. It was a system they'd worked out a few years ago.

The line rang and rang, which meant it wasn't Hailey. And if it wasn't Hailey, she didn't want to talk to them. Heck, she didn't even want to talk to Hailey.

"I don't know how to do this," she said. She stood up and moved into the kitchen to make more coffee. She wouldn't be working today, she knew that. She wanted to stay inside the walls of this cabin, curl up with hot drinks and buttery popcorn, and watch romance movies.

She wanted pizza too. And potato chips. Anything that would make her feel like less of a failure.

It was almost the beginning of August, and she and Hailey hadn't been able to save the camp. She'd pushed through day after day, telling herself it just took one person with the right kind of pockets to keep Clear Creek operating. But after weeks of trying to find a needle in a haystack, Toni just needed a day where she'd given up.

She wasn't going to shower, and she wasn't going to answer her phone. Or her door—either of them. Griffin had always come to the back door, but he hadn't come last night. She hadn't seen him since Friday night, when he'd crept under the drape of darkness to come see her.

She cried harder now, and she wasn't even sure why. She was as much to blame for the gulf between her and Griffin as he was. He didn't talk about much, and that bothered her. But she wanted to ask him more about his money and maybe if he could possibly donate to the camp.

And what kind of girlfriend did that make her?

Money-grubbing came to mind. *Opportunistic. Only likes him for his money.*

Toni didn't want to be any of those things. Things had

been going so well with him until she'd found out about his inheritance. And he knew it. She knew that was when things had shifted between them.

She wasn't proud of that fact, but she didn't know how to blot it out either. She sipped her coffee and then an herbal tea while the TV played quietly in front of her. She ate popcorn for breakfast and heated a frozen pizza for lunch.

She wasn't entirely sure when she'd fallen asleep, but someone knocking on her door woke her.

Jolting awake, Toni sat up, her heart sprinting around inside her chest.

"Toni," Griffin called from behind her. She spun toward the back door, dislodging her coffee mug from beside her on the couch. It landed on the floor with an ear-splitting crack, and shards of ceramic went sliding.

"Oh, no," she said, her face cracking from where her salty tears had dried. She couldn't open the back door in her current condition, but there was no way he hadn't heard that mug hit the floor.

"I know you're in there," he said next. "It's broad daylight out here, Toni. Open the door."

She got to her feet and quickly tiptoed past the carnage that was her coffee mug to let him in. "I was asleep," she said in her defense while she closed the door behind him. And she sounded defensive too.

Griffin's unhappy eyes met hers. "Why aren't you answering your phone?"

"I was taking a nap," she said, folding her arms across

her chest. Hadn't he heard what she'd just said? "I don't feel well." That much was true, at least.

He peered closer at her, and Toni wished he wouldn't. She stepped past him to get a roll of paper towels and her dustpan. "And I dropped a mug and it broke." She started sweeping up the bigger shards. "What do you need?"

"Oh. Nothing."

"Nothing?" Toni straightened and looked at him. "You came over here in broad daylight...for nothing?"

"Hailey said you weren't answering your phone. I thought you might...be...sick." He finished the sentence lamely, his voice dropping almost to a whisper.

"You were asking Hailey about me?"

"She couldn't get in touch with you," he said. "And I happened to overhear her talking to Kiki at lunch. That's all." He looked away too, almost like he didn't want to get too attached to Toni.

Fine, she thought.

But it wasn't fine. She had already grown extremely fond of Griffin. She was very attached. And she didn't know how to not be. The man was a North pole while she was a South. She craved him as much as he was her opposite.

"Oh, yes, Kiki. I suppose you were sitting by her." The jealousy and bitterness in her tone was plain to hear.

Griffin cocked his head anyway. "What does that mean?"

Toni's fingers curled into fists. It was time to have this conversation, though. Long past time, in Toni's opinion. "It means I know you went out with her last week."

"I did not," Griffin said immediately. "A *group* of people went to West Lake for chocolate and coffee."

"Why didn't you tell me?"

"I don't tell you everything."

"Exactly." Toni didn't want to fight with him. She'd already cried enough today. Enough for the whole month. She turned her back on him and wetted several paper towels. Then she got down on the floor and started wiping it, feeling the teeniest, tiniest pieces of glass rubbing against the wood.

"Toni," he said. "What's going on?"

"I don't know," she said. "You don't talk to me. You come over, but it's all camp talk and kissing, and I have no idea where you are." She stood up and smoothed her hair out of her face. "You're mad at me that I want you to donate to the camp. I'm not sure how to ask you to donate while still assuring you that our relationship isn't contingent on you donating."

The words just spilled from her like water pouring over a cliff. "And I don't know. Things feel really complicated, and I wish they weren't." Her chest heaved.

"I talk to you," he said.

"Name the last important, serious conversation we had." She tossed the paper towel in the trashcan and looked at him.

He said nothing.

"It's fine," she said. "I get it. It's been a weird summer with us—*because* of us—and maybe we should just quit while we're ahead." Ahead of what, she wasn't sure. Toni had already fallen for him—most of the way. She refused to admit she was in love with him. Otherwise, she wouldn't be ahead of anything.

"You want to quit."

"I want to stop guessing what I'm going to get," she said, pointing at the door. "When you walk in, who am I going to get? The Griffin who's smiling and takes me easily into his arms? The one who shares things with me and asks me about my parents? The one that's easy to be with? Or the one with a gaggle of gorillas behind him, making everything between us awkward?"

A dangerous storm entered his gaze. "You think *I'm* the one who makes things awkward?"

"I didn't say that. I know things are awkward between us, and that comes from both of us." She shook her head. "I never should've asked you to donate to the camp. That ruined everything." She paced away from him and looked out the window above the sink. "I'm sorry that ruined everything."

He didn't move. He didn't speak.

Toni just wanted him to speak.

"I'll answer my phone now that I'm awake," she said to her faint reflection in the glass. "Please just go."

"Toni," he said, and the word did carry some anguish.

She closed her eyes against the hot tears. "I'm not feeling well," she said, her voice much too high. "Please, just go. I don't want to get you sick too."

What she really wanted was a way to rewind time. Go back several weeks and keep the phone call about Clear Creek closing to herself. Griffin's support had been wonderful in the beginning, but even that had brought her humiliation and guilt when she'd learned that he had money and had been listening to her complain and worry for weeks.

Fresh embarrassment spiraled through her, and she swiped at her eyes.

Griffin hovered just behind her. "Will you answer if I text you?"

"If it's camp-related," she said. He just needed to go. She couldn't hold herself together for much longer.

"Fair enough." With that, he left through the back door. Toni collapsed, bending over the sink as everything broke inside her and the tears she'd been fighting won. They tracked down her face and dripped into the sink, leaving her exhausted and wrung out.

And then her phone rang again, buzzing against whatever table she'd left it on.

Steeling herself, she marched over to the end table by the couch and picked it up. Hailey's name sat on the screen, and Toni jabbed at the button to connect the call. She wanted to snap at her best friend, but instead she said, "Hey," in the brightest voice she could muster. "Sorry, I was taking a nap."

"Toni!" Hailey said, shrieking immediately afterward. "Have you gotten any of my messages yet? Or any messages?"

"No," she said, afraid to look at her phone now. "What's going on?"

"Are you sitting down?"

"No."

"Sit down. Tell me when you're sitting down."

"Hailey." Toni didn't have the time or patience for this right now.

"Just do it." Hailey giggled as Toni rounded the couch and sat heavily on it.

"Fine," she said. "I'm sitting down." Her heart felt like lead, but she was sitting.

Another shriek came through the line, and Toni whipped the phone away from her ear. Pure irritation ran through her, and she wished Hailey had employed the professional side of herself for this phone call.

"We got a new donor!" she yelled into the phone. "Recurring annually. For the cost of the entire camp!"

Toni couldn't believe her ears. Hailey was pulling a prank on her—and a very, very cruel one at that. "Who?" she asked, because she'd heard Hailey the first time. If there really was a donor, they'd have a name.

"A Mister Smith," Hailey said. "That's the name Eddie gave him. Mister Smith wanted to remain anonymous, so we don't actually know his name."

"Wow," Toni said, her mind whirring now. Spinning. Slowing down...

It landed on something she didn't want to believe. "When did the donor come in?"

"I don't know," Hailey said. "Eddie called me this morning when he couldn't get in touch with you. And then I couldn't get in touch with you, and we had a minor incident at lunchtime, and I sent Griffin over there to make sure you were still alive. Is he still there?"

Hailey spoke so fast that Toni had a hard time keeping

up with her. "No, he left already," she said, her heart growing an extra-heavy layer of cement around the lead.

They had a donor.

An anonymous donor.

And had she known, she and Griffin likely wouldn't have argued.

You wouldn't have had a crucial conversation, she corrected herself. The divide between them *was* about more than money.

"Okay, well, you're alive," Hailey said. "And the camp stays open!" She cheered, and a smile finally touched Toni's mouth.

She laughed and cheered with her friend, but her joviality dried up the moment the call ended.

"Mister Smith," she said with a scoff.

She knew exactly who the money had come from, and she wasn't sure why Griffin's donation made her so angry.

Oh, wait. Yes, she did.

Because he hadn't told her about it.

CHAPTER TWENTY-FOUR

G riffin placed his packed box of snacks on the front
seat of his truck in case he wanted some crackers
on the way home. Which was stupid, because the trip back
to Chestnut Springs was only an hour. He'd made it plenty
of times without a snack or a drink.

"Or Toni," he muttered to himself.

But this time, he was taking the snacks, the drinks, his
clothes, toiletries, everything he'd brought with him.

He wasn't taking Toni.

And if he were being completely honest with himself,
he wasn't taking a large piece of his heart, either. The piece
he'd given to Toni thumped out in the world somewhere,
but he didn't have it with him.

He'd texted her after leaving her cabin on Tuesday
morning. *I'm headed back to the ranch after this camp, if you can
survive the rest of the summer without me.*

We can.

Two words, and he'd quit his job a month early.

He couldn't bring himself to tell any of his brothers, who lived in such wedded bliss now. He didn't want to see them. He couldn't go back to the house he still shared with Rex. His brother would push and pry, and Griffin just needed some time to figure out why things between him and Toni had gotten so snarled.

Maybe if he knew why, he could unravel back to that point and straighten everything out.

You're being stupid, he told himself as he walked the path from the parking lot to his cabin one more time. He checked every drawer and every cupboard, just to make sure he hadn't left anything that would smell in a few weeks. The fridge was likewise empty. He'd made the bed and even swept the floor.

The cabin was probably cleaner than it had been when he'd first arrived, and he stood near the door, surveying it. A keen sense of sadness pulled through him. He loved Camp Clear Creek.

"That's why you donated to keep it running," he said to the empty cabin. Someone else would move in here and be a great counselor for the boys. The camp would stay open, making a difference in the lives of anyone who came to this patch of Texas.

It just wouldn't be Griffin who came back.

He sighed, turned away from the cabin he'd called home for the past two months, and stepped outside.

He locked the cabin door and flipped the key around in his hand. He hadn't arranged to check-out with Toni, and he wondered where she was. The boys had left a couple of hours ago, and everyone had the weekend off.

She'd probably go see her parents, or she and Hailey would be working on the packets for the new campers scheduled to show up on Monday morning. Two weeks ago, after she'd done that, Griffin had taken her to dinner and spent the evening on her couch with her.

How different tonight would be. He'd be on a couch, all right, but not Toni's. As if on cue, his phone chimed, and he looked at it to find a text from Darren. *You on your way?*

Leaving now, he tapped out and sent. *I can grab dinner on my way in, if you want.*

He was just grateful the cowboy who lived in a cabin along the lane that led to the ranch's homestead had agreed to let him stay there for a night or two. Just until Griffin figured out how to tell his brothers that he'd donated six hundred thousand dollars to Toni's camp but she'd broken up with him anyway.

Get whatever you want, Darren said. *I'm out at the fence line for another little bit, so I probably won't be home when you get there.*

Even better, Griffin thought, but he didn't send the message to his friend. He'd had plenty of alone-time this week; he didn't need more, especially when Darren was doing him the favor.

I'll get that cheeseburger pizza you like. Griffin didn't understand the concept of pickles on pizza, but Darren loved it. The man loved anything to do with burgers, and he actually made a really good cheeseburger kebob that had opened Griffin's eyes to what the concept of a hamburger really was.

Darren sent a thumbs-up emoji, and Griffin stuffed his phone in his back pocket. Back down the path one more time. Behind the wheel. Griffin drove down the street and to the other road that led to the main building. He couldn't just leave without checking out, and if he had to talk to Toni one more time, so be it.

His heart quaked as he walked into the building, but it was quiet and still. He hadn't seen her car in the lot either. In fact, with camp being over for the weekend, he was surprised the building had been open.

The lights were off, and he didn't encounter anyone as he walked through the big room and around the corner to the hallway where the offices were. Toni clearly wasn't in, but he went into her office and placed the key to his cabin on her desk. Thinking quickly—and acting before he chickened out—he found a post-it note on the table in front of her desk and wrote her a note.

Here's my key. Thanks for everything, Toni.

He stared at the letters, some of them swimming together as his vision blurred. "Stupid," he muttered, tearing off the top note. "Thanks for everything? What does that mean?"

He wasn't going to thank her for being his girlfriend. What a stupid thing to say.

In the end, he tried three times before he just wrote:

Toni,

Here's my key. Call me if you get in a tight spot and you need a counselor. I love this camp and hope it does well for you.

Griffin

He did want the best for her. He always had. He'd hoped *he'd* be the best thing for her, but in the end, he hadn't been. He made things awkward by not rushing to donate to Clear Creek, and she'd taken it as his way of saying he didn't want to support her.

He hadn't wanted to donate, because he'd been afraid she'd stay with him when she didn't like him, just to keep the money.

"She never said that," Griffin told himself as he left her office. "You didn't give her the chance to say that." There were so many arguments in his head, and he just wanted to stop thinking.

He got behind the wheel of his truck again, taking precious moments to adjust the radio and turn it up loud before driving away, probably for the last time.

Frustration built in him as he navigated the last twist before Horseshoe Bay came into view, and he slammed his open hand against the steering wheel. Once, twice, three times.

Then he reached for a box of crackers to keep him company on the drive back to Chestnut Ranch.

THE SOUND OF THE BACK DOOR OPENING AND COWBOY boots clunking against the hardwood floor got Griffin all the way to fully conscious. A moment later, Darren's face peered over the back of the couch. "You made it." He grinned down at Griffin, who had indeed made it.

"I brought pizza," he said, groaning as he sat up. "But I have no idea how long I've been asleep."

"It's just after six," Darren said.

So a couple of hours. He'd obviously needed the sleep, as Griffin wasn't a big napper and rarely slept during the day.

"What are you doin' out at the back fence?" Griffin asked as he stood up and stretched his back.

"Field maintenance," Darren said, opening the pizza box on the counter. "This looks so good. Thanks, Griffin."

"It's the least I can do," he said. "Thanks for letting me stay here." He sat down at the small bar where he'd put the pizza. There was only enough room for two barstools before the counter ended and the dining nook began.

Darren met his eye, curiosity in his. "Why don't you want to just go home? Sleep in your own bed?"

"Rex is there." Griffin wiped his hand down his face. "And I don't want to answer questions."

Darren nodded and turned to put his pizza in the microwave. "You drive an enormous, black truck. You don't think Travis or Seth is going to see it?" He faced Griffin again. "Or Rex, for that matter. The man drives right past here every day."

Just another question Griffin didn't want to deal with. "I'll park it behind the other cabin."

"We got a new guy," Darren said. "He took your place just after the Fourth. And we needed 'im too. We were getting pretty far behind."

Confusion struck Griffin. "Really? But you're now doing

field maintenance?" That always needed to be done, honestly. But the field maintenance in the middle of the summer was stuff cowboys did if everything else was caught up.

"He's a good worker," Darren said, turning his back on Griffin again. "We're getting caught up now."

"What's his name?"

"Samson." Darren brought his plate of piping hot pizza to the other barstool and sat down. "He got his own cabin, because he has a little boy who comes out here on weekends."

"Plus, you're an ogre and don't want to share," Griffin teased.

Darren chuckled and shook his head. "I know I'll have to share eventually," he said. "But you brothers haven't even furnished the loft."

Griffin looked up at the loft above the hallway that ran down to a bedroom and a bathroom. This was the smallest of the three cabins along the lane, and the other two had two bedrooms each, plus a loft.

"So where's Aaron? I thought he was in that third cabin."

"He moved into Brian and Tomas's place," Darren said. "So Sam could have the cabin to himself."

"Why not here?"

"It was a loft either way," Darren said. "I offered." He looked at Griffin, his dark eyes earnest. "I really did. Aaron said he much care, and the bathroom at the other place is bigger. Plus, it has a proper back deck, and—"

"Okay." Griffin laughed and waved off Darren's explanation. "I don't even care. You cowboys work out how you live."

Darren grunted, and he looked mildly annoyed. Griffin wasn't sure what he'd said to upset his friend, but he'd been doing and saying a lot of things lately that upset people. Darren finished his pizza and got up to put his plate in the sink. "How long are you going to be here?"

"I don't know," Griffin said. "I just need some time before I face all of them."

"They've all broken up with women before," Darren said. He cleared his throat. "We've all lost someone important to us."

Griffin whipped his head up, his nerves buzzing. "I'm sorry," he said. "I—I know that." He couldn't believe how insensitive he'd been. He'd asked Darren for a place to stay for a couple of nights because he'd broken up with Toni and didn't want to tell anyone.

And Darren had lost his wife. There was no getting back together when one party was dead and gone.

"How...are you?" he asked.

"It's a hard time of year," Darren admitted with a sigh. "Diana passed away in July."

Griffin felt the weight of fifty fools press down on him. "I'm so sorry. When?"

"Last week." Darren studied the countertop like it held a secret he needed. He seemed so...lost. He'd always been quiet, though he accepted every invitation to meals at the homestead. He said things in meetings if he felt he should. He was one of the hardest workers Griffin had ever met.

"Do you—?" Griffin cleared his throat. "Go to the cemetery or anything? Take her some flowers?"

"I have in the past," Darren said. "But I didn't get to it this year."

"We should go tomorrow," Griffin said. "Or your next minimal day. When's that?"

"Tomorrow," Darren said, lifting his eyes to Griffin's. "You'd go with me? It's a two-hour drive, one way."

"I have nothing better to do," Griffin said with a smile. "And even if I did, I'd go with you." He'd always liked Darren, and the man had been working for Chestnut Ranch for a little over four years now.

He'd found out about Darren's deceased wife quite by accident, and Darren had asked him not to tell anyone else. Griffin never had, and he wondered if Darren had ever confided in anyone else.

"Let's go then," Darren said. "You can drive, which will give you something to do, and you can tell me all about Toni on the way."

"Oh, boy." Griffin didn't like the sound of that. "I don't know if I can do that."

"Fine, I'll just take a nap." Darren grinned at him, and Griffin smiled on back.

"It's a plan," he said, getting up from the counter to find his cowboy hat. He'd left it on the dining room table, and he fitted it right back into place on his head. "But tonight, let's play cards. I'm feeling lucky now that I'm single again, and I think I can finally beat you."

Darren laughed, and Griffin let a ray of happiness slip through him. But he wasn't feeling lucky because he was single again. In fact, he felt the exact opposite about being single again. It was a curse, not a blessing, and there was no way he'd beat Darren at cards.

The man had many talents, and hiding his emotions was only one of them. Vowing to be more like him, Griffin studied his face as he decided how many cards to take on five card draw. Darren never gave anything away, and Griffin needed to figure out how to be more like that. Then maybe he could face his brothers, talk about his break-up, and move on with his life without feeling like he was one breath away from total asphyxiation.

CHAPTER TWENTY-FIVE

D arren feigned sleep when he knew the city limits of Hondo, where Diana was buried, were approaching. He loved the sight of the land, the water tower right downtown, the train tracks that ran parallel to the highway.

He could navigate any road in and out of Hondo, and he loved the tiny general store with the perpetually broken front door.

But he wasn't here for a trip down memory lane.

"I know you're not asleep," Griffin said a few minutes later. "Now sit up and tell me where to go."

Darren's heart beat out a staccato rhythm. He groaned and sighed as he sat up and straightened his cowboy hat.

"I've never been down to Hondo," Griffin said. "Take me around town."

"Am I a tour guide now?" Darren growled. He never should've agreed to this trip. Griffin had just caught him in a weak moment. He did normally take Diana's favorite flowers to her grave every summer. And this year...he'd just felt depleted.

And now he was lying to himself.

He hadn't come last week, because to do so would've meant he wouldn't have been able to see Sarena. They'd been meeting along that fence a couple of times a week for over a month now. On his last minimal day, he'd taken lunch, and she'd climbed the fence like she'd been doing it her whole life. He'd spread a blanket on the ground and they'd enjoyed a bona fide Texas picnic together.

And Darren liked the woman a whole lot.

A slash of guilt cut across his heart, and if he stepped foot inside the cowboy church he and Diana had used to attend, he'd have to confess that he was cheating on his wife.

Your wife is dead, he told himself. And she'd want him to be happy. So why shouldn't he go out with Sarena? The brunette was incredibly pretty, competent around a ranch, loved horses and dogs, and she knew how to make potato salad—with mayonnaise, not Miracle Whip.

His relationship with her was still very new, and they hadn't gone out in public yet. He hadn't mentioned her to anyone around the ranch, keeping her close to the vest exactly the way he had Diana.

"Turn left up here," he said. "Go over the tracks and past the store."

"I'm thirsty," Griffin said. "Can we go in that store?"

"Sure." Darren made it sound like no big deal to go back inside the store where he'd bought the ingredients for

Diana's last meal. Panic gripped his heart in a vice, and he pulled in a breath.

Griffin heard it, and he looked over at Darren. After several long moments, he said, "We don't have to go in the store."

Darren nodded and looked down the street. "There's a church right down there we went to." He could still feel the spirit of this place. Feel his wife with him.

"You don't have to take me on a tour." Griffin turned up the radio. "Just tell me how to get to the cemetery."

He said nothing, and somehow Griffin managed to get them to the cemetery without any directions from Darren.

Diana was everywhere here, from the lane where her parents still lived, to the road that led out to Lantern Hollow. Darren had never felt her presence so strongly in the past, and he wondered what it meant.

He managed to take the flowers he'd bought in Boerne to her headstone and look down at the letters. Five years ago, he'd been here too. He knew, because he'd come everyday for the first couple of months. He'd brought flowers and trinkets of hers he'd found as he slowly went through her stuff. He'd brought her favorite sandwich from Polo's, and the pumpkin latte when that season hit all the coffee shops in town.

Eventually, he'd stopped going every day. He'd sold their ranch and moved away. But he'd always come every year in July.

"Hey, sweetheart," he said, everything inside him softening as he crouched in front of her headstone and cleared away some dirt from the letters of her last name. His last name too. He sighed as he set the flowers along the bottom of the stone. "I sure do miss you. I'm a little late this year, but I still made it."

All at once, he was glad he was there. Glad Griffin had suggested it. He told Diana about why he hadn't come, and he asked, "So what do you think? She seems nice."

His wife didn't answer, of course. He hadn't been to church in a while either, and he thought maybe if he found one in Chestnut Springs, he'd get more direction for his life.

He straightened and looked out across the cemetery. "Sure is pretty here, baby," he said. "You'd like the sunrises, I bet. I love you, Di." With that, he turned and walked back to Griffin's truck.

He looked up from his phone when Darren got in the cab. "All set?"

He just nodded, because Darren felt like another chunk of his heart had been ripped out and left on Diana's grave.

"All right," Griffin said. "Let's get to that chicken place you mentioned earlier."

Darren smiled, because he didn't think there was a man alive who liked food more than Griffin Johnson. The mood lightened, and Darren glanced at the cowboy church as they passed it once again.

Yes, it was definitely time for him to get back to church. Get his life back on track. Get on with living.

Darren had more "field maintenance" to attend to

on Monday morning, and he left Griffin showering in the cabin so he wouldn't have to go over his daily itinerary. He'd never had to explain himself to any of the Johnson brothers. They gave him work. He did the work. Everyone was happy.

No one needed to know that he'd added about ninety minutes to his day a couple of times a week to see Serena Adams. No one needed to know that he heard the sound of her voice at night just before he fell asleep. No one needed to know that he'd gone to church yesterday, praying to know if starting a new relationship with a woman was the right thing to do or not.

When the fence came into view, he found Sarena sitting atop it. And what a vision that was. His pulse fired through his chest at the rate of a machine gun, and a smile curved his lips.

Thankfully, by the time he got close enough for her to see him, he'd tamed the goofy grin into something a little less hormonal.

"Mornin'," she drawled, her own smile sitting easily on her face.

"Mornin'." He swung off the four-wheeler and approached her. She sat on the top rung of the fence, her legs crossed, and he wondered how on earth she'd positioned herself like that.

"Look what I found." She held up a small, brown rectangle, and it took a moment for Darren to register what it was.

"My wallet." He climbed up onto the fence too and took it from her. "Well, I'll be."

"I didn't peg you for a liar, Mister Dumond."

He looked from his wallet to her, realizing in half a heartbeat that she was teasing him. Her eyes sparkled like fool's gold, and Darren really wanted to ask her to go out with him. He bit back the words though, because they sounded stupid in his head.

"A liar?"

"Your driver's license says you weigh one-eighty." She scanned him. "Honey, you're at least two-twenty."

He burst out laughing, and Sarena did too. It felt so good to laugh, and Darren felt something get cleansed from his soul.

"Also," she said, quieting. "That thing is expired."

"I had to get a new one anyway," he said, reaching into his back pocket and pulling out his wallet. "And look." He retrieved his new driver's license and pointed to the weight.

"Two-twenty," they said together.

Their eyes met, and Darren could've sworn a thunder-storm materialized, with huge bolts of lightning there was so much electricity between them. He hadn't felt anything like it since...since he'd met his wife.

"Darren?" Sarena asked.

"Hm?" He dragged his gaze from her lips with some difficulty.

"Would you like to go to dinner with me?"

Pure horror shot through him, replacing the raging hormones and the happiness that had settled right behind his wounded heart.

She'd asked him.

How embarrassing. He cleared his throat, trying to figure out what to say. He wanted to explain that he was going to ask her, and she'd just jumped the gun.

Then he thought that was stupid and would just make him seem like he was making excuses for not asking her first.

"Okay," she said, twisting to slip down off the fence. "Forget I asked."

And now he'd waited too long.

"Wait," he practically shouted at her, and she was only a few feet away from him. She looked up at him again, and Darren was so far out of his element, he felt like he'd gone to a different planet.

He reached for her, leaned forward, and the next thing he knew, he was kissing the gorgeous, funny, and smart Sarena Adams.

CHAPTER TWENTY-SIX

top kissing him! Sarena told herself. But she couldn't make herself do it. Darren cradled her face in his hands, and wow. Just wow. She wasn't sure what his romantic background was. For all she knew, he could have a girlfriend in town while kissing her out here on the ranch.

She didn't think so. Darren was a gentle giant of a cowboy. Tall, and broad, and strong. His whiskers whispered against her skin as he kept kissing her too. At first glance, the bearded man could inspire a blip of fear in a woman.

But he barely spoke loud enough for her to hear, and he had plenty of thoughts about the sunrise, and why he did what he did for a living, and great advice for what she should do with a sick cow.

And he kissed like a pure gentleman, leaning further and further into her as if he couldn't get close enough.

He finally pulled away, and Sarena sucked at the air

while she found her bearings. She opened her eyes, and the sun seemed to be ten times brighter before. The sky bluer. The birds tweeting in the nearby trees.

"I'm sorry," he said, jumping down from the fence in the next moment.

Sarena blinked a couple of times, trying to catch up to the situation. "Wait," she said. "You're sorry?" She quickly climbed back up the fence and slid down to the ground on his side, but she wobbled on her feet. She hadn't been kissed like that in a long time.

Ever, she amended in her mind. And she didn't want the man responsible for it to walk away from her.

"Darren," she called.

He finally paused and turned toward her. His chest rose and fell in great gulps of air. "I don't know what I was thinking." He took off his cowboy hat and ran his hand through his hair. Thick, brown hair Sarena wanted to thread her fingers through too. She couldn't believe she hadn't done it while he was kissing her. But she'd just been trying to keep up with him.

"Pardon me?" she asked.

"I shouldn't have done that." He threw his arm toward the fence.

"Hey." Sarena stepped closer to him, almost like she was approaching a small animal she didn't want to scare off. "It's fine. I...liked it."

"You what?" He searched her face, and his surprise was honestly really cute.

She smiled at him. "I asked you to dinner, Darren. Do you think I hike out here for exercise?"

He blinked, realizations finally entering his eyes. His arm dropped to his side, and a scoff escaped his mouth. "Well, I don't know what to say now."

"You say yes," Sarena said. "To dinner." She reached up and touched one of the buttons on his shirt. "Tonight?" She wanted to take their relationship off the ranch. Or at least into a building, if he was a good cook.

She felt like she'd laid everything on the line. If he said no, she wasn't sure what she'd do. She had a fence to climb, and plenty of open space before she could duck behind a tree on her own property. She hadn't been out with anyone in so long, and maybe he'd kissed her to see if she was any good at it.

Maybe she wasn't.

The seconds ticked by, and Sarena's face continued to heat. Last time she'd reached this point of embarrassment, she'd said something. Darren had kissed her. Every cell burned with that need again, but she refused to let herself speak.

"Okay," Darren said. "I can take you to dinner tonight."

"We could eat at your place," she said. "If you cook."

"Nope," he said, maybe a little too fast. "I can't at my place tonight."

"I thought you said you lived alone." She furrowed her brow, trying to see more than what he'd said.

"I do," he said. "But I have someone sleeping in my loft for a few nights, and he just broke up with his girlfriend..." He trailed off. "Do you cook? Want me to come to your ranch?"

"Oh, we can't do that," she said. "My sisters will be all

over you." She grinned up at him. "So come pick me up, and I'll meet you at the mailbox. Say, seven? We'll go get something in town."

Darren swallowed and nodded, and Sarena wondered how long it had been since he'd been on a date. She was about to ask when his phone rang. He practically dove into his pocket to get it, saying, "It's my boss. I have to go."

She nodded, and he fled from her. Sarena watched him get on the four-wheeler, the phone attached to his ear. He took off a moment later, without ever looking at her again, and all of Sarena's adrenaline from the kiss and asking him out faded.

Her muscles sagged as a trail of dust lifted into the air as Darren left. "Well, that could've gone better." She turned back to the fence. "But he did kiss you." A smile touched the same lips his had, and she made it over the fence easily, a new bounce in her step as she returned to the ranch—and her chores for the day.

"What are you doing?" Sorrell stood in the doorway leading into Sarena's bathroom, a horrified look on her face.

"Putting on makeup." She looked away from her sister, her heart pounding beneath her breastbone.

"Why?" Sorrell committed to coming into the bathroom, and she reached for the curling iron on the bathroom counter. "What is going on? You're curling your hair?" She sucked in a shocked gasp. "You have a date."

Sarena rolled her eyes, which in her opinion, looked pretty amazing. She'd watched a few videos that afternoon in the barn on the perfect smoky eye, and she had all the makeup from her earlier days. Days when she cared what she looked like, even if she was just going out to feed the goats and check on the bulls.

But that was back when she had free time for things like curling her hair and putting on makeup. She did a lot more around the ranch now, and she had been for years. She knew that was her choice, and for a while there, she'd thought she'd take up Daddy's habits of never going to town.

The hermit life had helped her heal after the accident, that was for sure. She pressed her lips together, wishing her tumultuous thoughts would go as easily. She hadn't told Darren about the accident yet, and her indecision raged inside her.

But it shouldn't be a big deal. She was still mostly made of human parts, and she'd made a full recovery. And if he hadn't noticed her prosthetic yet, he probably wouldn't unless she pointed it out.

Something in her mind whispered that she'd been sure to wear jeans and boots, or shorts and high socks every time she went out to the far fence. She pushed those thoughts away and realized Sorrell still stood in the bathroom, gaping at her.

"What?" Sarena put her old tube of lipstick down and checked her lips again. It was the wrong color, though she'd worn it a lot in years past.

But she wasn't the same person she'd been back then.

Pulling a makeup remover wipe from the box, she found it dry and wrinkled. She ran some water on it, squeezed out the excess and carefully started removing the lipstick.

"Who is it?" Sorrell asked. "And when in the world did you meet him?" She gasped again, definitely the more theatric of Sarena's two sisters. "Don't tell me you've been using one of those apps."

Sarena scoffed and rolled her eyes, even as a pinch of pain pulled through her. "Of course not." She wasn't stupid, and she tried really hard not to repeat her mistakes. The last man she'd been out with—Joey—she'd met on a Christian singles app. He'd been nice, charming, and good-looking.

And always looking for the next handout, too. Sarena had paid for most of their dates, and she hadn't realized what a narcissist he was until *he* did something to upset her —draining her bank account without her permission—and *she* apologized for getting upset about it.

"Then who is it?" Sorrell put her hands on her hips. "I find it highly suspect that you won't say, and I've asked a million times."

Sarena turned from the mirror, deciding she could go to dinner with Darren without wearing lipstick. She didn't like how it tasted anyway. "Darren Dumond," she said.

"Who?" Sorrell asked.

"He's a ranch hand at Chestnut Ranch," Sarena said. "And I'm not answering any more questions right now. I'm going to be late." She pressed past Sorrell and reached for her purse. She couldn't remember the last time she'd used it, but it was probably to put in her credit card information to a website. She bought almost everything she needed online, and what she didn't, Serendipity picked up in town when she went.

She exited her bedroom and went down the hall, Sorrell's displeased tuts behind her. "I'll be back later," she said. "You girls have a good evening."

"What's going on?" Serendipity asked from the kitchen.

"She's going out with Darren Dumond," Sorrell practically spat.

"What in the world?" Serendipity said behind her. Sarena didn't wait to see her youngest sister's reaction. She wasn't nearly as dramatic as Sorrell, and she'd calm down the middle sister, feed her some warm cocoa, and all would be well when Sarena returned from her date.

She stepped outside, the evening sun baking the Texas landscape. But she loved it, and she thanked the Lord above for the fact that she'd been born in a warm climate. She practically skipped down the steps, though she couldn't actually do that with her prosthetic foot, and hummed to herself as she started down the lane.

It was a half-mile walk to the mailbox, and she'd barely started when her phone rang. Her heart sank all the way to the bottom of her cowgirl boots. She'd paired those with a skin-tight pair of black jeans and a tank top with the colors of the ocean swirling across it. She thought she looked bright and fun.

And until she'd seen her father's lawyer's name on the screen, she'd felt bright and fun too. But she couldn't ignore Janelle Stokes. "Hello?" she asked as if her phone hadn't told her who was calling.

"Sarena," Janelle said, a happy edge in her voice. And why shouldn't she be happy? She'd gotten remarried a few months ago. "How are you tonight?"

She'd be better if she wasn't talking to Janelle. No offense against the woman, but she rarely called with good news. The last time she'd called, it had been to tell Sarena that Daddy owed fifteen thousand dollars in back taxes. The ranch had paid it, and Sarena had sent over boxes of paperwork for the law firm to go through.

"Just tell me," she said, pausing in the shade of a juniper tree. "Is it something bad?"

"Depends on your definition of bad," Janelle said.

Sarena's heart melted into the gravel beneath her feet. She tipped her head back and started a mental prayer. *Please, Dear Lord*, she thought. *I just need one good day*. And today was supposed to be the best one of her life so far. A date with a new man. A stolen kiss atop a fence...and...

"I've just gone over your father's will," Janelle said, the sound of some kids laughing in the background. She'd probably taken Sarena's files home with her. "And I'm afraid there's a stipulation that was never amended."

"What kind of stipulation?"

"I've been on the phone with Jones and Jones, and they can't find a newer will, so what we have is going to stand."

"Okay," Sarena said, beginning to lose her patience. She needed to keep walking. She didn't want to stand Darren up or have him come down the lane. Then he'd have to go all the way to the house to turn around.

"It seems that your father put in his will that the only way one of you girls could inherit the ranch was if you were married."

The cartoony sound of bombs falling filled Sarena's ears. "Married?" she asked.

"It can be any one of the three of you," Janelle said. "Then the ranch can be retitled to that person, who has a legal obligation through the will to split the ranch with the other two."

Sarena turned in a full circle, looking for a camera crew of people to jump out from behind the trees and tell her this was just a big joke. "I—I—" She had no idea what to say.

"Do any of you have any prospects?" Janelle asked.

Sarena looked down the lane as if she could see Darren's truck there. "Well—no."

"Well, there is a consequence," Janelle said, and she didn't sound happy. Nothing she'd said had been delivered with any emotion at all. "If none of you get married within the first six months after your father's death, the ranch goes to his brother, Dale."

Sarena automatically hissed through her teeth. "That will never happen," she said. "Why would Daddy do that? He didn't even talk to his brother." Not for the last five years of his life, at least.

"I'm so sorry," Janelle said, and now she infused some emotion into her voice. "And I wish we'd seen this sooner. We've lost some time."

Sarena thought of her two sisters. They hadn't been out with anyone seriously in a while, though they did have the opportunity to meet more men than she did. Out of all of them, Serendipity went on the most dates, but they were casual. Cups of coffee or lunch dates with a co-worker.

She thought of Darren next, and the way he'd kissed her on that fence.

"How long do I have?" she asked, determination filling her from top to bottom and floating her heart back into the right place in her chest.

"Legally, until almost Christmas."

"Who else knows about this?" She raised her chin and kept walking, faster now.

"No one," Janelle said.

"Good," she said. "Let's keep it that way for now. I'll talk to my sisters. I know Sorrell was seeing someone a month or so ago."

"Okay," Janelle said. "Let me know. I just need a valid marriage certificate as soon as you have it."

"How long do I—does one of us—need to stay married?" she asked.

"There's no stipulation for that," Janelle said. "But Sarena...you don't need to do anything crazy."

"I know," she said, though there was absolutely no way she was letting Fox Hollow go to her uncle. What had Daddy been thinking? Why hadn't he amended his will?

"Okay," Janelle said, apparently satisfied. "Sorry to not have better news."

"It's fine," Sarena said, almost convincing herself. "I'll talk to my sisters and get back to you." The call ended, and Sarena marched on toward the mailbox.

Around the last corner, she saw Darren had already

arrived. He drove a blue pickup truck with a white stripe down the side of it, and it was a few years old. He'd obviously washed it very recently—maybe that morning—and that care made Sarena's heart do a little tap dance.

The thoughts streaming through her head made her want to run for the hilliest hills in the Hill Country. *You can't ask him to marry you*, she told herself. *You can't, you can't, you can't.*

But she really needed to.

CHAPTER TWENTY-SEVEN

Toni couldn't take another mindless night of TV-watching. Especially not on her parents' old, dilapidated couch. They needed a new piece of furniture, but her mother said it was fine.

Her mother never sat on the couch. But Toni's back ached like the Dickens when she stood up, groaning. "I have to get back to camp," she said, and her father immediately started to protest.

"Daddy, I have to." She gave him a small smile and patted his hand. Thankfully, things with them had calmed down since the beginning of the summer. Toni came to refill their pill boxes every week, and there had been no more disappearing scares.

She'd spoken to them about calling her for what they needed, or using the grocery delivery service around town, and they'd reluctantly agreed not to drive unless it was an emergency. To her knowledge, the car had sat in the

driveway all summer long, and she brought them choco-
lates and fresh fruit from the stand on the highway leading
into town every weekend.

As she hugged her mother and then her daddy, Toni
realized what a pathetic life she now led. Griffin-less, she
didn't have much to look forward to.

Being a good daughter is not nothing, she told herself as she
left. Twilight had fallen, but there was still easily an hour of
light left in the day. She'd make it back to Clear Creek
before full dark, but the camp didn't hold the same magic
as it once had.

It seemed like everyone around her knew it too. No
one had been able to articulate why, but Toni knew why.

Griffin was gone.

And Griffin wasn't coming back.

She'd thought about him every day, every hour, since
he'd left last weekend. Sometimes she'd find herself staring
at something on her computer, not knowing how much
time she'd lost as she thought about him.

She arrived back at Clear Creek, and she had no idea
how. She hadn't paid attention to the traffic or the turns,
and she realized she'd just lost more time to Griffin Johnson. She sat in her car, tears filling her eyes. She thought
she'd probably given him her whole heart, and she couldn't
figure out why she'd broken up with him.

Men didn't talk about things. He wasn't that abnormal.
And yes, things had been awkward, because of *her*. Because
she'd made up some stupid thing about asking all the counselors to donate.

"So what do I do?" she asked. She couldn't face getting

out of the car, because then she'd have to walk to her empty, dark cabin. And there was no prospect of Griffin showing up in an hour, a soft rap on her back door, and a big smile on his face.

Toni wept for several minutes, feeling as helpless now as she had when Jackson had kicked her out of their home. Toni had wanted to leave then anyway, but she hadn't had the spine to do it. Now she had the guts and the strength, but she wanted to use them to get Griffin back, not run away.

In the end, she trudged up the path to her cabin, arriving out of breath and so consumed with her own troubles that she didn't notice there was a light on in her front window until she reached the porch.

She froze, because she hadn't left the lights on for herself.

Someone was in her cabin.

Her heart pulsed and skipped, almost shouting that it could be Griffin. Perhaps he'd returned to Clear Creek and was waiting just behind the door, worried about her. Ready to apologize and kiss her until everything between them was all right.

But she'd been having fantasies about him all week, and none of them had come true. Still, hope was a cruel thing, and she opened her front door slowly, calling, "Hello?"

"There you are," Hailey said. "I was just about to call you." She rushed toward her. "Where have you been? It's almost ten o'clock."

All the air rushed out of Toni's lungs, and those blasted

tears returned. "Visiting my parents," she said, her voice breaking on the last word.

"Oh, dear." Hailey guided Toni into the house and straight to the sofa. She hurried to close the door and then returned to her. "It's Griffin, isn't it?"

"Why would it be Griffin?" Toni asked, a bit defensively. "I just came from my parents' house. It could be about one of them."

"Oh, honey," Hailey said. "I know your different cries, and this isn't over your mom and dad. This is about Griffin." She stood up and went into the kitchen. "I'm going to make tea. Wait, I already made tea. I'm going to heat up these cinnamon rolls Dalton left for you this morning, and you're going to tell me all about it."

"I don't want to," Toni said. "Besides, I told you everything earlier this week." She slumped against the back of the couch and waited for Hailey to bring her a cup of tea. She did, and Toni wrapped her hands around the hot cup.

A minute later, Hailey extended a plate with a gooey cinnamon roll on it. The frosting was partially melted, and she'd put a dab of butter in the middle of the roll before heating it in the microwave.

"Bless you," Toni said, swapping the teacup for the cinnamon roll. She took a bite, and everything in her world got better for just a moment.

But only that one moment, and she couldn't spend the rest of her life with butter and sugar in her mouth.

Hailey returned to the kitchen, got her own tea and sweet, and came back to the living room. "Okay, Toni, here's what you need to do."

Toni really needed a life coach in this moment, so she perked up, her ears open.

"You're going to call Griffin—"

"Nope," she said.

"Toni, you're miserable. Anyone with even one eye can see it."

"I can't call him."

"Why not?"

"I just can't." She didn't want to accuse him of being their anonymous donor. Besides, it wasn't really an accusation, though it burned that he couldn't just tell her.

"I'm going to call him then," Hailey said, but Toni knew she wouldn't. "We know he's the donor."

"We don't know," she said. "And I think the main reason he didn't tell me is because he doesn't want me to be with him out of obligation."

Hailey nodded. "I agree. So how do you tell him you want to be with him, no matter what? Money or no money? Camp or no camp?"

"Is that what I want?" Toni asked, but she already knew the answer.

Yes.

"Please," Hailey said with a laugh. "You fell for him so fast, *I* almost got whiplash."

Toni straightened her back and shook her hair over her shoulders. "Well, we don't all wait until the sixth date to kiss a man."

"Hey," Hailey said, shock in her voice.

"I'm kidding," Toni said with a smile. "How are things going with Leon?"

"Great," Hailey said with a sigh and a smile, and Toni could see her friend falling too. Had she seen Toni with that soft, cinnamon roll smile on her face when she so much as thought about Griffin?

Probably.

They finished their treats, and Toni leaned back into the couch and sipped her tea. "Thank you, Hailey," she said. "I don't know where I'd be without you."

"With a pint of ice cream, sniffling in bed." Hailey grinned at her.

"Don't think I'm not going to do that once you leave," Toni said. "I think I have some butter pecan in the freezer."

"Nope," she said. "I checked."

They laughed together, and Hailey leaned down and hugged Toni. "Love you, Toni. Just think about calling Griffin, okay? I don't think he'd ignore you."

She nodded and watched Hailey walk out the front door. The clicking of it sounded much too final, and Toni hated being alone.

She'd thought if she never let another man into her life, then she'd be happy.

She'd been wrong.

She'd thought if she could just get the money she needed to keep Clear Creek open, then she'd be happy.

She'd been wrong.

She stayed on the couch for a long time, thinking through the last couple of months with Griffin. They'd definitely been the happiest times of her life in the past decade.

And the week without him had been terrible.

Call him.

The thought lingered there, and she tried pushing it away. It wouldn't go, though, and Toni scrambled for what she might say to him.

But then her fingers were dialing, and the line was ringing, and Toni couldn't breathe.

And Griffin didn't answer anyway. "Hey, it's Griffin Johnson," his voicemail said. "Leave me a message, and I'll call you back."

Toni closed her eyes as that luxurious voice flowed through her eardrums. And she knew in that moment that shew as in love with him.

The beep sounded, jerking her eyes open.

"Griffin," she said. "It's Toni." Nothing came to her mind. Then she remembered the note he'd left for her.

Call me if you get in a tight spot.

"I'm in a tight spot," she said, struggling to keep her voice even. "Call me back, would you?" She hung up quickly, taking several quick breaths to get her head to clear.

She looked at her phone as the screen darkened. "Did you really do that?" Before she could open her phone and look at her call history, her device rang, right there in her hand.

She bobbled it, dropping it on the floor before she could see the caller. "Shoot." Hurrying, she picked it up, and her vision went white when she saw Griffin's name and smiling picture on the screen.

Answer it!

She swiped on the call. "Hello?"

"Toni," he said, and his voice in person was so much better than a recorded message. And saying her name? That was like magic. "You called?"

"Did you get my message?"

"No," he said. "I just called back." He sounded a bit groggy. "It's late, sweetheart."

"I'm sorry," she said, glancing at the clock on the microwave. Almost eleven. Yikes. "I wasn't paying attention." And he'd been in her cabin this late before, plenty of times.

"It's fine," he said softly, almost like he was sharing a room and needed to whisper so he didn't wake the other person. "What's going on?"

"I—" Her throat closed, and all the wrong words streamed through her mind.

I miss you.

I love you.

I'm sorry.

It's not you. It was never you. It's me.

You're the anonymous donor, aren't you?

The money means nothing.

I just want you.

Griffin didn't say anything either, and they just breathed together on the call. Finally, Toni said, "Would you take me to breakfast on Sunday? I can deliver your last paycheck in person, and I have something...I mean, I want to talk to you."

Without hesitation, he said, "Yes."

Just like that. Toni wondered if he could love her too,

but she didn't dare let that hope into her heart. She'd already been disappointed by love, and she had a lot to make up for with Griffin as it was.

"Great," she said. "I'll meet you at Stegg's?"

"You don't like Stegg's," he said.

"I know," she said. "But you do. Ten?"

"Toni—" He exhaled heavily. "I have direct deposit."

Her heart paused. He'd already said yes. Would he back out?

"I'll come to you," she said. They'd driven by his house once, but she didn't have the address memorized. "If you text me your address, I'll come to you."

"All right," he said. "Sunday at ten, my place."

Toni repeated it to him and hung up. That dreadful, dangerous hope crept into her heart, and she closed her eyes as they started to burn with unshed tears again. But she could do this. She'd done much harder things in her life, that was for sure.

And she wanted Griffin in her life, through the good, the bad, the hard, the easy, all of it. She just had to go get him.

"Sunday," she whispered to herself, suddenly thinking through the many things she needed to do before then.

CHAPTER TWENTY-EIGHT

Griffin spent Sunday morning scrubbing every inch of the bottom floor. Rex had been living in the house alone for months, and the man seriously didn't know how to turn on a vacuum cleaner.

By the time he emerged from his bedroom, it was almost ten. He yawned as he walked into the kitchen wearing a pair of gym shorts and nothing else.

"Dude," Griffin said, annoyed already. He'd hardly slept last night, and he couldn't believe he'd agreed to host Toni at his house. "Toni's going to be here any minute."

"I forgot about that." Rex looked down at his bare chest. "Are you sure you don't want me to stay?" He grinned at Griffin, who wanted to knock the smile off his face. He'd finally come back to the house on Wednesday, his tail tucked between his legs and ready to answer Rex's questions.

His brother had been...less Rex-ish than normal, and

he'd just welcomed Griffin home with open arms. He'd hardly asked anything, and they'd talked about Griffin's donation to the camp more than the woman it directly affected.

"Go get dressed at least," Griffin said, throwing away the last antibacterial wipe. "And you say hello and leave, like we agreed." He scanned Rex's body. "Isn't Holly waiting for you?"

"We're not getting together until eleven," Rex said. "I'll jump in the shower real quick." He took a cup of coffee with him down the hall, and Griffin frowned at his retreating back.

The doorbell rang, and Rex called, "Good luck, Griff," before he disappeared into his bedroom.

Griffin spun toward the front door. "She's early." He slicked his hands down the front of his pants, wishing he'd stopped cleaning an hour ago so his hands wouldn't be so dry and smell so chemically.

With nothing to be done about it now, he strode toward the front door and opened it in one swift movement. The door nearly banged into the wall behind it because of the force he used, and he caught it just in time.

Toni stood there, her dark hair curled and framing her face in the most beautiful way. She carried a brown paper bag, which she thrust toward him. "I brought you a sandwich."

Griffin didn't move to take it. He couldn't believe she was here. Their last conversation had been full of tension and hurt feelings, and he wanted a do-over. He wanted to take her into his arms and breathe in the scent of her hair.

He wanted to touch those bare shoulders and run his hands down her arms to her back.

She wore a sleeveless shirt with a loud floral print that screamed her style, and a pair of blue jeans. Typical Toni. Stylish, yet practical. Organized, and detailed, and smart.

"Come in," he said, backing up.

She kept the bagged sandwich in her hand and did what he'd said. He closed the door behind her and took a deep breath of her lingering perfume. He couldn't help how he felt about her, and he followed her into the kitchen.

"This is a nice place," she said, facing him. She wore a timid smile, and Griffin wanted to turn it into a full-blown, joyful one. He'd seen that look on her face and in her eyes before, and he hated that it wasn't there now.

"Thanks," he said. "Full disclosure. Rex is a late riser, and he's in the shower. He's promised to say hello and go as soon as he's done."

Toni glanced down the hall and put the bag on the kitchen counter. "Okay." She faced him again, pure anxiety in every crease of her face. And Griffin knew them all. "I just came to say I'm in love with you."

Shock punched him right in the nose. "What?"

"I mean, I'm sorry." Her eyes widened too. "I meant to say I was sorry."

A smile spread through Griffin's whole soul. "I listened to your message," he said. "You said you were in a tough spot." He ducked his head, glad he'd put on his cowboy hat so he could hide his face. He didn't want her to see him smiling yet.

"I am," she said.

"Because you're in love with me?" He lifted his head and looked right into her eyes. He couldn't hold back the smile now.

She opened her mouth, presumably to protest. But instead, she just shrugged one of those sexy shoulders and said, "Yeah."

Joy filled him and filled him. "I love you too, Toni." He wanted to sweep his cowboy hat off his head and toss it into the air, whooping. Instead, he approached her slowly. "So now what?"

She sniffled and wiped her eyes. "I don't understand you."

He frowned, his fantasies drying up on the spot. "I don't know what you mean."

"You love me?"

"So much," he said.

Tears streamed down her face. "I don't see how that's possible."

He took her into his arms then, wishing she could see herself the way he did. "Oh, it's possible, sweetheart. And it's because you're good, and kind, and loving. You take care of people, and your parents. You have a soft heart, and a strong will." He touched his lips to a spot just under her ear. "And you're beautiful, and you make my heart beat so fast. And you make me want to be a better man than I am, all in the hopes that you'll never realize how much better you are than me, so you'll never leave me."

Toni cried harder, and Griffin just held her while she did. He wanted this good, strong, sexy woman in his life. And for that, he had to tell her the truth.

"I got up at the crack of dawn to clean the house," he said as she quieted. "So you wouldn't know how big of a slob I can be. And I got those onion bagels you like, with the strawberry cream cheese, though that combination makes no sense to anyone on this planet but you."

She laughed through her tears, but Griffin wasn't finished. "And I know it took everything you have to come here, and I want you to know—I don't want there to be any secrets between us."

She fell back a step and looked at him through her tears.

"I'm your anonymous donor," he said, quickly adding, "And I didn't tell you, because I didn't want the donation to have any place in our relationship. If you don't want to be with me, you can walk away. At any time. I'm not going to pull the funding or anything."

She wiped her face and nodded. "I knew it was you. I mean, I suspected."

He nodded. "If it's about the money, Toni, I'm not interested."

"It's not about the money," she said. "It's never been about the money."

"Yeah?"

"Yeah."

He believed her, and his gaze dipped to her lips. "Then I guess you better kiss me now."

Toni giggled, sniffled, and wiped her eyes one more time. "You think you're so smooth, cowboy."

"I am," he said, grinning at her. He took his hat off and set it on the counter, gathering her close again. "And I have never lied to you, Toni. When I say I'm in love with you, it's the truth."

Their eyes met, and he could see every teeny tiny drop of water on her individual eyelashes. "I know," she said. "And I'm going to work on believing it."

"I believe you love me."

She nodded. "I know you do." She tipped up and touched her lips to his, and Griffin let his eyes close and his instincts take over. Oh, how he loved kissing this woman. He'd never been as complete as he was when he was with her, and he wanted to keep her in his life for a good long while

"Oh, wow," Rex said, and Toni broke the kiss to look at him. "Had I known you'd make up so quickly, I would've taken longer in the shower." He grinned at the two of them, and Griffin could only grin back.

"Hey, Rex." Toni laughed as she moved over to embrace him. "How are you? Griffin says you're engaged."

Rex exchanged a look with Griffin, who moved over to take the sandwich out of the bag. He knew exactly what it would be, and he'd never been happier that a steak and egg sandwich had brought the woman he loved back to him.

Rex chatted with Toni for a few minutes, and then he left, just as he promised he would. Griffin had gotten out the strawberry cream cheese and the onion bagels, but before she could take a bite, he said, "Let me kiss you again before you have onion bagel breath."

And she did.

Two months later:

"What if they don't like me?" Toni asked, worrying her fingers around each other.

"Impossible." Griffin kept her tucked right against his side, expecting Rex to arrive with their parents any minute now. Not only would Toni be meeting them, but Griffin had a very important question to ask her too.

Rex was getting married in three days, and Griffin really wanted to be her fiancée at the wedding. It seemed only fitting to go from reuniting with her at Russ's wedding to dancing with her and kissing her at Rex's.

"They're here," Russ said, coming in the back door. "Rex just pulled up."

The excitement and anticipation in the air was almost more than Griffin could stand. He'd missed his parents— particularly his Momma—more than he wanted to admit. But the way Seth kept grinning, and Travis had his arm around Millie, they all had too. Momma was a special lady, Griffin knew that.

And he also knew she'd love Toni. Heck, she'd forgiven Holly for lying about Sarah for five years, almost in a heart-beat. He'd told Toni over and over that Momma's only wish was for her sons to be happy, and Toni made him blissfully happy.

The past two months with her had been amazing. Hard, but amazing. He hadn't gone back to work at Clear Creek, but she had. The hour between them was easily managed, especially because he didn't have to work. But he couldn't drive up there and stick by her side every day, and he couldn't sit around the house and do nothing all day either.

He craved being busy, and he'd gone back to work on the family ranch. It had become apparent quite quickly to him that Darren was seeing someone, and he and Griffin made a pact—Griffin would pick up any slack Darren created by sneaking off to see his girlfriend. He wouldn't name her, and he never said a word about what they did.

But Chestnut Springs was a small town, and Griffin lived right downtown. It hadn't taken him more than a couple of times standing in line at the bakery or coffee shop to hear someone say that Darren Dumond was dating Sarena Adams. And the consensus was that it was quite remarkable that she left the ranch at all, her daddy being a hermit and all.

Griffin thought both of them dating was pretty remarkable, especially Darren.

He blew into the kitchen next, and Griffin immediately knew something was wrong. The man was very good at hiding how he felt, but he wore a storm cloud above his head, and Griffin wanted to go ask him what had happened.

But Momma called, "Hello! We're home!" and shouts of joy and welcome filled the homestead. All the boys crowded around her and Daddy, but Griffin hung back just a little. "See?" he said to Toni. "If you don't fight for your place, you get shoved out."

She just smiled, and the gesture looked a little fake to him. He finally got his turn with Momma, lifting her right off her feet as he hugged her. "Oh, my baby," she said, though Griffin was not the baby of the family. She took his face in both hands and gazed at him, her smile so full of love and emotion. "I hear you have a special woman here."

"That's because I told you that." He grinned at her and led her over to Toni. "Momma, this is Toni Beardall. Toni, my Momma, Sally."

Rex helped Daddy over, and Griffin hugged him while Momma exclaimed over how pretty Toni was and asked her if she was sure she liked Griffin.

"Yes, ma'am," Toni said, laughing. "I think he's the one."

Griffin turned back to her and introduced Daddy to her. "My father, Conrad."

"It's my pleasure, sir."

"Oh, sir." Daddy chuckled. He looked tan and rested, though how that was possible, Griffin wasn't sure. Their letters from the Dominican Republic had been filled with work and activity—and sunshine. Lots of sunshine.

"I like her."

"I do too," Griffin said, reaching his hand out. Rex put the ring box in it, as they'd rehearsed. "And I have a question for her while everyone is here."

"All right, quiet down," Rex said, and since he was the loudest brother, everyone heard him. And surprisingly, everyone complied.

Griffin's nerves made his stomach quake and his hands shake. "Toni," he said. "I'm in love with you, and there's nothing I want more than to be your husband."

"Oh," Momma said with a sigh. "Get down on your knees, Griffin."

"Momma, let him do it," Rex said.

"She's right, though," Russ said.

Griffin grinned at Toni, who clapped both hands over her mouth. He got down on both knees and cracked open the ring box. "If I can do it right, I guess this is me asking you to be my wife."

The very homestead seemed to hold its breath. Everyone looked at Toni, but she held Griffin's gaze, plenty of surprise in hers. Then she calmly lowered her hands and said, "Yes."

Cheers and congratulations lifted into the air, along with plenty of advice about how Griffin should put the ring on her finger. He did while he was still on his knees, and then Rex pulled him to his feet. He hugged Rex, then Toni, kissing her—his fiancée—while everyone clapped.

"Good group effort," he said to everyone. "You guys would think I'd need your help to get dressed in the morning."

"Oh, come on," someone said.

"You should've gotten down first," Travis said. "Not our fault you didn't."

Griffin just rolled his eyes, noting Darren as he slipped out of the kitchen without fanfare. His heart twisted, but Janelle drew his attention with a hug for him and Toni, and Griffin told himself he'd catch up with his friend later.

He'd just gotten engaged. His parents were home. Life was grand.

He pressed a kiss to Toni's temple and caught her admiring the ring. "How'd I do?" he asked. "If you don't like it, we can go pick out a different one."

"Are you kidding?" She looked up at him, the softest expression of love in her eyes. "I love it. I love you."

"I love you too." Griffin kissed her, not even caring that there were too many people watching. "I guess I get to marry my boss, huh?"

"Or am I marrying mine?" Toni giggled and kissed him again.

Keep reading for Rex's and Holly's wedding, as told by Darren Dumond, ranch hand at Chestnut Ranch.

THE END

SNEAK PEEK! CHAPTER ONE OF A COWBOY AND HIS FAKE MARRIAGE

D arren liked the quiet stillness of the ranch early in the morning. He'd just come in from feeding the horses, and he needed to hurry. But he took a moment on the back porch, as if waiting for his new golden retriever puppy to bobble his way up the steps.

But Koda had already made it to the door and he was just panting, waiting for Darren to open the door. He took one last look out over the land, the bubbling of the river barely audible in the distance. He breathed in deeply, because he needed today to be a good day.

"It's going to be great," he told himself. "Rex is getting married, and I have a new suit to wear." He bent down and ruffled the dog's ears. "Even you have a bow tie, bud. Let's go get ready."

He opened the door then and went inside, repeating the words, "It's going to be a great day," over and over.

He desperately needed it to be, because he hated weddings with the heat of a thousand suns. But he couldn't just not show up. He was friends with Rex, and the man had asked Darren to be in the wedding party.

Griffin was the best man, and he'd gotten engaged a few days ago too, when the Johnson parents had returned from their service mission to the Dominican Republic.

Darren blinked, and he saw Conrad Johnson lying on the ground, his leg bent unnaturally underneath him. Panic reared, and everything that had happened after Darren had found the man thrown from his horse streamed through his mind.

Conrad was an experienced horseman, but the horse he'd been working with was young, and unbroken, and wild. Conrad couldn't remember what had happened to spook the horse, but Darren had found it running free on the ranch and known immediately that something was wrong.

Conrad had never walked the same again, and he couldn't ride anymore. Darren's compassion for the man had doubled as he watched him fight for every inch of mobility he had, and he wasn't too tough of a cowboy to say he'd shed a few tears the day Conrad and Sally had left the ranch for a single-level home in the center of Chestnut Springs.

Then he could get to his doctor's appointments easier, and the grocery store was closer. Life was just easier when they didn't have to drive fifteen to twenty minutes for everything, especially as Conrad couldn't drive anymore.

So much had been taken from him in just a split

second, and Darren understood exactly how that felt. He'd lost everything he cherished in the same amount of time, and he was still reeling and trying to figure things out.

Which was why he'd had to break-up with Sarena Adams. He couldn't shake the feelings of infidelity he had, though Diana had been gone for a long time now.

He sighed as he soaped up, wishing the negative thoughts and emotions swirling inside him could wash down the drain as easily as the suds.

"It's a good day," he told himself as he tipped his head back into the shower spray. "I have hot water."

As he continued getting ready, he named all of his blessings. "The cabin has air conditioning."

"I have an amazing pup." He grinned at Koda as he got the dog dressed for the wedding. "And good friends."

He thought of the family he'd left years ago, and he determined he'd call his mother that night. Maybe if he talked to her, she could help him see how unreasonable he was being.

The thing was, he *knew* he was being unreasonable. But he couldn't rid himself of the feelings. But his mother had a way of saying things in a way that Darren hadn't thought about before, and maybe...

He held onto maybe's these days like they were anchors. He needed some of them to be true.

Maybe he could have another loving relationship with a woman.

Maybe he could tell Sarena about Diana.

Maybe he could be happy again.

He bent down to leash Koda when Aaron came in the back door. "You two ready?" the other cowboy asked.

"So ready." Darren stood up smiling, sure of one thing: He could smile through this day. *It's going to be a great day...*

✿

AN HOUR LATER, HE HELD THE LEASH LOOSELY IN HIS hand as he waited for the ceremony to start. Holly and Rex had wanted to get married in their backyard, and Rex had hired Millie to make it look like paradise.

A huge tent filled almost the whole thing, with lights and flowers hanging from the ceiling. Chairs had been set up inside, and Millie bustled around straightening the bows and reserving seats as the first guests started to arrive.

Darren told himself it was almost over, because he knew Rex had given Holly what she wanted—a simple ceremony with just family and very close friends.

So he was more than surprised to see Sarena Adams enter the backyard through the gate, both of her sisters with her. She wore a long, pale pink dress that brushed the grass and made it impossible for Darren to know if she was wearing shoes or not.

The sight of her almost made it impossible for Darren to breathe. She was gorgeous, with the dress swelling in all the right places and tying around her neck, leaving her shoulders and some of her back bare.

She stepped right over to Janelle, Russ's wife, and hugged her hello. All the sisters did, and then they looked around for a place to sit. At least that was what Darren thought initially. But he soon realized they were looking for someone.

As all four of them continued to whisper and search, Darren watched Sarena. Kissing her had reintroduced magic into his life. Holding her hand reminded him that he wasn't alone in this world, even if he had put up some walls to keep people out. She'd started to break those walls down, and he'd let her.

They'd dated until about a week ago, when he'd told her he wasn't sure he could do more than be friends with a woman. She'd wanted to know what that meant, and he had no explanation. She'd said he didn't kiss her like they were friends, and he couldn't argue with her.

He had not told her about Diana, and even now his tongue felt too thick inside his mouth. He'd only told two people about his late wife—Griffin and Conrad Johnson. And he'd only told Griffin because the man had come across Darren while he was looking at his wedding pictures on his phone—and crying.

Griffin had been nothing but kind and compassionate, and as far as Darren knew, he'd never told anyone about Diana.

Darren's heart pulsed too many times, too closely together, and that somehow made Sarena look in his direction. She froze, her eyes widening. Janelle said something to her, but Sarena didn't even react.

Janelle was one of the smartest women Darren knew, and she followed Sarena's frozen gaze. Her eyes landed on Darren too, and she stared at him for a moment as well.

Then she stepped in front of Sarena, breaking their connection.

Darren cleared his throat and ducked his head, his face heating quickly. "We're ready for you and Koda," someone said, and he turned toward Travis. He'd been keeping an eye on his pregnant wife and helping with the setup, so Darren followed him back into the house.

Rex stood there, and he looked more agitated than usual. Travis said, "Okay, we're ready to get Rex out there. Momma you come too." He looked around. "Where did Millie go?"

"Right here," she said, panting as she bustled into the house. "The seats are almost full. Let's get the family out there. If you're in the wedding party, you stay right here. Griffin, you're going to lead them down the steps and escort a lady down the aisle. The women are waiting at the bottom of the steps."

Griffin nodded and smiled. "We practiced this, Millie. We've got it."

"And Seth's back with Holly?"

"I sent him back a few minutes ago," Travis said.

Millie nodded and looked around at the crowd. "Okay, everyone knows what to do. Rex, you're with me." She took the groom with her, and they went outside. Darren waited in the dining room, the scent of frosting and rose petals floating in the air.

Everything was happening right here at the house. First, Rex and Holly would be married. Re-married, technically. Then they were serving lunch, and Darren had volunteered to move chairs and help set up tables in the same space under the tent.

After they cut their cake, they'd leave on a honeymoon, something they'd never done when they'd gotten married the first time. Rex had wanted to go big with the wedding, Darren knew, but he was secretly on Holly's side.

Smaller was always better, and if he ever got married again, he'd want it to be a private ceremony with just him and his bride. Maybe her family, if she wanted them there. And probably the Johnson's, as they'd done so much for Darren over the past four years.

His thoughts migrated right to Sarena, but he told himself that was because she was the only woman he'd been out with since Diana's death. He thought about her as he took his place in line. As the excitement mounted as they went down the steps. As he linked arms with Jenna Johnson, Seth's wife, and kept Koda at his side. People pointed and smiled at the dog, and pride swelled within Darren.

He smiled through it all, and he steadfastly watched the woman dominating his thoughts. The ceremony was short and simple, but absolutely beautiful.

"I will love you forever," Rex said, his voice catching on itself. "I've never stopped loving you, and I'm glad to be yours."

Darren had never stopped loving Diana either, and he didn't think it was fair to Sarena to not give her his whole heart. Surely she understood that and didn't even want someone who couldn't give her everything. Right?

He cheered and clapped when Rex and Holly kissed,

and he helped set up tables like he'd agreed to do. Lunch was served, and he lost track of Sarena. Maybe she and her sisters hadn't stayed for lunch.

He let Koda roam the yard with Holly's dog, and he stuck close to Aaron, Brian, and Tomas as they got their food and found a table. He'd barely taken a bite of his rosemary chicken when someone sat beside him.

The scent of the woman pricked his attention. He didn't have to look to know Sarena had just sat next to him. "Is this seat taken?"

"No, ma'am," he muttered, twisting his shoulders slightly so he was turned further away from her.

She didn't say anything else, but her sisters started talking about the ceremony and how perfect Rex and Holly were for each other. The chicken stuck in Darren's throat. He couldn't sit here like this.

This was torture.

Absolute torture.

He got up and took his plate with him.

"Hey," Aaron said. "Where are you—?"

But Darren walked away before he could finish. He couldn't breathe. He couldn't swallow. He hurried up the steps, almost knocking down a waiter in his haste to get out of Sarena's sight.

He burst into the house, sucking at the air. He'd felt this wild and out of control just once before, and that was the day he'd buried Diana. He waited for the episode to pass, but when it did, he was left sweating and exhausted.

Thankfully, it only took a few seconds too, and he thought maybe he could make an excuse about needing to use the restroom. The house was quiet while the yard was noisy, and it seemed like everyone had been served now.

He put his plate on the counter near the sink and turned, trying to decide where to go.

Sarena stepped into the house, locking the door behind her. "Darren," she said. "I know you broke up with me. I don't understand why, and I just have to say this. Then you can decide what you want to do."

She pressed her palms together and looked over her shoulder. When her eyes came back to his, she looked nervous yet hopeful.

"I really like you," she said, her voice throaty and oh-so-sexy. "I don't know why you don't...no, that's not what I want to say." She drew in a deep breath and steadied herself. "I want you to know that you can trust me."

She looked like she might say something more, but she just nodded. "That's it. You can trust me with anything." She took a step toward him. "Your secrets. Your past. Your hopes and dreams and future." She moved with every item she said, and soon she was only a couple of feet from him.

She reached out and touched his chest, right over his heart. A shock moved through his body, and she whispered, "Your heart." She looked up at him. "Okay?"

He nodded as an automatic response, but he couldn't get his voice to work.

She nodded too, and with those beautiful eyes sparkling at him with need and desire and hope, she tipped up on her toes and swept a kiss along his cheek. "Okay."

With that, she turned and left the way she'd come. The

door opened, letting in the noise from outside, and the moment between them broke.

She left, and Darren couldn't breathe again.

She left, and Darren's world didn't make sense anymore.

She left, and Darren immediately wanted her back.

He just didn't know how to have her and Diana at the same time.

SNEAK PEEK! CHAPTER TWO OF A COWBOY AND HIS FAKE MARRIAGE

"Maybe I should go," Sorrell said.

"We're all going," Sarena said as she plucked another errant eyebrow hair from her brow line. "Why aren't you dressed yet?"

"I really thought you talking to Darren would work." Sorrell wrapped her arms around herself, her nerves pouring from her expression.

Sarena had thought that too. But in the two weeks since Rex Johnson's wedding, he had not called her. She'd walked out to the back fence every morning and every night, and he did not come. The notes she left for him there had not been picked up.

He'd gotten a puppy, and maybe that was all he needed in his life. Puppies were easy to talk to. Puppies were warm at night.

But Sarena didn't want a puppy. She wanted Darren

back in her life—and not just because her time to tie the knot or lose the ranch was dwindling.

But it was, and that was why she was going to the speed dating event during the town's Octoberfest tonight.

And Sorrell should be as well, but one more glance at her sister, and Sarena knew she wouldn't be going.

She'd told her sisters about the stipulation in their father's will the same day Darren had broken up with her. They'd immediately started brainstorming other men any of the three of them could go out with, but the choices were slim.

It had only taken an hour for them to come back to Darren, and they'd started devising a plan for Sarena to get him back.

But the relationship was about more than the ranch, and she knew it. Sorrell and Serendipity didn't need to know.

And he hadn't called. She couldn't make him call.

So while her heart continued to beat, it was a shell of what it had once been. Without him, Sarena didn't feel half as alive, and she doubted that she'd ever be able to be her authentic self with someone.

The worst part was how lonely she was. She sighed as she finished her makeup and smiled as Sorrell helped her into her dress. "You're going to get a ton of dates," Sorrell said. "You don't need me to come."

"I knew you wouldn't." Sarena smiled at her sister. She'd always known it would be her that would get married to save the ranch.

She just needed to find someone.

Tonight, she told herself. She was going to find someone tonight. Janelle had become a good friend over the past three months, and she said Jenna and Seth had started dating in the fall and been married by Thanksgiving, so it was definitely do-able.

Armed with that hope, Sarena drove herself to town and parked in the community center parking lot. Though it was October, it certainly wasn't cold in the Hill Country, and she hoped her boots wouldn't be too noticeable.

She'd never told Darren about her prosthetic foot, and she was glad about that. She didn't need his pity on top of the other humiliation.

She'd arrived early, and the men were still getting instructions and getting set up. She waited with the other women in the room, quickly realizing that all of them were hoping for the same thing she was—a wedding by Christmas.

Her stomach revolted, and she almost bolted from the room. But there were easily sixty or seventy men here, most of them wearing cowboy hats. She needed to meet someone if she was going to get married, and there weren't a lot of men knocking on the door at Fox Hollow.

She steeled herself as the emcee got behind the mic. "And we're ready. Ladies, you were given a number when you got here. You'll start at the table with the matching number, and we'll start the clock in five minutes." She smiled down at everyone from the small stage at the end of the room. "Everyone grab a drink and get ready to talk!

The rounds are three minutes, and we hope you'll make some great connections tonight. You'll go in ascending order, with table seventy-six rotating to number one."

Sarena was hoping for that too. She'd brought a tiny purse with her driver's license, a credit card, her phone, and a couple of mints. She put one in her mouth, took a bottle of water from the table, skipping the coffee and sweet tea, and faced the sea of tables where the men waited.

After a quick glance, she started looking for table sixty-five. She caught the eyes of several men as she wove through the tables, and she earned herself more than one smile. She started to relax before she'd even reached the sixty row.

Maybe this would work.

She almost tripped when she saw Darren's face. One of her feet stopped, and the fake one kept going, and she had to steady herself against the nearest table, which was number fifty-one.

Darren sat at fifty-seven.

She wouldn't make it to him during the speed dating.

His eyes wouldn't leave hers, even when his first date sat down in front of him and introduced herself.

Sarena wondered what in the world he'd been thinking when he'd broken up with her. The spark and chemistry between them was insanely hot and powerful. Could he not feel it? Did he not care?

And now he was here?

Hurt and humiliation flooded her throat, and Sarena gagged against it.

"Are you okay?" someone asked—the man whose table she still used to support herself. He stood up and put one hand on her back and the other on her forearm. He said something else she didn't catch, because when she and Darren were in a room together, he was the only one she could see and hear.

So he just didn't like *her*. He didn't want to be more than friends with *her*.

For a week or two after he'd broken up with her, she'd reasoned that he just wasn't ready. He'd told her that he hadn't dated in a long time, and that was the best reason she could come up with by herself.

But he was here. So he obviously thought he was ready.

He just doesn't like you.

Sarena couldn't see straight, and thankfully, the cowboy from table fifty-whatever had helped her to a seat along the side of the room and opened her bottle of water for her. She drank with a shaky hand. The emcee chirped into the mic. The room spun.

Everything hurt, and while Sarena knew her time was running out, and she desperately needed to meet someone soon, she couldn't stay here. Not with *him* here.

She stood, glad her feet supported her, and headed for the exit. She'd suffered enough humiliation at the hands of Darren Dumond. She reached the doors and went through them. Just across the lobby, freedom lay.

She wanted to run, but she wasn't great on her feet when she moved too fast. So she settled for walking.

"Sarena," a man called behind her, but the sound of Darren's voice only spurred her to go faster. Tears streamed down her face now, and she would *not* let him see her like this. He would not get the satisfaction of knowing that he'd broken her heart all over again.

She burst through the doors, taking huge gulps of air, and kept on going.

You're being ridiculous, she told herself.

She was stronger than some cowboy who'd kissed her a few times. Though, she knew it was a lot more than a few times, and that each time Darren had touched her, she'd felt cherished and alive in a way she'd never felt before.

But she'd been running the ranch nearly single-handedly for over five years. She could handle a little heartbreak.

"Sarena," he said again, and he was much closer now.

Sarena broke into a stilted jog, her right leg throbbing with the effort it took to keep the left one from buckling. She knew the moment she was going to fall, and she flailed her arms out, trying to find something to latch onto.

Only open air met her fingers, and she twisted to land on her hip.

"Sarena." Darren reached her a moment later. "I'm sorry. I'm sorry." He put those big, warm hands on her arms, his eyes searching for where she was hurt. But he couldn't see through skin and bone to her wounded heart beneath her ribs.

"You're bleeding." He touched her knee, and Sarena winced. "Where else does it hurt?"

Everywhere, she thought. Just having him so close was like the most brutal form of torture she could imagine.

He met her eyes. "I'm sorry," he said again. "Let me take you home and get you fixed up."

She shook her head, swallowing her emotion. "No," she said. "You should go back inside. You're going to miss all of your dates."

He gazed at her again, so many things streaming through those dark, deep eyes. "I don't care," he finally said. "I don't want to go out with any of them anyway." And with that, he picked her up and started toward his truck.

"Darren," she protested, though it sure was nice to be in his arms again. "I have my own truck."

"We'll come back." He wasn't taking no for an answer, and Sarena didn't want to give him those two letters anyway.

"You don't have to do this," she said as he set her on the bench seat in his truck.

"I have a first aid kit right here," he said, opening the glove box. He looked at her again. "And I want to do this." He stilled, and the whole world fell away. "I trust you, Sarena."

Those stupid tears filled her eyes again, and she brushed them away quickly. "You didn't call."

His throat worked, and then he opened the first aid kit and got busy looking at her scraped knees. He cleaned them up and put a couple of Band-aids on them. "What else hurts?" he asked.

She didn't answer, because she didn't want to tell him all of her secrets. *She* didn't trust *him*, at least not yet.

But she didn't have much time, she knew that.

She reached down and touched her left ankle, her fingers meeting the hard plastic of her prosthetic through her sock. "Here," she said, her voice hardly her own. "And here." She touched her own chest, just above her heart.

Surprise filled Darren's expression, but it was quickly overtaken by something softer and then more anguished. "I've made a huge mess of things, haven't I?" He ducked his head, which was just adorable. He'd done it many times over the last few months they'd been seeing each other, and he usually did it when he was embarrassed or scared.

Which was he right now?

Probably both, Sarena reasoned.

"I miss you," she said, employing her bravery.

He lifted his eyes to hers. "I miss you, too."

"Why are you here?" She gestured toward the community center and the speed dating.

"I—I—" He cleared his throat and swallowed hard, but he didn't look away from her. "I think I'm ready, Sarena."

"But you just don't want to go out with me."

"I do," he said. "You're the *only* person I want to go out with."

"Then *why* are you *here?*" She didn't understand, and she really just wanted to stop thinking about him.

"Because I was too embarrassed to call you."

Sarena searched his face, trying to find any evidence of a lie. But Darren was as humble as he was handsome, and she wasn't even sure the man knew how to lie. Her foot ached, and she really needed to adjust it. She reached down and said, "Okay, listen, I have to fix this, and I don't want you to freak out."

"Freak out?"

She didn't answer as she took off her ankle boot and sock. "I have a prosthetic foot." She stuck her fingers between the silicon and her skin, breaking the seal there. A sigh escaped her lips when the false part of her foot released, and she took it all the way off.

"I was in an accident about ten years ago," she said as Darren fell back a step. "And I crushed the bones in my foot. We were able to save the ankle and some of the heel, and now I wear this."

Darren looked at the prosthetic in her hand and then looked at her. "Wow, Sarena." He wore compassion in his eyes. "Do you—can I help you with it?"

"No, I just don't run well, and I need to adjust it." She made quick work of getting the prosthetic back where it should be, covering it quickly with her sock and then her boot. "All good."

But she'd exposed herself completely to him, and she wondered if he knew that. From the wide-eyed look on this face, he did.

The silence stretched between them, and Sarena knew to simply let it. Darren was a brilliant man, hardworking and kind. But he tended to take a while to order his thoughts before they came out of his mouth.

"I need to tell you something," he finally said. He took a step closer to her, filling the space between where she sat on the seat and the open passenger door.

"Okay," she prompted when he didn't say anything.

"I broke up with you, because my feelings for you were starting to get out of control." He swallowed, but his words made Sarena feel like singing praises to the sky. "See, I've been...married before, and I lost my wife five years ago."

"Oh, no," Sarena said, reaching out and cradling his face in her palm. He leaned into her touch, and the moment between them was so sweet.

"I didn't mean to hurt you," he whispered. "I felt disloyal to her, and my knee-jerk reaction was to break-up with you."

Sarena just looked at him, this handsome man she wanted to spend more time with. "But you think you're ready now?"

"I honestly don't know," he said. "So this is probably really selfish of me, but would you like to go to dinner with me?"

"Right now?"

A slow smile crossed his face. "Yeah, right now."

Sarena couldn't think of anything better in the whole world, so she said, "Yeah, I'd like to go to dinner with you."

"Great." His smile turned into a full cowboy grin, and he leaned toward her as if he'd kiss her.

She sucked in a breath and froze, and Darren did too. "I guess...uh...yeah, let's start with dinner." He backed out of the doorway, and she turned so she was sitting in the seat the right way. He closed the door and started around the hood of the truck, muttering to himself.

Sarena smiled and tucked her hair, because Darren Dumond had almost kissed her. She was going to dinner with him. And maybe, just maybe, they could pick up where they'd left off a month ago.

She hoped so, because the clock was ticking.

֍

Can Sarena save her ranch by getting Darren to marry her? Find out in **A COWBOY AND HIS FAKE MARRIAGE**.

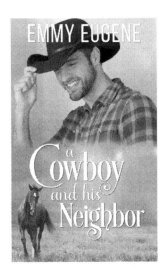

A Cowboy and his Neighbor (Chestnut Ranch Romance Series, Book 1): This is why cowboys should never kiss their best friend...

Can best friends Seth and Jenna navigate their rocky pasts to find a future happily-ever-after together?

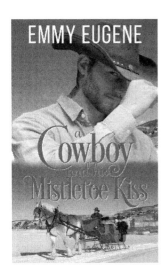

A Cowboy and his Mistletoe Kiss (Chestnut Ranch Romance Series, Book 2): This is why cowboys should never kiss under the mistletoe.

He wasn't supposed to kiss her. Can Travis and Millie find a way to turn their mistletoe kiss into true love?

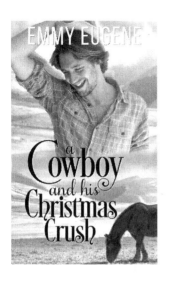

A Cowboy and his Christmas Crush (Chestnut Ranch Romance Series, Book 3): He's the foreman for the family ranch. She's broken up with him once already. Can their mutual love of rescuing dogs bring them back together?

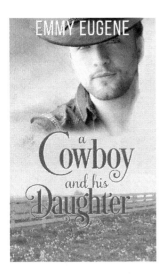

A Cowboy and his Daughter (Chestnut Ranch Romance Series, Book 4): They were married for four months. She lost their baby...or so he thought.

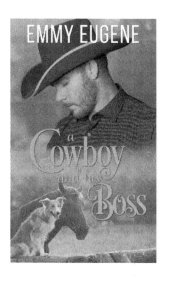

A Cowboy and his Boss (Chestnut Ranch Romance Series, Book 5): She's his boss. He's had a crush on her for a couple of summers now. Can Toni and Griffin mix business and pleasure while making sure the teens they're in charge of stay in line?

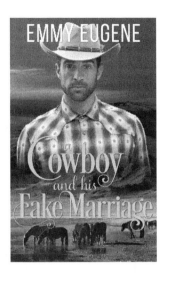

A Cowboy and his Fake Marriage (Chestnut Ranch Romance Series, Book 6): She needs a husband to keep her ranch. He lost his wife years ago and isn't interested in real love. But he can help a friend...

ABOUT EMMY

Emmy Eugene is a Midwest mom who loves dogs, cowboys, and Texas. She's been writing for years and loves weaving stories of love, hope, and second chances.

Made in the USA
Columbia, SC
07 January 2022

53810781R00195